CRIMINAL INTENTIONS

SEASON ONE, EPISODE TWO
"JUNK SHOP BLUES"

COLE MCCADE

[TABLE OF CONTENTS]

[CONTENT WARNING]

CONSIDERING THAT *CRIMINAL INTENTIONS* IS serialized in the form of episodic novels akin to a television series, I think it's safe to rate this using U.S. FCC television standards and mark it TV-MA. *Criminal Intentions* follows multiple homicide investigations and, at times, can graphically depict the act or aftermath of attempted or successful murder.

While it's a given that a series about homicide investigations will describe actual homicides, it may be wise to review content warnings regarding the specifics of cases depicted in each episode.

Content warnings for Season 1, Episode 2, "Junk Shop Blues," include:

- Graphically depicted murder by stabbing.
- Blood and gore.
- Graphically depicted forensic autopsy procedures.
- Depicted sessions with a therapist.
- Flashbacks to murders of queer characters.

- Discussion of drug trade, use, and addiction.
- Discussions of divorce and infidelity.
- Alcohol consumption.
- Use of firearms.
- On-page cis male/cis male penetrative sex.

Content warnings for the afterword include:
- Discussions of mental health.
- Discussions of police brutality.

Please read at your discretion, and make whatever decisions are best for you regarding content that may or may not be safe for you.

Take care of yourselves, loves.

–C

[READING NOTE]

THE CHARACTER SADE MARCUS USES the pronouns they/them/their as their preferred gender-neutral pronouns for a genderqueer and two-spirit person from the Lumbee nation.

[0: MOTIVE FOR MURDER]

MARION GARVEY HAS A LONG and storied history of people trying to kill him.

It's a hazard of the business. A hazard of success, too. Scum always want to go for the heavy hitters at the top. The big dogs. And he's proud of being the kind of big dog who doesn't have to be afraid of showing underbelly, because even his underbelly is armor-plated and bulletproof. He is untouchable. When Marion Garvey looks at himself, he sees the definition of a self-made man. The phrase "too big to fail" was *made* for him.

When you're on top of the world, it's inevitable the small fry will try to take you down.

Tonight, though, he's hardly expecting an attempt on his life. Tonight is *special*. He's been waiting for tonight for weeks, and after he went to the trouble of booking a honeymoon suite at the Wellington everything had better damned well go off smoothly. He's thrown enough money at the valets, the bellboys, the fucking *maids* to make sure he'll get the VIP experience. He wants nothing but the best.

And he damned well intends to give nothing but the best, tonight.

The jewelry box in his pocket weighs heavy. That weight is a sense of satisfaction, of pride, of promise. Of wealth. He can buy the things other men only dream of.

Whoever said money didn't buy happiness was just trying to make the best out of his sad lot in life.

Money can buy anything, including happiness on demand.

But his happiness comes from a more immediate source, as he hears the door slip open, the faint beep of a keycard unlatching echoing from outside. He takes one last look around, taking in the champagne cooling in the ice bucket in perfect reach between the catering cart and the bed, wherever this might happen to take them. The roses, spread in splendor all across one wall, over three hundred fine red blooms without a single blemish, every last one hand-chosen and spilling their lush fragrance to fill the room. The petals of hundreds more roses still, turning the floor into a sea of blood.

He's bought happiness, all right.

He's bought it, and he won't let it go.

Marion turns, a smile on his lips, and smooths his hands over his perfectly tailored suit, hand-made to his specifications. Only the best, always. Only the best.

"Darling," he says, and spread his hands—only to stop as a strange wet feeling spreads in the center of his chest, dull and heavy.

He looks down. His chest is red, he thinks numbly. What an odd shade of red, thick and somehow more vivid than other reds. The smell of the roses is so strong. So strong he can hardly pick out another smell, hot and thick and strangely metallic.

Blood.

Oh.

That is his blood.

He should feel pain, he thinks. He should feel pain, but there is only a sort of heavy numbness. His body doesn't want to move. His head is a balloon detaching from his body, taking his consciousness with it until he is separate from the shell of meat and blood and bone that had formed a man for over thirty-seven years. Thirty-seven years in which he'd made himself into everything he'd wanted to be.

Only to be unmade in a single stroke.

The handle protruding from his chest is black. The metal inside his flesh is cold. That, he can feel. Every inch of the blade lying against his insides, this flat cool sheet of stainless steel icing his flesh. Still no pain.

That is a kindness, he thinks. That is a kindness money can't buy.

He stares at the face wavering in his vision. At the resolute stare. At skin spattered in blood, his blood, blood that had been cut out of his chest in splatters and still soaks warm down the front of his shirt.

Why, he tries to ask, but when his head is floating and only tethered on by the thinnest thread, his lips don't want to move.

[3]

He's going to die on a bed of roses.

He falls, and the last thing he hears is the rustle of leaves. The last thing he feels is the bite of thorns, hooking through his suit to find skin.

The last thing he sees is the shower of petals, as rich and velvety red as his blood.

He is cold, so cold.

And still those familiar eyes stare through him, watching his life ebb away.

[1: WHEN THE LEVEE BREAKS]

SEONG-JAE YOON SAT STIFFLY in the plush leather chair of the departmental counselor's office and stared fixedly straight ahead.

The counselor stared right back.

They'd been like this for the last half-hour: staring off across a room paneled in pleasantly honey-toned wood, festooned with so many plants that the light through the windows filtered green through their leaves. During the first ten minutes the counselor had asked him questions such as *how do you feel* and *do you want to talk about what happened* and *have you been sleeping well at night?*

I feel fine, Seong-Jae had answered. *I do not want to talk about it. My sleep patterns are normal.*

The answers had been honest enough.

The counselor had not seemed particularly pleased with them, nonetheless.

And so she had asked again.

And again.

Until Seong-Jae had stopped answering.

Repeating himself was a waste of breath, a waste of time. Dr. Ryusaki seemed to feel the same, for the dark-eyed, plump little sparrow of a woman had only pursed her lips, crossed her legs, and rested her pad on her knee, tapping her pen against the paper thoughtfully and regarding him as if he were either some alien species or a particularly stubborn child she was determined to wait out.

Finally she sighed, shoulders slumping slightly, sagging inside her cashmere blouse. "Detective Yoon, I can't force you to talk to me. But many of the BPD officers have found it beneficial. I know you're new to our division, but you stepped into a particularly gruesome case. One that involved seeing gay and bisexual young men murdered in heinous ways. Considering that you asked to be on the case because you yourself are gay, it's not unreasonable to think the case would have had a psychological and emotional effect on you regardless of the extent of your experience." Her gaze searched him as if she was searching for a crack inside him, anywhere she could pry in deep. "I'm not going to pull you off duty if you admit a moment of vulnerability."

"Then what is the point of this? Are you not attempting to determine if I am fit for active duty?"

"It's required, after such a shocking case. I need to at least see you. I haven't seen anything that would mandate sidelining you from active duty." Ryusaki drummed her pen back and forth between her fingers. "That doesn't mean I'm not concerned about you as a person."

"I told you. I am fine."

"Are you?"

Seong-Jae sighed. "Do you think if you ask in a different way, I will answer differently?"

She half-smiled, rather sadly. "The thought might have crossed my mind." She shook her head. "Your job has a way of eroding at your humanity. Honestly, I worry more when people are fine than I do when they aren't. If you're indifferent to the idea of—"

"I did not say I was indifferent," Seong-Jae cut in. "I said I am fine."

"Ah." She exhaled heavily, tapping her pen against her lower lip, before tucking it into the glossy slick of her black hair, pulled back into a neat chignon and just beginning to show signs of silver streaks throughout. "If you have your own coping methods, that's less worrisome. But I'll still check in on you in a week. For now, our time's up. Battle stations down, Detective Yoon." She offered him a smile.

He did not answer it.

He only stood, shrugged into his coat, and headed for the door.

But as his hand fell to the doorknob, she called after him. "Detective Yoon?"

He stopped, glancing over his shoulder. She grinned wryly.

"Tell your partner he's got three more days to avoid me or I'm benching him for real this time."

Seong-Jae considered. Then nodded.

"As you say," he said, then twisted the doorknob and escaped Dr. Ryusaki's den.

MALCOLM KHALAJI SAT AT HIS desk, restlessly flicking a pencil between his fingers. He didn't want to be here, sprawled back in his chair and staring blankly at his computer screen. He had places to be. A new case to investigate.

And a partner to wait for, keeping him tethered on a leash when if not for Seong-Jae, Malcolm would have been out the door half an hour ago.

He hated waiting.

He hated waiting for someone else even more.

The homicide bullpen was almost empty, at this time of morning. They'd already been through the morning briefing, everyone scattered to follow their own leads, only a few people left behind doing desk work—and Sade, their voice drifting merrily from their spider's lair of cables, singing in a language Malcolm couldn't pick up. It was a different one every time, and he was really starting to wonder just how many Sade *knew*. And why.

Not that he'd ever get an answer out of the cheerful little monster.

The door to the hall swung open. Seong-Jae cut into the room like a knife, all sharp edges covered neck to toe in black, his black button-down half-untucked from his jeans, sleeves cuffed to mid-forearm against golden skin. A pair of unused vinyl gloves sprouted from the front pocket of his jeans, dangling against the denim.

The day after they'd closed the Park case, he'd shown up with a shopping bag full of several boxes of sterile vinyl surgical gloves. Without a word, he'd unceremoniously dumped them in a drawer of Malcolm's desk, then ripped one box open and filled his pockets with several pairs.

Malcolm had tactfully chosen not to say a word.

If he did Seong-Jae might switch back to latex out of spite, and Malcolm didn't need a full-on case of hives just because their hands brushed in passing.

Hands, or anything else.

Not that he was thinking about that kiss. That kiss had meant nothing. Felt like nothing.

Nothing at all.

Seong-Jae threaded through the clusters of desks to Malcolm's, angled black eyes locked on him unerringly, his red bruise of a mouth set in a thin, irritated line, the tousled mess of black hair shadowing his gaze.

"I take it it didn't go well, then," Malcolm said as Seong-Jae drew within earshot.

Seong-Jae worked his jaw, stopping next to Malcolm's desk with militant precision, hands tucking into the pockets of his jeans. "It went."

"What did she say?"

"That you have three days, or you are suspended."

Malcolm groaned, dragging his hand over his face, thunking his head against the back of his chair. "...I'll go. When I'm ready."

"Are you?"

"No." He sighed. "But I was asking what she said about you."

"She said nothing about me."

Malcolm eyed Seong-Jae. "...Ryusaki will suspend you. Don't find out the hard way like I did."

"Why would she suspend me when I attended my mandated counseling session?"

Because you're a stubborn asshole who won't bend enough to admit that maybe, just maybe, that last case was too much for us.

Too much for anyone.

But Malcolm was learning the art of grit-toothed silences, with Seong-Jae. And he ground his teeth together for a moment, giving himself that indulgence, that second to be irritated, before he sighed and levered out of his chair, catching up his suit coat and draping it over his arm. "We have a case. Downtown. Forensics beat us there."

He strode for the door. Seong-Jae followed, the gliding

raven at his shoulder, always there like some prophet of doom. "You seem agitated," Seong-Jae said mildly.

"Your appointment was long."

"And your paperwork backlog is quite extensive."

Malcolm pinched the bridge of his nose. "Stop that."

"Stop what?"

With an annoyed sound, Malcolm stopped just past the door, turning in the hallway to glower at Seong-Jae. Calm, implacable Seong-Jae, standing tall and unflappable in the doorway, his head cocked in that curiously inquisitive tilt that could mean *I have no idea what you mean* or *I do not understand why you are so emotional, human, but I find the phenomenon quite fascinating.*

"I know," Malcolm growled. "I turn my shit in to you now. I *know.* You don't have to grind the rank thing in."

"I was not aware I was doing any such thing."

"Sure you weren't."

Seong-Jae's expression didn't change, but something snapped in his eyes, unreadable and dark. "As far as I am concerned, you and I are equals."

"Are we?" Malcolm bit off—then reined himself in.

He didn't know what was wrong with him today. Why he was so irritable. Everything grated on his nerves, particularly Seong-Jae. That implacable, icy calm and aloof elegance were getting under his skin more and more every day.

It had been tolerable, though, while they were just working through old backlog on cold cases, identifying those that still had potential and familiarizing Seong-Jae with what was on their docket for the last six months. Tedious work that bordered on clerical. Something Malcolm could deal with, even with Seong-Jae always perched on the corner of his desk like a black-feathered vulture, leaning over him and bringing in that hot scent of diesel and smoky musk and maleness until Malcolm's space was starting to smell more like Seong-Jae than like Malcolm himself.

But of course he'd picked the day when a new case had landed on their desk to reach break point, until just the sight of Seong-Jae's coolly unruffled stare was enough to push Malcolm to snarling.

There was an easy fix for that.

And Malcolm turned away, giving Seong-Jae his back and heading for the stairs.

The stairwell door banged open, echoing. Malcolm clattered down, Seong-Jae silent in his wake but still *there*.

"Would you like to educate me on the case we are pursuing?"

"I'll brief you in the car," Malcolm muttered. "When we get back, put in a requisition for your own desk. If you had your own desktop, you'd already have the prelims by now."

"But I like your desk," Seong-Jae pointed out.

"Of course you do." Malcolm tried to bite his tongue, but then added under his breath, "...asshole."

"Jot," Seong-Jae countered without missing a beat.

With a sour look over his shoulder, Malcolm clattered

off the bottom step and pushed through the door to the parking garage. "I know what that means now."

"Of course you do." And for all his dispassionate detachment, there was no missing the maddening, entirely frustrating note of amusement coloring Seong-Jae's voice. "Because I told you."

Malcolm said nothing, only stalking toward his car.

If this kept up, there'd be another homicide on his desk within twenty-four hours or less—and he wouldn't regret a single damned thing.

[2: SAY THAT YOU LOVE ME]

WHILE MALCOLM DROVE THEM TO the crime scene, Seong-Jae leaned against the window and read the notes from police dispatch. A 911 call had come in approximately an hour ago from a downtown hotel—one that was, according to Malcolm, owned by one of the richest families in Baltimore. A housekeeper had unlocked a suite to clean it, and found a body face-down in the bed. Male. Not young, but not yet middle-aged. Fit. No identity, but then they'd been warned not to touch the body, not even to get an ID.

There's blood everywhere, the housekeeper had sobbed, per dispatch's notes. *So much blood.*

He grimaced. Honestly, was it entirely necessary for criminals to be so *messy?* The disorganized killers always made such a splatter everywhere, hasty and quick to depersonalize the body to separate themselves from the reality of their crime and any attachment to the victim as a *person.* Organized killers *could* be neater when they chose—but the ones who were neat enough not to make a mess were also neat enough not to leave an evidence trail linking their kills, unless they were narcissistic enough to want the attention and enjoy

[14]

the game of flirting with the police. Which left the organized killers who deliberately made messes of the body as a fetishistic ritual.

He supposed he would find out which one they were dealing with, once they reached the crime scene.

At his side, Malcolm was tense—more tense than usual, his slate blue eyes fixed tightly on the road, sharp gaze occasionally cut by a few tendrils of silver and chestnut hair drifting loose from its tie. Seong-Jae pondered asking why, but the old wolf would only bare his teeth and raise his hackles. Not particularly productive, and Seong-Jae needed his mind on the case and not on thinking back to just why Malcolm might be so very irritable with him.

It was simply because he didn't want a partner, of course. No more than Seong-Jae did, though they made do while stuck with each other.

No other reason.

No other reason would be logical.

Even if in the tension between them, that hot buzzing feeling that made Seong-Jae's blood feel alive, threatened to overwhelm him—filling his head with a slow and pounding throb.

He hated it. Hated that it never wholly left him, never fully left him at peace.

It was just easier to ignore when things were not so tense between them.

The address from the dispatch notes turned out to be a

high-rise building paneled in glossy, reflective black lined in gold, tinted windows throwing back the sun to create a towering onyx obelisk that spoke of ostentatious wealth, class—and pretension, with the name blazoned down the side of the building in story-high gold letters. *Wellington*. Just that, as if that name alone was recognizable enough that anyone hearing it should know their brand, their products, their market.

Seong-Jae had no idea who they were.

People in luxuriant clothing strode down the gold-lined front walk of white marble, not even sparing a glance for the invisible valets who brought their cars around and handed them over. Malcolm parked the Camaro a block back from the front drive of the hotel. At Seong-Jae's inquisitive look, he grumbled.

"I'm not giving them my keys."

"You are possessive of your car?"

"Something like that." Malcolm tossed his head, shoulders rolling tensely beneath the crisply pressed shoulders of his suit. "Come on."

Seong-Jae held back a sigh. Malcolm was even more impatient than usual today, and Seong-Jae only hoped it would not impact his ability to focus on the case.

Together they strode up the walk to the hotel. A few people flung curious, disdainful glances their way. Seong-Jae supposed even Malcolm's rather nicely tailored suits were considered inferior here, and his own jeans were not the particular sort of couture scruff that wealthy starlets indulged in. People were…so bizarre about such things. Such affectations.

He did not quite understand the point.

And it was hardly a surprise when they reached the glass-fronted, gold-framed front door—only to be cut off by a man in a crisp red waistcoat before Malcolm could even reach for the handle. The small, trim man's hair was hair slicked back and pomaded into a shell, his thin pinched moustache waxed down until it was barely a dash on his upper lip, like two calligraphic ink strokes.

He eyed them, his pinched nose wrinkling. "Good morning, gentlemen. Are you visiting guests of the hotel?"

Seong-Jae cocked his head. "Are you not aware that a murder occurred on your premises?"

The man hissed, leaning toward them, eyes narrowing. "If you could *please* not publicize this. We're trying to maintain calm, and the Wellington has a *reputation*."

Seong-Jae exchanged a glance with Malcolm, before Malcolm arched one bushy, skeptical gray brow and flipped out his badge. "BPD. The faster you let us in, the faster we get this sorted so you can go back to business as usual."

The man stared at them icily, eyeing Malcolm's badge as if searching for signs of forgery, then staring at Seong-Jae as if waiting for him to produce his badge as well. Seong-Jae remained silent. The man held his gaze in a blatant attempt to stare him down, then wrinkled his upper lip and looked back to Malcolm, clearly hesitating.

Malcolm sighed. "We can't investigate a crime from outside the building," he said with weary patience. "And you can't exactly toss the body down the laundry chute."

The man's eyes widened with such utter offense that if Seong-Jae were so inclined, he might almost crack a smile. Then the man lifted his chin, tossing his head—not that it did anything for the little waxed curl of hair laying against his brow—and pushed the door open wider before stepping back. "This way."

They ducked through before the door could close. He led them through a massive lobby with arched ceilings so high they faded into shadow, lit only by golden lights dotted among the darkness like lanterns hanging against a still and quiet night. Even though the lobby was filled with people, from guests to concierges, it was as quiet as an opera hall before a show, something about the grandeur of the reflective golden-ivory flooring and tall, stately columns lining the walls seeming to demand silence of even the most boisterous guests.

The loudest sound in the entire room was the steps of their escort, clicking swift and sharp and accusatory, as if he needed to *announce* exactly how offended he was with every busy stride.

He led them past the shining polished wood doors of the main elevators and ducked through a side door hidden behind a tall potted ficus, gesturing to them impatiently. Seong-Jae met Malcolm's wry glance, then followed the man into a narrow hallway of dingy gray-white walls and old, ratty gray carpeting, the fluorescent lights cold and flickering dimly, stark contrast to the opulence, elegance, and grandeur of the main lobby. Just to one side was a set of double steel doors, and the man pressed the *Up* button next to the doors impatiently.

Malcolm stopped just behind him, his thick bulk looming over the other man. "You're taking us through the service elevators?" he growled.

The man turned on Malcolm, glaring up at him. It was like a mouse staring down a wolf, and in some bizarre way the mouse was winning.

"I," the man said firmly, "have a duty to my guests, and do not want to cause a panic if any of them should see you and realize something is amiss." He drew himself up, as if he could puff up enough to outdo Malcolm's bulk. "When your...*people* arrive to take photographs and dispose of the body, I would appreciate if they did not attempt to enter through the front door. There is a side entrance for staff."

Malcolm stared at him with the most incredulous expression on his face. Seong-Jae found it quite fascinating; for all his rough edges, Malcolm often gave off a subtle air of one who appreciated finer things, from the well-tailored cut of his suits to his taste in Greek restaurants—yet he countered it with disgusting filthy pub dives like Swabbie's and an apparent complete and utter disdain for purveyors of finer lifestyles such as this man. His preferences were as much at opposite extremes as the deadly, rough-edged aura he gave off, paired with the gentleness and patience he so often showed to witnesses.

They had barely been working together for a week, but Seong-Jae only found Malcolm increasingly more contradictory, puzzling, and intriguing.

The elevator doors swung open. Malcolm stepped forward, forcing the man backward one step at a time, until they stood in the elevator with the narrow little man's back against the wall. Seong-Jae slipped inside just before the doors closed.

"Those *people*," Malcolm growled, a dangerous undertone in his voice, "are the forensics team and county medical examiner, and they'll come through whatever entrance will fit their equipment." Penetrating slate blue eyes narrowed. "You got something to hide, Mister...?"

"Brixton." He drew himself up with pride, officious and haughty, and leaned around Malcolm to jab one off the numbers on the elevator plate. The elevator hitched upward, a jolt of high-speed lift making Seong-Jae's stomach drop out. "I am Caldwell Brixton, the General Manager of the Wellington."

"Good for you," Malcolm bit off, as the elevator doors swung open on one of the upper floors, revealing glossy marble and wood paneling and lights subtly spaced among rich velvet hangings. "Now show me the body."

SOME DAYS, MALCOLM THOUGHT PEOPLE actually forgot he was actually here to *help* them.

It was in the goddamned police officer's creed, for fuck's sake. *To protect and serve.* Then again, with the state of police affairs in this country lately, he couldn't blame people for being mistrustful.

That didn't excuse Brixton being outright contemptuous and rude, as if they were somehow inconveniencing him by coming to look at the dead body sullying his hotel.

While Brixton swept ahead, Malcolm hung back, walking at Seong-Jae's side. "Can you believe these people?" he muttered, half under his breath.

Seong-Jae inclined his head. "His priorities do seem a touch...skewed."

"Does it bother you?" Malcolm asked. "Knowing he's judging us."

"No." Seong-Jae shrugged lightly. "He does not know me. He does not know my background, or what culture or privilege I have experienced, or my tastes, or my education. That he judges based on my occupation and clothing is his problem, not mine."

Yet every word made Malcolm starkly aware that *he* didn't know those things about Seong-Jae, either. He knew nothing about his partner, as if the man had simply come to exist the day he'd shown up at Malcolm's crime scene with no past or present beyond what little he wore readily apparent on his glass-smooth façade.

Malcolm shouldn't want to know.

They were here to do the work, nothing else.

He didn't need to know Seong-Jae for that.

He just needed to put up with him, and accept that the strange gestalt energy between them when they hit up on a case was some kind of *something*.

Tearing his gaze from Seong-Jae's coolly impenetrable expression, he fixed his focus on Brixton's back while the man fussed in his breast pocket, fishing up a master keycard.

"That's not a bad outlook," Malcolm murmured. "Sometimes your ice queen act can be useful."

"Why are you under the impression that my behavior is an act?"

Malcolm sighed. "Wishful thinking, I suppose," he said, then cut off, stepping forward quickly and raising his voice. "Stop. Don't move."

Brixton froze, tossing a sharp, annoyed look back at him. "Excuse me?"

"You're about to walk on evidence." Malcolm caught up in three quick strides and brushed past Brixton to nod down at the polished marble floor under his feet. "Look."

Brixton looked down. Just at his toe-tips was a rusty spatter of blood: small, but in a distinctive arcing pattern of trailing, ever-smaller droplets that said a finite amount had fallen from someone's person, likely from their hand as they fled. A secondary blood smear in the shape of fingertips, on the wall outside a room door marked with *1408*, corresponded.

Brixton went pale, his fingers tightening on the key-card. "O-oh."

Malcolm crooked a finger to Seong-Jae. "Come look at this."

Seong-Jae drifted to his shoulder, a hovering blackbird looking down at the blood spatter, then sank down into a crouch, cocking his head and staring keenly down at the blood stains. "Perpetrator's or victim's?"

"Likely victim's," Malcolm said. "But I won't know until I get a look at the crime scene. Brixton?"

Brixton shook himself, working his lips in a sad little stammer. Malcolm had a feeling he'd not even gone inside the room. Just the sight of blood had knocked all that hauteur out of him, and Malcolm sighed. Goddammit, he hated feeling sorry for the annoying little asshole, but he was a fucking civ and civs never really understood how *real* things could get until the blood was right there and a body was staring at them.

A little perspective changed their attitudes real fast.

In his own way, he wished they never had to learn that perspective. He'd rather have Brixton snotty and offended than traumatized and dreaming for the rest of his life of the blood spatter surrounding a dead, waxy, stiff-pale body.

"I...o-oh, yes," Brixton blurted. "The room."

He stared down at the blood spatters for a moment longer, then skittered to one side, giving them a wide berth. From the side of the door he leaned over, stretching to reach, and fit his key card in the slot. It flashed green, the latch unlocked, and he gave the door a ginger little push with his fingertips before casting Malcolm an uncertain look.

"I...I will wait here. I'm sure you wouldn't want me contaminating your crime scene."

Malcolm nodded briefly. "That might be best," he said, and nothing else. Let the man hold on to his pride. It was the safest, gentlest option he could offer, right now.

But there was nothing safe or gentle about the scene that unfolded as the room door swung open.

Red everywhere. An explosion of red, and for a moment Malcolm saw an ocean of blood scattered across the floor before his vision resolved and he picked out the finer details.

Rose petals.

Rose petals all across the floor, the bed, the tables, the chairs, even the windowsills, scattered about in a floral massacre of red. A disarrayed trail ran through them, as if someone had kicked them aside—or as if something had been dragged toward the bed.

The bed where a motionless man lay face-down on sumptuous sheets of white satin, their subtle gilded sheen turned dull by the drying, crusting blood soaked into the threads. His face was obscured, buried against the sheets, nothing but a shock of swooping brown hair. Even from the doorway Malcolm could tell his suit was expensive, likely at least a few thousand dollars from the crisp cut of the fabric and the texture of the wool, and Malcolm filed that little detail away as he stepped inside, moving carefully so as not to disturb too much.

Room service cart. Champagne floating in a steel bucket half-filled with water, glass sweating. No condensation down the side of the steel, but wet spots soaked into the paper doily underneath. Note card folded against the bucket, untouched. A few more roses in a vase. Covered dishes for two. A faint aroma of…was that lobster?

He stepped in further, then glanced back, tossing his head to Seong-Jae. Seong-Jae followed him inside on ginger steps, his hands in the pockets of his coat. He scanned the room, black eyes flicking back and forth as if recording data in an ever-processing stream, before he brushed past Malcolm and stopped at the edge of the bed, leaning over to study the body.

"Malcolm," he murmured.

Malcolm followed him, tracking his gaze not to the bed, but to just beyond the foot of it. Half buried in rose petals, the gleam of silver. He rounded the bed, then crouched down, eyeing the long, triangular knife resting on the floor, its wooden handle carved with grips. Blood crusted all along the point, halfway up the blade, farther along the edge, congealed in splatters like jelly. Cutting weapon, but from the blood pattern it had likely been used for stabbing.

"Murder weapon?" he murmured.

"Likely," Seong-Jae answered.

"That looks like a kitchen knife."

"I believe that *is* a kitchen knife."

Malcolm glanced over his shoulder at the room service cart. "Do we want a member of the staff for this?"

"It would depend on motive."

"Which we, right now, do not have." Malcolm sighed, pushing himself to his feet and reaching into his pocket for his gloves. "We don't even have a name. I—fuck." He came up empty, no gloves in his pocket. "I forgot—"

Smoothly, Seong-Jae produced a pair of clear vinyl gloves from his coat pocket and offered them.

Malcolm blinked, then took the gloves. "Thank you."

"You need only ask."

Snapping on the gloves, Malcolm fought the urge to roll his eyes. "That's better than 'as you say.'"

"Pardon?"

"Nothing."

Malcolm circled to the edge of the bed again, bracing his gloved hand to the bedsheets so he could lean over to get a better look. A rip in the back of the suit offered glimpses of blood congealed against flesh underneath, past the shreds of a blood-soaked shirt—and showed the source of all the crimson soaked across the bed. A gash, the cut fairly neat. No chance he was still alive and just unconscious from blood loss, not with a hole in him like that. Malcolm delicately lifted the hem of the victim's coat. One back pocket was raised, and he slipped his fingertips in to retrieve the victim's wallet.

"Let's see who this is." He flipped the wallet open, scanning the ID. An overconfident smirk full of white veneers looked back at him, below a swoosh of brown hair with a white streak so deliberate it had to be bleached. That white streak tugged at his memory, as did the name on the ID. "Marion Garvey. That name rings a bell."

Seong-Jae withdrew his phone from his pocket, thumb tapping lightly, swiftly, before he said, "Google states that he is a night club owner in downtown Baltimore."

Malcolm frowned, then groaned. "...fuck. I remember him now. I ran into him a few times during a stint on narcotics, years back, before transferring to homicide." He eyed the corpse. "High roller. He keeps his clubs legal, but tries to slip a few loopholes now and then. Claims it's for tax purposes, but really he's just trying to put more money in his pocket. I've had to bust him a few times for deals happening on his properties, but he always wiggles out of it." He flipped the wallet closed and slipped it back into place in the victim's pocket. He liked the crime scene completely intact for his initial assessment, down to the smallest details. "Not this time, I guess. He's an obnoxious jackass. Oily. Constantly circling between a superiority complex, inferiority complex, and just plain textbook narcissism. One of those 'bootstraps' types who wouldn't know bootstraps if he was strangled with them." He frowned. "That would be more ironic if he actually *was* strangled."

Seong-Jae lifted his head from his phone, but his gaze fixed on Malcolm, not the body. "That is an interesting habit you have."

"What?"

"Referring to the victims in the present tense even while handling their dead bodies."

Black irritation flashed through Malcolm. He growled. "If you don't stop psychoanalyzing me, you can take the fucking bus back to the office."

"I would prefer a taxicab," Seong-Jae retorted mildly.

"You are deliberately fucking missing the point." Malcolm flipped him off. "Asshole."

"You are rather on edge today, Malcolm."

"I fucking wonder why." Malcolm shifted to gingerly turn the corpse's head, gripping the back of his skull. The neck moved stiffly, already locked in rigor, but he managed to turn it enough to confirm that the victim was, in fact, Garvey and not someone with Garvey's wallet in his back pocket. Same smug face, even frozen in shock and locked in the waxy white rigidity of death, with that perfectly cultivated five o'clock shadow that Malcolm had always secretly thought Garvey sprayed on daily. "Glove up and help me lift him."

"Should we disturb the body before forensics has a

chance to photograph him?"

"I want to confirm something." He pointed to the wound in the victim's back, circling it in the air with his fingertip without touching. "Look. This is an exit wound, not an entry wound. It's too small for the amount of blood. But it matches the width of the kitchen knife around the depth it would reach if plunged fully into his chest."

Seong-Jae snapped on a pair of gloves, then edged past Malcolm and gripped one of the victim's wrists, lifting his arm and exposing his palm. Slashes, crusted over with dried blood, cut across his palm in erratic overlaps. "Here," he said. "Defensive wounds."

"So he was stabbed from the front. The killer slashed at him first, he held up his arms to defend, and that was when the killer stabbed him in the chest from the front."

"But did he fall onto the bed on his own, or was he placed there?"

Malcolm straightened, scanning the room, biting at the inside of his cheek as he tried to reconstruct the scene in his head. The roses, scattered everywhere. Disarrayed in a burst by a fall. "Placed," he said. "In a hurry."

He stepped back, gesturing to the floor at their feet. "Look. The carpet is soaked here, but not so much as the sheets. He was stabbed..." He followed that track through the rose petals, some crushed, back to the room service cart. "...here. By the champagne. He turned to face his attacker, held up his hands, then the big plunge."

He could picture it in his head, and he searched until he found what he was looking for: the blood splatter against the wall, just behind the cart and over a bureau. So Garvey had been standing there, and then…

"He falls forward. The attacker catches him. Maybe stumbles, looks like the body could've hit here—" He gestured toward a bare patch in the rose petals. "—then lifted up again. Most of the initial blood flow soaks into the attacker's clothing. Some drips as he's dragged to the bed." He backed up, following that track backwards. "The killer's movements are hasty, and between that and the victim's dragging feet we've got a clear path through the petals, to the bed. A few drops on the way there." The backs of his calves hit the edge of the bed. "The perpetrator hits the bed, hauls him over, dumps him face-down, dropped almost vertically from above. Look at the wrinkle pattern in the sheets. If he'd fallen face-forward they'd be more skewed from an angled approach."

Seong-Jae folded his arms over his chest. "So we are looking for someone with enough upper body strength to drag a corpse, who managed to escape the hotel in bloodied clothing, leaving the murder weapon. Someone who now has evidence to dispose of."

"If they even left the hotel." Malcolm shook his head. There was something…off, here. He couldn't put his finger on it. "Might've been a guest. We'll need to review the security tapes. And get prints off that knife."

"A member of the hotel staff might have worn gloves."

"But we don't know if we're dealing with staff." Malcolm turned back, eyeing Garvey. Fuck, this was going to be a pain in the ass to figure out. He could think of a good dozen people off the top of his head who would have a reason to kill Garvey, and the means to do so. But they wouldn't be this...*sloppy*. "This isn't premeditated. So we might get a good print off the handle. Crime of passion, frantic escape, no time to wipe the murder weapon. The blood smear on the wall outside, too. Might have retained a residual print." He glanced at the body. "Skip lifting him. We'll let forensics handle that. We can inspect the body on the autopsy table if need be."

Seong-Jae inclined his head, considering, but he seemed distracted. His gaze scanned the room, before he settled on the victim once more. He cocked his head, studying Garvey, then leaned over and plucked something from his coat pocket. A jewelry box, black velvet, small and square and rimmed in gold. He flipped it open, before arching a brow.

"Malcolm."

Malcolm leaned in, peering over the lid, then whistled softly. A diamond ring nestled against the black velvet bedding. The ring had to be a solid fifty carats, framed by multiple smaller diamonds in a gleaming platinum setting. The killer hadn't even tried to take it, that he could tell. They probably hadn't even known he'd had it, so the killing couldn't have been motivated by financial gain.

"That's a serious rock," he murmured.

Seong-Jae frowned, eyes narrowing as he cast a searching look about the room again. "Is this a honeymoon suite?"

"Think so. We'll have to confirm it with the manager, but..." Malcolm folded his arms, stepping back to take in the room once more—big picture instead of smaller details. "So he set up a proposal. The roses, the champagne. He'd wanted to propose, then spend the night together to celebrate."

"But with whom?"

"That's the question, isn't it?" Malcolm said. "Whomever it was, they either didn't show, or found him and left without reporting it. If they didn't show, I have to wonder if they knew in advance."

"Or they are the perpetrator."

"I'm trying not to draw too many conclusions at this stage." He pulled off one glove so he could rake the few loose strands of hair that had escaped their tail back from his face. "Something about this scene feels messy. Wrong."

"It does somehow feel...incomplete," Seong-Jae agreed, carefully placing the ring box back into the victim's pocket.

"So where do we start?"

Seong-Jae said nothing at first, cocking his head left to right in that way that made Malcolm think of a bright-eyed, sharply intelligent crow, all gleaming black feathers and razor edges, before he crossed the room to the room service cart. He flipped the card leaning against it over. A name was scrawled on it in looping letters.

"We could start," he said, "by finding out who Lillienne is."

"That's not a name you forget easily." Malcolm pulled his other glove off and tossed his head toward the door. "Which means the best person we can ask? Is our good friend Brixton."

[3: CONSTANT CRAVING]

SEONG-JAE HAD WANTED TO STAY at the crime scene for a little while longer.

Malcolm didn't seem inclined to stay in one place for more than five minutes, and had nearly paced out of his skin while waiting for forensics and the team of uniformed officers to arrive.

The man's restlessness was almost infectious, crawling under Seong-Jae's skin until he was hard-pressed to keep from snapping. He didn't know what was bothering Malcolm, but if it interfered with Seong-Jae's ability to do his job they just might have to have *words*.

But for now he bit his tongue, eyeing the balcony of the suite, the blinds drawn back on bright midmorning light, before he turned and followed Malcolm from the room.

He always seemed to be *following* Malcolm.

But he had to admit that at least Malcolm was familiar with the city, while to Seong-Jae Baltimore was still a place of alien colors and spoken accents that dragged in ways that sometimes ate at his nerves. At least people here were more straightforward and businesslike than the more relaxed

[34]

denizens of the West Coast, though he would admit that he often found the feeling of Baltimore's close, clustered city streets rather oppressive after the more urban sprawl of Los Angeles. There was a certain *dryness* to Baltimore, an arid feeling of concrete and cityscapes.

He would adapt, he supposed.

He always did.

Brixton paced in the hallway outside, making a marked path around the blood spatters on the floor. Malcolm tossed Seong-Jae a significant look, then nodded toward Brixton as he fished his phone from his pocket and lifted it to his ear. The signal wasn't hard to interpret:

Malcolm wanted Seong-Jae to use his particular methods to extract necessary information from the already-nervous man, because it would likely be more effective than Malcolm's particular hard-edged patience.

Seong-Jae sighed.

He really rather wasn't overly fond of human interaction.

They were much easier to deal with when they were dead.

But Malcolm was already on the phone, Seong-Jae would assume to forensics with the mention of Stenson's name, Malcolm's gaze glazing over into distant clouded slate blue skies as he moved a few steps down the hall, broad shoulders tight against his suit coat. He glanced back at Seong-Jae once, lifting his bushy brows, that long scar over his left eye quirking. Seong-Jae closed his eyes, pinching the bridge of his nose with a sigh.

Fine.

But they were going to have a *talk*, once this was over.

He opened his eyes and pivoted toward Brixton. The man froze as Seong-Jae's gaze landed on him, as if Seong-Jae had pinned him like a butterfly to a board. He stared at Seong-Jae with his eyes wide and glazed, his hands fretting together.

"Well?" Brixton asked. Gone was the officious, snooty man who'd led them inside. "You'll take the body away soon, won't you?"

"That is not our decision."

Brixton looked horrified, his face seeming to stretch to accommodate his widening eyes. "Whose decision *is* it?"

"The forensics team. I believe, if my colleague's phone conversation is any indication, that they are on their way."

With a frown, Brixton folded his arms over his chest, huffing, trying to wrap himself in the cloak of his shattered dignity. "I cannot have this interrupting my business operations. You must end it quickly."

"An investigation takes as long as may be required. If you rush the procedure, there may be mistakes that delay the process." Seong-Jae cocked his head. "Who is Lillienne?"

Brixton jerked as if he'd been slapped, darted a glance at Seong-Jae, then immediately looked away. "I've no clue," he said stiffly, drawing himself up. "You'll have to excuse me if I don't memorize the names of all our guests."

"I find that very difficult to believe," Seong-Jae said.

"You operate the type of establishment that provides highly personalized service to important personages. I imagine that you not only memorize your current guest roster, but also require your employees to as well. Correct me if I am mistaken."

"Why does it matter?" Brixton snapped.

"Because you know who Lillienne is, and you are lying to me." Seong-Jae took a step closer. "Do you know the charges for lying to an officer of the law and obstructing an investigation?"

A scowl darkened Brixton's features. "You don't have a warrant, and I have a right to protect the privacy of my guests."

"So you admit that Lillienne is a guest here."

Brixton opened his mouth, froze, then snapped his lips shut with a glare. "I admit nothing."

"Then perhaps while you are admitting nothing, you would like to give us access to the security footage for the last twenty-four hours."

For a moment Brixton looked as though he would argue. Seong-Jae could practically follow the thoughts flittering behind his eyes, the debate, before he settled on the lesser of two evils.

"If you *must*," Brixton said tightly.

Interesting. And likely an indication that Brixton was, in fact, hiding something. Perhaps even protecting someone, that he had chosen to accept giving up the security tapes to avoid yielding information on this Lillienne.

Why was he so eager to protect her, then?

Did he know more of the murder than he let on? Was he even now feigning his distress, that film of sweat above his upper lip, the agitated jerking of his pupils?

No, Seong-Jae thought. He wasn't feigning upset, too pale and clammy to be pantomimed, but he was most certainly nervous for reasons other than the dead body in the suite. The longer Seong-Jae watched him without speaking, the more uncomfortable Brixton grew, shifting from foot to foot and twitching his shoulders.

Seong-Jae let the silence stretch onward, punctuated only by the quiet sound of Malcolm's voice in the background, that low rumble that had become so familiar it was almost soothing, a physical texture like touching sandpaper and raw velvet. Seong-Jae tilted his head, listening for a moment, caught a few mentions of *diamond* and *bag and tag* and *murder weapon, prints* before he drifted his attention back to Brixton, who was darting his gaze left, right, anywhere but at Seong-Jae.

"The footage, then," Seong-Jae said softly, and was rewarded by an agitated jerk of Brixton's shoulders.

"Yes. The footage," he repeated, an odd shrill edge to his voice, before he bobbed his head and turned to march toward the elevator. "This way, if you please, *gentlemen*."

Seong-Jae closed his eyes, exhaling slowly, then opened them again.

Humans.

Malcolm hung up his phone and drifted to stand next to Seong-Jae, his gaze following Brixton. "He spill on Lillienne?" he murmured.

"Not yet. But he is concealing something about her identity."

Malcolm arched a brow. "So why is he walking away?"

"Because," Seong-Jae said, "we are going to view the security footage."

"That sounds exciting."

"It is part of our job."

"Thanks for informing me of that, Lieutenant Detective."

Seong-Jae's hands curled into fists inside his pockets. "I was not attempting to, as you would put it, 'pull rank.'"

"No?" Malcolm shrugged, but that tightness in his shoulders was back. The old wolf had his hackles raised, and there as an unspoken growl of warning in everything he did, everything he said. "That's fine, then."

This was why Seong-Jae hated dealing with people.

Particularly when that person was his irascible, snarling jot of a partner.

And especially when one of the most frustrating things about Malcolm was how hard he was to read. He gave off so many surface signals that he seemed entirely transparent, and yet there was something always hidden behind the shadowed blue of his eyes, something veiled, his snarl and apparent grouchiness a façade.

Seong-Jae was getting tired of trying to figure out what it was a front *for*, so he could work out the pattern of Malcolm Khalaji and how best to work with it—and around it.

But whatever retort rose to his tongue was cut off, as Brixton stepped inside the service elevator and beckoned impatiently, his hauteur seeming to return the farther removed he was from the body. "If you will *please*, gentlemen."

Malcolm swept forward without another word, leaving Seong-Jae standing in the hallway, watching his tight, loping strides, the wisps of hair that fell loose from its knot drifting around his face and shoulders.

Jot, he thought to himself, then straightened his coat and followed Malcolm into the elevator.

THE RIDE BACK DOWN TO the lobby was marked by silence and tension. Seong-Jae leaned his shoulder against the wall and tried to ignore Brixton's stiff, sweating stillness and Malcolm's radiating hostility, but both in such a small enclosed space were nearly enough to choke him. He closed his eyes and counted until the elevator stopped, and had hit eighty-four by the time the chime dinged and the door slid open.

He followed Brixton and Malcolm out into the lobby. Another detour through the waves of haute couture sailing through the lobby on marginally human legs, and then Brixton was leading them through another service area far dingier and dirtier than the customer-facing areas of the hotel, into an office cluttered with so much paperwork it was hard to even find the desk buried somewhere underneath it.

An entire wall was taken up with a shelf full of DVD cases. Brixton bustled around the desk and to the shelf, running his fingers along the spines of the cases. "We pull the DVDs every morning," he explained. "The security guards record via the CCTV computer banks, and change out the burnable DVDs every twenty-four hours."

"So you think the murder occurred last night?" Seong-Jae asked.

Just the words *the murder* made Brixton flinch. "I don't know." He pulled down one DVD case and flipped it open, his gaze tracking back and forth over the handwritten liner inside. "I only know that the tape swap was at nine AM, and the housekeeper had already come screaming down the elevator by eight thirty AM."

Seong-Jae frowned. "And who was the one who found the body?"

Brixton tilted his head back. "Ah…" His mouth thinned into a thoughtful line, before he snapped his fingers. "Kiara. Kiara Jacobs."

"Where is Miss Jacobs now?" Seong-Jae prodded.

"Obviously I let her go home for the day, with full pay." Brixton made an offended sound. "I'm not *heartless*. She was quite traumatized, poor girl."

Malcolm's brows drew together. "We'll need her address and phone number." He nodded toward the DVD. "The security footage?"

"Ah. Yes." Brixton fumbled the DVD out with shaking hands and inserted it into the optical drive of the laptop buried among the clutter covering his desk. He beckoned to them imperiously with two fingers. "Come."

Seong-Jae glanced at Malcolm. Malcolm looked back at him. They both raised their brows, before moving together to circle the desk and stand behind Brixton's chair as the man settled into the rolling leather seat. He pulled up the contents of the DVD drive, and selected one marked *FL14CAMB.MOV*. "This one gives the clearest view of the room."

He double-clicked it. It opened into a media player, and he set it to play in fast-forward, people zipping up and down the hallway at triple-time. Strangers came in and out of rooms. Housekeepers pushed carts up and down. Vacuums ran over the hall. Not long after nine PM, the victim's room was the subject of a great deal of activity, people entering with bouquet after bouquet of roses and leaving empty-handed, all of them in uniform shirts from the same flower shop. Then a bellhop in full dress uniform, wheeling a cart with champagne and two covered trays.

Seong-Jae tensed, though, when he caught sight of the victim. The timestamp said it was just after ten PM when he came swaggering down the hall. A slight hitch and reel to his step indicated he was somewhat but not overly intoxicated. He used his keycard to open the door of the room, and vanished inside. The DVD zoomed forward.

And then went blank, the screen turning a flat dull gray while the timestamps continued ticking forward.

Seong-Jae had unconsciously leaned in, but now he straightened, exchanging another look with Malcolm before asking, "Why is this section blank?"

"I…I don't know." Brixton fretted his hands together. "There must have been some kind of problem with the DVD."

Malcolm made a skeptical sound. "Right at the approximate time of the murder."

The video skipped, the gray flickering—before the image resolved once more. The door to the victim's suite was open now, that fingerprint-shaped smear of blood on the wall, spatter on the floor.

"Look," Seong-Jae said. "It is working again."

A moment later, a woman came backing out of the room, her hands clutched over her mouth, her eyes wide and streaming with tears. Malcolm leaned in sharply.

"Slow it down," he snapped.

Brixton fumbled to obey. A click and the video playback slowed to normal speed. The woman stood just in the hallway, her hands clasped over her mouth. The image was in black and white, but it wasn't hard to figure out what the dark smears on her fingers and the lush white fur of her coat were; wasn't hard to project red onto the smudges of gray. She was a tall, lean woman with a tumble of dark hair falling down her shoulders and back, her face aquiline with haughty brows and lips that had been shaped by hand into perfect, precise bows. Her chin was stubborn, her hands angular.

And after staring into the room for long moments she turned and scurried away, her coat trailing behind her, her gaze darting fearfully over her shoulder as she strode down the hall and off camera.

"Who is that?" Malcolm demanded. "Is that Lillienne?"

Brixton said nothing. He only stared at the screen, his face ashen, his mouth a tight line. His thin little moustache quivered.

"Interesting," Seong-Jae said. "You would not reveal her identity to me, but the fact that you were willing to allow us to review the security footage says that you did not expect us to see her on the video." He folded his arms. "So you likely arranged to have a specific portion of the footage wiped during the time when she entered and left the room."

Brixton's shoulders jerked. His head hung for a moment—a guilty tell, but still he remained mutinously silent, only clicking the pause button on the video, leaving the image frozen with the wall smeared with blood in streaks that could very well match the shape of slim, delicate, feminine fingertips.

"Were you aiding and abetting a murder, Brixton?" Malcolm growled. "How much did she pay you?"

"And who is she?" Seong-Jae added.

Malcolm let out an almost jovial snort. "That information would be useful, yeah." He jerked his chin at Seong-Jae, but his drilling, hard eyes never left an increasingly small, hunched Brixton. "I know my partner here already warned you about charges for obstructing an investigation. What do you know about the charges for aiding and abetting, Seong-Jae?"

"I am rather certain that Mr. Brixton would not fare well in a maximum security prison."

Malcolm spread his hands as if that were the most reasonable thing in the world. "So really, we're looking out for your well-being. Prison's a rough place. Hate to see anything happen to you in there." He let his hands drop, that jovial air disappearing to leave only cool, steady calm, grim iron certainty. "You tell us what's really going on, though, and maybe we've got grounds to just look right past all of this."

"All right, all *right!*" Brixton almost shrieked, before letting out an irritable sound and dragging his hands over his face, scrubbing against his cheeks. "The two of you are bullies of the worst kind, are you aware of that?"

"Are we?" Malcolm tossed Seong-Jae a mild glance. "Am I a bully, Seong-Jae?"

"You have your moments."

"I'll take that as a compliment."

But for a moment Malcolm lingered on Seong-Jae, and something unreadable flickered in his eyes. Something almost like question; something almost like warmth; something almost like neither, strange and impossible to decipher.

Then Malcolm turned his gaze away, focusing on Brixton.

"Come on, Brixton. Talk to me. Who is she, and why is there a fifteen-minute chunk of security footage missing?"

Brixton made an irritable sound. "Because *she*, detective, is Lillienne Wellington, the daughter of Maximilian Wellington, owner of this hotel and the entire Wellington empire of which the Madame is heir to."

Malcolm whistled under his breath. Seong-Jae arched a brow.

That certainly changed things.

"Then what," Seong-Jae asked, "was she doing in the suite with Marion Garvey?"

"Engaging in her private business," Brixton snapped. "And as the general manager of this hotel, part of my job is making sure that the Madame's business *stays* private."

"So you make arrangements when she's fooling around with Garvey, and have the guards shut off the recording for that floor in the windows she asks for," Malcolm concluded, then nodded at the laptop. "Do you have any other cameras with an angle on that room?"

"Yes, but…" That little curled moustache twitched. "They were also temporarily out of service at the time."

"Of course they were." Flat, weary cynicism darkened Malcolm's gaze, his voice. "Show me where she went next. Does she stay here in the hotel?"

"She occupies the penthouse suite at her leisure." Brixton scrolled through the folder of video files, then opened another marked *PHCF.MOV*. A steady image of the lushly appointed door to a suite, the only door in a small entry area outside an elevator, appeared. "We don't have cameras inside the penthouse, per orders of the Wellington family."

"Fast forward," Malcolm ordered.

Brixton clicked to increase the playback speed. Seong-Jae kept his gaze on the ticking numbers in the lower right, watching for the timestamp to match up to the moment the woman had fled the scene of the crime. A few minutes after the timestamp passed she came tumbling out of the elevator, her face streaked in tears and mascara, her hands still dipped in blood and her coat still filthy.

Brixton slowed the playback to normal speed without being asked. Together they watched as the woman scurried to the door of the penthouse suite, still looking over her shoulder as if afraid she was being followed, before fumbling with a keycard, smearing blood all over it, the key plate, the doorknob, and the white lacquer of the door. She hunched, her lips moving soundlessly as if begging, then finally got the card to work, the reader flashing. She burst into the suite, and there was one last glimpse of her squirming desperately out of the bloodied coat before the door shut.

"Is she still in her suite?" Seong-Jae asked.

"No." Brixton shook his head. "She always informs us when she leaves. The valet called a private car for her at seven thirty this morning. She seemed perfectly composed when she departed."

He sounded almost puzzled, as if he couldn't conceive how the woman on the camera, shaking and frightened, could be the same woman he'd seen this morning. But he fast-forwarded the tape again, until the timestamp rolled forward several hours, the light from the windows changing, the shadows moving in arcs. Lillienne Wellington emerged in a complete change of clothing, including a high-collared trench and dramatically large sunglasses. She carried a garbage bag tucked under her arm, puffy and bulging with something inside, something soft enough to compress in the shape of her arm, clamping it against her side.

Likely the bloody coat, Seong-Jae thought.

She looked about furtively, latching the door behind her, then scurried off-camera and to the elevator. "Here," Brixton said, closing the player and then opening another video on a view of the lobby. Brixton himself was on the video, standing officiously behind a wide standing desk of curving, polished oak.

Lillienne emerged from the elevator and into the lobby. Quickly she skittered across the lobby, pausing to speak to

Brixton, whose smile and ingratiating gestures made it fairly easy to work out the conversation despite the silent playback. On the video Brixton picked up a desk phone, spoke into it briefly, then said something else to Lillienne, at which point she nodded fervently and went stalking out of the lobby through the front doors, hair bouncing behind her in a luxuriant trail.

"So that's perfect composure?" Malcolm asked dubiously.

"The Madame has always been a touch...high-strung, particularly on days when she made arrangements for her privacy," Brixton said. "I saw nothing out of the ordinary."

"Not even the fucking trash bag under her arm."

Brixton sniffed. "Part of my job is learning to mind my own business."

"And part of our job is figuring out that business," Malcolm said. "Where would she go? Does she have a residence off-site?"

"She is known to stay at the Wellington family home in Chinquapin Park."

"If," Seong-Jae said, "you could supply us with the address?"

Brixton made that rather officious face again. "I absolutely will not violate the Madame's privacy so flagrantly!"

"You really need to get your priorities together. The *Madame* may be a murderer." Malcolm reached inside his suit coat for his phone, then returned for another delving moment before he emerged with a small USB charging cable. He fit the micro-USB end to the charge port on his phone, then thrust it at Brixton. "Forget the address. I want all the security DVDs for the last three days. Physical copies. But for now, copy the contents of that one to my phone. Don't skip a single video."

Brixton's eyes widened. "That's nearly ten gigabytes of data."

"And my phone is practically a palm-sized computer. Just do it. Use the SD card." Malcolm left his phone in Brixton's fumbling hands and glanced at Seong-Jae, though his attention seemed mostly on Brixton. "Google the Wellington residence in Chinquapin. It's like trying to find the White House. The richest family in Baltimore isn't hard to track down."

For a moment, something inside Seong-Jae bristled in mute rebellion. Something about Malcolm's sharp, impatient tone, something about the way the man was already turning away from him as if assuming his obedience. He grit his teeth, biting back a retort. It wasn't an unreasonable request. It was part of their job.

It was just getting under his skin because Malcolm was being such a jot today, for no good reason at all.

So Seong-Jae bit back his protests. All he said was, "As you say."

If only because he knew it irritated Malcolm no end.

Before he turned away, already withdrawing his phone from his coat and pulling up a new Google search.

There was a faint growl at his back, nothing more.

Jot, he mouthed, before entering in the search.

[4: CAN'T YOU SEE, CAN'T YOU SEE]

MALCOLM ONLY WAITED LONG ENOUGH for Brixton to copy the files—watching him the entire time to make sure he didn't skip anything to protect the *Madame*—before he was out the door and heading for the service stairs. He'd taken the elevator to keep Brixton calm, but right now he didn't want to be trapped in a moving metal box.

Especially not when it would be a small, enclosed space with only him and Seong-Jae.

Seong-Jae who kept giving him strange looks, while Malcolm was trying to avoid looking at him at all.

Seong-Jae who was currently a shadow at his back, hovering a little too close, almost stepping on Malcolm's heels with only a single stride between them.

They emerged into the lobby just as the forensics team was bullying their way past a few valets and bellboys, Sten and her crew armed with badges, equipment bags, and a stretcher while various guests milled around, staring and whispering and snapping photos on their phones. Brixton would probably be down here in thirty seconds or less having an aneurysm, but that wasn't Malcolm's problem. Stenson could handle him, probably better than Malcolm had, and he needed to get moving.

"Witness or Wellington first?" Seong-Jae said at his shoulder, as they spilled out onto the sidewalk.

"Let's see what we can squeeze Wellington for first." Malcolm fished his keys from his pocket. "This might be an easy confession. We might not even need the witness."

"Is it ever an easy confession?" Seong-Jae asked dryly.

"No," Malcolm admitted, then sighed. "But let's get the obvious avenues out of the way." He strode toward the Camaro. "Otherwise we're going to have to go chasing down some pretty dark alleyways into Marion Garvey's world."

He let them into the car, then leaned over and peered at the address Seong-Jae offered on the screen of his HTC before tapping it into the GPS and pulling out into traffic. Seong-Jae settled in that lazy sprawl in the seat, elbow propped on the window frame, knuckles curled against his temples, dark gaze fixed out the window. Then,

"She seemed very distraught," he murmured.

"Most people are, after flying off the handle and murdering someone in a fit of passion." But after a moment Malcolm sighed, relenting and glancing at Seong-Jae sidelong. "You aren't feeling her for this, are you?"

Seong-Jae shook his head minutely. He was like that, Malcolm thought. All small things and subtleties, speaking volumes in the slightest motion—until he was all extremes

[53]

and unexpectedness, and Malcolm never knew what he would do next.

He didn't like things he couldn't predict.

"No," Seong-Jae said. "I would surmise she arrived for the meeting with Garvey, then discovered him dead and fled the scene without thinking."

"Probably." Malcolm shifted gears, heading for the turn-off that would take them toward Chinquapin Park. "But she fled the scene of a crime without notifying the police. Her coat is probably evidence, with all the blood on it—even if it's not enough blood to fit with the scenario. Something isn't adding up here, and it's not just being scared her rich Daddy will find out she's been fucking a sleaze like Garvey." He shrugged. His shoulders ached, and he realized just how much he'd been balling himself up into knots of tension and forced himself to relax. "So we've got to squeeze her until we get a better lead."

"Do you think she knows something?"

"Garvey had…connections." Malcolm pressed his lips together, searching for the right words. "It's one of those things you get used to once you've been around long enough. There are people who'd be happier if he was dead. She might have been around to overhear something that could have escalated into motivation for murder."

"I see," Seong-Jae said flatly, yet there was something unsaid on the end of it. Malcolm sighed.

"*What?*"

Seong-Jae arched a brow and slid a mild look toward him. "…I am uncertain as to what you are questioning."

"You're doing that—that *thing* again."

Seong-Jae blinked. "What thing?"

"Nevermind."

They were here—pulling up in front of a gated estate large enough to be a subdivision in and of itself, a massive marble-columned house surrounded by several other outbuildings spread across lush, carefully-tended grounds shaded by tall trees. He glanced over his shoulder, checking traffic, then reversed and eased half a block down. Paranoid suspicion didn't want his car anywhere near the gated security cameras. Not to mention if they drove in they would be expected to drive away—and if he could get the freedom to slip away and walk the grounds, it would be easier on foot rather than with them watching his car like a hawk.

He put the Camaro into park, then slid out of the driver's seat. "Just nevermind," he repeated. "Let's go."

He heard the slam of the car door behind him, and pressed his key fob in his pocket to activate the alarm.

"Malcolm," Seong-Jae called. Then the particular not-silent silence of his steps, catching up quickly, his voice closer, long fingers against Malcolm's arm. "*Malcolm.*"

Malcolm jerked back, pulling out of that grip before he even realized what he was doing. He didn't know what was wrong with him, but he suddenly didn't want those long, elegant fingers touching him, didn't want Seong-Jae looking at him with that odd flicker in his eyes, that crack in that stark, smooth black shell of dispassion that almost hinted there were feelings under that icy façade.

He couldn't deal with it right now.

He just couldn't.

"Don't," he bit off, and turned away, striding down the sidewalk.

"Malcolm?" drifted after him. "What did I *do?*"

Malcolm stopped in his tracks, closing his eyes, sighing. Fuck, this wasn't like him. None of it was like him, and he couldn't even say *why* he was lashing out like this.

Part of him wanted to say it was that kiss.

That kiss that still, after over a week, burned under his skin and ate at him, while Seong-Jae had already dismissed it as nothing as if he'd been *toying* with Malcolm.

But the kiss was only a part of it. A part of the million things weighing on him, a vicious pack of little mental rats tearing at him from all directions, and he couldn't even name one as the primary culprit when they spoke in a thousand voices, each trying to drown each other out. The accusatory, hollow voices of a half-dozen dead queer boys he hadn't been fast enough to save. The silent curse in Nathan McAllister's tired, broken stare. The hard cases always stuck to him, but this one…

This one was riding his back like Satan using him for his broken and whipped hobbyhorse. Malcolm couldn't handle it.

Any more than he could handle the memory of

Gabrielle's voice whispering through the phone, broken and on the verge of tears.

I'm not okay, Mal. I'm not okay and I don't know what to do about it.

Do you want me to come?

No—no. Don't. You have your life there, don't drop it...not for me...

Gabrielle...I'd do anything for you. You know that.

Yeah. He could hear her smile, even around her choked tears. *That's part of the problem.* Then a long pause, heavy and trembling, before she'd asked, *Would...I...would it upset you if I moved back to Baltimore? I feel like I ran away. I want to be home. Trying to be somewhere else feels like trying to be someone else, and that's just hiding.*

He hadn't had an answer.

Not then. Not now.

And he didn't have an answer for Seong-Jae, when Seong-Jae asked *what did I do?* with a sudden and raw honesty and uncertainty that cracked that icy mask in ways Malcolm had never wanted to. There was a part of him that wanted to know Seong-Jae, to understand what was behind that coldness, to at least be comfortable with him by picking up on his cues and unspoken things and those long, meaningful silences.

He didn't want to do it by punching holes in the goddamned man.

He sighed, glancing over his shoulder and tossing his

head. "C'mon. We'll talk later."

"Later?"

"When we're not standing on a suspect's doorstep." He forced a smile. "I'll treat you to dinner."

"If it is Swabbie's again, it does not qualify as a treat."

A bark of laughter came out before Malcolm could stop it. "Oh fuck you. What do I have to do to get you to admit you actually like the place?"

"There is little you could do to coerce me to lie, Malcolm," Seong-Jae said, but there was a faint glint in his eyes, and the tension in his shoulders eased. Malcolm grinned.

"You're lying if you say you don't like the fries. C'mon. Let's go find us a murder suspect."

Together they approached the tall, wrought-iron gate set into the brick fence ringing the property. A guard station was set to one side of the gate, and the man inside slouched in his seat, doing a crossword in red ink. He didn't even glance up as Malcolm and Seong-Jae drew close, just popping his gum and muttering out of the corner of his mouth.

"This is a gated property," he recited. "Unless the Wellingtons are expecting you I can't allow you in, and I already know I don't have any arrivals on the schedule today."

Malcolm sighed and glanced at Seong-Jae. Everyone had an attitude today. Malcolm fished his badge out and held it up.

The security guard didn't even look up.

Malcolm rapped his knuckles against the glass enclosing

the station, then pressed his badge against it. "Badge," he growled.

The guard glanced up, blinking owlishly, seeming to see them for the first time, before sighing and unclipping his walkie from his belt. "I'll call it in." He turned away as if he was having a private conversation in the middle of a glass-fronted booth on the sidewalk, muttering a few things into the crackling walkie, then listening, then muttering again before swinging his chair back around and eyeing them balefully. He hit a lever, and the gate started to creak open. "You can go in. You have half an hour."

Malcolm stared. "Permission and a time limit. Fuck me."

Seong-Jae slipped through the opening gate and beckoned to Malcolm. "I suppose they are accustomed to ordering their world," he said, his voice dropping to a low murmur as Malcolm caught up with him. "You seem to hold them in a great deal of contempt."

"I just can't connect." Malcolm tilted his head back as they set off down the long, winding drive, almost the full length of a city block; he fixed his gaze on the trees overhead, the way the diamond-shaped leaves turned into translucent green-gold spidered with veins as the sun shot through them in winking bursts. He shook his head, sighing. "People like them, the ultra-wealthy? They live in a wholly different world. It's a mindset I can't even begin to comprehend. They see everything through such a skewed lens."

"That sounds personal," Seong-Jae observed.

"It's not," Malcolm bit off.

Anything else he might have said was cut off as a man in a valet's uniform seemed to materialize out of the bushes, popping out from just behind the guard station before they'd made it more than a few steps down the drive. Malcolm jerked away from the motion in his peripheral vision, hand instinctively reaching inside his suit coat, before he stilled as he took in the thin, pallid man blinking at him with a bland and pleasant smile.

Seong-Jae's fingers brushed his shoulder, as if to say *calm*. Malcolm took a deep breath, dropping his hand from inside his coat and straightening.

Fucking *hell*, he was jumpy.

The valet smiled brightly. "Sir, I noticed you left your car on the curb. If you'd like me to bring it around—"

"I'll keep my keys, thanks," Malcolm growled.

"But—"

"Look. We're only allowed in for half an hour. By the time you get the car in, we'll be leaving. The damned thing can stay where it is." He eyed the valet balefully. "I'm serious. Don't touch my car. I haven't been to temple in weeks, and I'm not telling my chazzan I punched a valet in the face."

Then he turned and walked away, turning his back on the valet's dismayed, offended look.

For fuck's sake, Khalaji. Get yourself under control. You're taking your shit out on the goddamned hired help.

Seong-Jae fell into stride with him once more; despite his blank expression, there was no mistaking the amusement radiating off him. "I thought you were non-practicing," he said obliquely.

"If I don't show up to temple at least once a month, my father will guilt me into my grave."

"That sounds…pleasant."

"I work too much. It gives me a reminder to visit with my parents."

Malcolm glanced up—and caught Seong-Jae watching him rather than the path, head cocked inquisitively, gaze searching.

"Are you an only child, Malcolm?"

"Yeah. You?"

"Younger sister. She is still in high school."

"Back in L.A.?"

That inquisitive gaze shuttered, and Seong-Jae directed his gaze forward again. "Yes."

Malcolm smiled slightly. "She must be pissed at you right now."

"I imagine she will forgive me for moving in a year or so." That seemed it might be the end of it—but with one of his slow, considering sighs, Seong-Jae melted enough to add, "I have not often been present in her life because of the difference in our ages. By the time she was beginning to walk, I was already in university. I also traveled a good deal for the BAU."

[61]

"One day you'll have to tell me what that was like, working for the BAU."

"No," Seong-Jae murmured as they drew up on the broad, terraced marble steps fronting the palatial house, "I do not think I will."

Malcolm eyed him sidelong, then shook his head and pushed the doorbell. Less than five seconds later the broad front doors swung open grandly, with a flourish so elegant it had to be practiced. Malcolm fought the urge to roll his eyes as a tall man dressed in a butler's swallowtail, his gray-and-black hair swept back with a stark layer of wax and his moustache almost identical to Brixton's, came striding out with his arms spread, gripping either door as if he would spread his entire body as a barrier to entrance.

"Is there something I can do for you?" he demanded in a droning voice with a thick New England accent.

You could try not being such a fucking cartoon stereotype of yourself, Malcolm snarled mentally.

Fuck, this was bringing up too many memories.

He forced himself to impassivity, taking a page from Seong-Jae's book, and kept his voice as neutral as he could as he flashed his badge again. "BPD. We'd like to speak with Lillienne Wellington."

The butler somehow managed to pinch his nose without even touching it. It just narrowed on its own, nostrils sucking in. "Do you have a warrant?"

Malcolm stared at him flatly. "If you make me get one

when I already have probable cause, I'll tell her it's your fault we perp-walked her out of here in cuffs."

The butler fixed him with a disdainful look that bordered on pure loathing, then made a disgusted sound in the back of his throat. "One moment, please," he said icily.

Then slammed the double doors in their faces.

"You are relying rather strongly on intimidation tactics today," Seong-Jae said.

"Sometimes it's necessary."

"Is it?" Seong-Jae's reflection watched Malcolm thoughtfully from the doors' glass insets. "I cannot help but observe that it is very much unlike you."

"A week and a half, and you already know what's *like me?*"

Anything else either of them might have said was cut off by one of the double doors opening. The woman from the video stepped out, looking considerably calmer and more composed, pleasant and harmless in a modest and notably blood-free white sundress and a pair of sandals. Freckles stood out on her sun-browned shoulders. She looked between them quizzically, offering a polite smile.

"Excuse me?" she asked. "You requested my presence? May I help you, gentlemen?"

Malcolm considered her. No, she didn't have the look of someone who'd just committed murder and was trying to play it off for the cops—but she *did* have the careful, forced politeness of someone with something to hide, a façade that would likely crack with one light hit.

Right to the point, then.

"You can explain," he said, "why we have you on security footage fleeing the scene of a homicide."

She blinked, her lashes fluttering a little too falsely, but there was a delay in the disappearance and then puzzled reappearance of her smile. She was selecting reactions like she was selecting a shade of bronzer from her vanity, deciding what she'd put on or take off second to second. "I...I have no idea what you're talking about, sir," she said.

Seong-Jae cocked a brow. "I must say that your poker face leaves something to be desired, Miss Wellington."

She flicked her slightly too-wide eyes to Seong-Jae, before a transformation passed over her features. The mask fell away and suddenly they were looking not at the careful mask of curious innocence, but at the real Lillienne Wellington.

And the real Lillienne Wellington was afraid.

Her pupils jumped, her mouth creased at the corners, her brows crumpled, and she glanced over her shoulder furtively before leaning in close to them with a hiss.

"I cannot have this conversation here," she said tightly.

Malcolm shrugged. "Then we can have it down at the station."

She stared at Malcolm and retreated back a step. "You're arresting me?"

"We're asking you to come with us for a conversation.

It's not an arrest. Yet." He stepped back, sweeping a half-bow and extending his arm toward the steps and the drive. "Our car's waiting on the curb, if you wouldn't mind accompanying us."

Lillienne Wellington worked her lips helplessly, then glanced over her shoulder, where the butler hovered just on the edge of foyer, watchful and protective. She offered him a faint, almost wistful smile, then turned a more mistrustful look on Malcolm and Seong-Jae, before nodding. She lingered for a moment while the butler disappeared and reappeared seconds later with a white leather purse, pressing it into her hands. She tucked it under her arm and offered a shaky smile.

"I'd be happy to join you, gentlemen," she said, already sweeping past them and toward the steps. "And perhaps then we can clear this up."

Malcolm watched her for a few moments, then shot Seong-Jae a look and smiled thinly. "Less intimidating, then?"

Seong-Jae just fixed him with a long, almost disapproving stare, then shook his head and turned to follow Lillienne Wellington down the steps.

WELLINGTON WAS QUIET ON THE drive back to the station, sitting primly in the back of Malcolm's car with her hands folded in her lap, her gaze trained out the window, her charm school stare and smile fixed perfectly in place—but when Malcolm caught her eye in the rear view mirror, her subtle gasp and that faint tremor of her lashes gave her away.

She'd come with them willingly, yes.

But she was clearly terrified of what they would find out.

Though Malcolm still couldn't peg her for murder. Maybe he was relying too much on his intuition again, but it just wasn't coming together in his head. He wouldn't say she looked too soft for murder. People who looked soft often had hidden reserves that led them to do things no one ever expected they were capable of.

She just didn't have it in her to *hide* murder, he thought. She'd either be perfectly icy and composed, or falling apart and confessing at a single hard stare.

Instead she was jittery, trying so hard to maintain her calm, but too damned *obvious*.

She had it in her to hide secrets.

Not bodies.

And she was almost docile, as they arrived at the station and Malcolm guided her inside and upstairs with a light grip on her arm. She kept her hands clasped in front of her as if she was already cuffed, her head bowed, her hair falling forward to hide her face. Everything in her body language whispered guilt.

What are you guilty of, Lillienne?

He led her to an interrogation room and nudged her gently into a chair. Seong-Jae took up his usual position by the door, the vulture standing guard, watching as if circling a dying thing and waiting hungrily for its last gasp. Malcolm eyed him. Maybe Seong-Jae shouldn't be here for this, when Lillienne might crack under that sharp scrutiny and dissolve into a useless mess—but Malcolm couldn't do a suspect interview alone, he didn't feel like finding anyone else, and it wasn't as if he was much better himself right now.

He felt like he was all sharp edges, and he'd forgotten how to blunt himself.

But he tried, taking a deep breath and settling on the edge of the table, before reaching over to start the recording. "So you want to talk, Miss Wellington?"

Lillienne drew herself up, lifting her chin. "I have nothing to talk to you about."

That was interesting. Complete change in demeanor the moment they were on the official record. Malcolm folded his hands against his thigh. "You said we were going to have a conversation, so let's have a conversation. I'll start. Marion Garvey is dead."

She flinched. Her lips quivered, then tightened into a thin line, but she said nothing, only staring glassily straight ahead.

No. Not glassily.

That was a wet sheen in her eyes, gleaming bright.

Malcolm raised his brows. "You don't look surprised."

"Perhaps," Seong-Jae pointed out, "because she saw the dead body hours before we did."

Lightning crackled in her eyes, snapping her silence in a single strike. She flashed a furious gaze toward Seong-Jae. "Don't you dare," she bit off, her voice choking. "Don't…don't talk about him that way. 'The dead body.' He was a person."

Maybe having Seong-Jae here was useful, after all.

"So you admit to being at the scene," Seong-Jae pressed.

"I don't admit to anything!" she cried.

"No?" Malcolm asked, then spread his hands. "I've got to say, I'm liking you more and more for this."

Her gaze flew back to him, staring at him with a combination of incredulity and fury—but beneath it was pain, stark and true. "I didn't do anything! I loved Marion!"

That, Malcolm thought, was likely the first truly honest thing she'd said in the last half hour.

But he was going to have to break her and make her confess what she was hiding, if he wanted to rule her out for murder. Otherwise, she was all they had.

"Of course you did," he said. "Except you wouldn't be the first person to kill someone they loved in a crime of passion."

She shook her head, her eyes welling. "You think I'm strong enough to kill him? Especially like…like *that?*"

Seong-Jae made a thoughtful sound half under his breath. "Like what? We had not yet informed you of the nature of the murder."

"I *saw!*" she spat through quivering lips, the rasp of impending sobs in her voice. "I saw what that monster did to him! You honestly think I could stab someone all the way through? A man that size?"

"Hey, I'm equal opportunity. Anything a man can do, a woman can do just as well." Malcolm caught her eyes and held them. "Including putting a knife through a lover's chest."

Break, he begged her silently. *Break. I don't want to do this to you. You're hurting. You're afraid. Just give me what I need to rule you out.*

But all she said was, "I'm telling you, I didn't do it."

"We've got you on camera leaving the room. Not to mention the blood on your clothing." Malcolm retrieved his phone and thumbed through the videos Brixton had copied over, then pulled up the one from the night before and let it play. He slid it across the table to her. "Here. That's a very nice coat you've ruined."

She stared down at the phone, her eyes widening in horror as her gaze tracked the miniature of herself, her black-and-white doppelganger stumbling out of the room, blood everywhere.

"I...I..." She worked her lips helplessly, tears spilling down her cheeks, and she stared down at her hands in her lap as if she could still see the blood on them. "I...I walked in and saw him like...like..." She swallowed, gulping back a harsh sound. "I didn't kill anyone! You can look at the tapes and see

[69]

I just got there!"

"Actually, I can't." Malcolm leaned over and stopped the playback, frozen on her stiff form, her wide eyes staring through the door. "Because you told Brixton to shut the camera off on that floor for a fifteen-minute window. And I understand this was a standing agreement between the two of you."

He could see the moment hope deserted her. The moment she realized she was the only viable suspect at the moment, and the more she denied it the worse she looked. Her face fell, those welling tears beginning to bead, then drip, her shoulders slumping.

"I...don't..."

Malcolm pushed just a little harder. "So we've got you at the scene. We've got a premeditated attempt to conceal your arrival right before the murder." He paused, letting that sink in, then added, "And we've got the fact that you ran and didn't report the crime. Tell me again how that doesn't make you look guilty?"

She stared down at the phone screen, then looked away sharply, fixing her gaze on the far wall. Her brows knit, her mouth twisting up, and she sniffled furiously, scrubbing at her nose, then knotted her fingers together in her lap.

"I'm married," she muttered, nearly subvocally—then seemed to come to a decision. She lifted her head, glaring at them both defiantly, repeating herself clearly: "I'm married, all right?"

Suddenly it came together. The secrecy. The hidden trysts, taking place at the family hotel. The lies to protect someone, but not herself.

It still gave her motive.

But it gave them another potential suspect, too.

"So you were having an affair," Seong-Jae said.

Lillienne sighed, but then actually smiled, weak and tired and pained. "We were in love. I promise you, we were in love and I would *never* hurt him." She lifted her gleaming, liquid eyes to Malcolm, that smile struggling and trembling. "We were supposed to meet last night. I was going to tell him I'd finally decided to go through with the divorce. I was going to leave my husband to be with Marion. I'd had the lawyers draw the papers up and everything. I even left them for my husband to find, and went to meet Marion." Her smile faded, the trembling in her lips deepening and seeming to spread to her entire body. "I swear he was dead when I got there!"

"That's a convenient story to set your husband up for the crime," Malcolm said.

"Why would I do that?" she demanded. "What kind of horrible person do you think I am?" She shook her head, gaze darting between the two of them as if looking for mercy and not sure where to find it. "Don't you get it? My husband…my husband's a good man. He is. We're just…not in love anymore. I don't want to hurt him any more than I have to."

Malcolm said nothing. He thought silence might be best. Let her string herself out. Get it all on tape to analyze later.

[71]

He didn't think she was lying, not by a long shot, but he could only trust his gut so far.

And his gut wasn't admissible in court.

But it was Seong-Jae who broke the silence, driving home a single pointed question:

"What did you do with the bloody clothing?"

"I..." She cursed softly under her breath, then closed her eyes. "...I burned it."

Malcolm came close to swearing himself. "What in the— Why? Why would you do that if you aren't guilty?"

"I panicked!" she flared. "I knew you'd try to put this on me, and I panicked!" She wrung her hands together. "I'm not trying to set my husband up. It's not that I don't care about Paul, it's just that we want different things. That's all. That's all it had to be!" Her gaze begged him to believe her. "I would've left him a huge divorce settlement!"

Malcolm had to look away from her. Maybe he was being too soft. Maybe his head was on too goddamned sideways for this. She was sitting here basically incriminating herself, and for some reason he'd decided he didn't want her to be guilty, so he was looking for every reason for her not to be when it was staring him right in the face.

Was he really that far off his game right now?

Seong-Jae interjected with another of his soft, pointed questions. "Would have?"

"I..." Lillienne lowered her eyes. "I got the papers before he did. I destroyed them."

"Second choice is better than nothing, huh?" Malcolm bit off.

"Don't," Lillienne snapped back. "Don't you judge me." Offended pride made her shoulders stiff, and she drew herself up. "You don't know what it's like growing up the way I did. I had nannies and servants, and no one to be close to. I don't...I don't like being alone."

"What about your parents?" Malcolm asked.

"As if they saw me," she answered bitterly, shrugging. "All they saw was another thing to pay for, and a doll to dress up in Wellington family branded fashion before hiding me away behind lock and key until I might as well not have existed." Her lips creased in a thin, humorless line, so raw and ugly it was almost terrible. "Life kind of sucks when you own half of Baltimore, did you know that?"

Malcolm shook his head. "Can't say it's something I've ever experienced."

"So you think because I'm rich, I can't possibly have any problems?"

"I'm saying because you're rich, you have a skewed view of those problems versus the problems other people face." He searched her face, the tremors in her body language. "...but you're still human. You're allowed to have pains and losses. You're really upset over Garvey's murder, aren't you?"

"I told you. I loved him. I know how other people saw him, but...but...he was always kind to me." She sounded resigned, defeated. "I was leaving my husband for him. Why would I kill him?"

"That's what we're trying to figure out. Motive."

"I don't have a motive. I don't have...anything." Her voice hitched. "Just...just find who did this. Find who took him away from me. I'll pay you whatever it takes."

"Some problems you can't just throw money at," Malcolm said. "And we don't need extra money for doing our damned jobs."

She parted her lips—but then stopped as the sound of demanding, angry voices came from outside the interrogation room. One demanding, angry voice in particular stood above the rest, masculine and sharp with cultured inflections and the air of one accustomed to being obeyed. Lillienne Wellington's face went white, her eyes stark and wide. Her gaze locked on the door, but Malcolm had eyes only for her, and the way she sat utterly petrified, frozen to her seat.

A moment later, the door swung open sharply enough to knock into Seong-Jae, kilting him off balance and against the wall. Two extremely large men in black suits over black shirts entered; they wore the suits as if they were military uniforms demanding conformity and utter obedience. They both scanned the room, glanced at each other, then nodded, squaring off to either side of the door.

Four more men and one woman entered, geese moving in an arrowhead formation with the two men flanking one side and the man and woman to the other side, each carrying themselves with that pinched rigidity that screamed *lawyers*—while the man at the head of the arrow was recognizable from billboards, newspapers, gossip rags, and magazines all around Baltimore.

Maximilian Wellington was aging, but not old; he stood with the solid stance of a bulldog, squat and strong and barrel-chested inside a suit that probably cost half Malcolm's annual salary. His hair was swept back in a perfectly polished steel-gray buttress, gelled into place, and if his body was that of a bulldog then his face was that of an eagle. Give him wings and he'd be a gryphon, Malcolm thought, predatory and ferocious.

And that gryphon was currently staring at Malcolm as though Malcolm had walked up to him and spat on his polished shoes.

Malcolm tilted his head, sweeping a look over Wellington from head to toe. "Don't recall inviting you."

Wellington beckoned imperiously to Lillienne. "This conversation is done. Come, Lilli."

Lillienne flung herself from the chair and to her father's side, clinging to him and burying her face in his shoulder. "Daddy!"

So Wellington himself wasn't the reason she'd gone pale.

Had she been expecting her husband to be with her father? Was that why she'd looked so afraid?

Was that who she was protecting after all?

Wellington drew himself up. He was rather short, but he still managed to find a way to look down the bridge of his hawkish, hooked nose at Malcolm. "How dare you?" he demanded. His voice rolled and boomed, commanding with authority. "How dare you treat my daughter like some kind of common criminal? Do you know who I *am*?"

Malcolm sighed. "Don't really have any choice, do I."

Wellington's eyes narrowed. There was ice underneath that bullish exterior, cold and calculating. His eyes were a particular shade of gray, shining like a razor's edge. "Name and badge number," he ordered coolly.

Malcolm laughed.

Short, harsh, and he managed to rein it in, but it slipped out nonetheless. He slid off the table, rising to his feet, and slipped one of his cards out of his inner breast pocket. He offered it to Wellington between two fingers. "Here. It's right there on the card. Have fun with it. Call me if you want to pull the stick out of your ass."

Wellington stared at the card as if it was too filthy for him to touch. After long moments one of the lawyers flanking him scurried forward and took the card almost apologetically, before retreating with it folded between his fingers and palm. The entire time Wellington held Malcolm's eyes as if making a point. Malcolm arched both brows, looking right back at him, waiting.

"I," Wellington said flatly, "will have your job if you come near my family again. You'll never recover from the lawsuit. I'll see you in the poorhouse."

He started to turn on his heel, ushering Lillienne with him, but stopped when Malcolm said, "Did you know your daughter is a murder suspect?"

"If you think my daughter would ever harm anyone, you aren't particularly good at your job, are you?" Wellington's voice dripped contempt. "If you wish to pursue this line of questioning, you should come with a warrant." Another disdainful glance, before he slipped his arm around Lillienne's waist and ushered her toward the door. "Come, darling."

Together they swept from the room, the entourage of lawyers in their wake, the bodyguards bringing up the rear. Seong-Jae had retreated to the corner, unobtrusive, yet Malcolm doubted those keen black eyes had missed a single thing. Now Seong-Jae pushed off from the wall, drifting closer to Malcolm.

"Do you think he is serious?"

"Possibly." Malcolm sank back down onto the table, exhaling heavily and hitting the pause button on the recorder. "I'm not overly concerned."

The Captain's voice preceded her from the hallway. "You should be."

Captain Anjulie Zarate y Salazar leaned around the doorframe, her short black hair spiked into a mess from her fingers raking through it—as they did again now, as she gave Malcolm a flat look and propped her angular shoulder against the door.

"Explain," she said dryly.

Malcolm lifted a hand. "Morning, Captain."

With an exasperated sound, she rolled her eyes and pointed a warning finger at him. "Be careful. The Wellingtons have deep pockets, and a lot of hands in them. Maximilian Wellington golfs with the District Attorney."

"And my father plays shuffleboard with a former dictator." At her fierce look, though, Malcolm groaned. "Fine. *Fine*. I'll cross off the Wellingtons for now. We'll check out a few other leads and circle back to this."

"Let's hope you find someone for it and don't have to circle back. If you ruffle feathers, I'm the one stuck smoothing them." She flicked her fingers at them. "Go. Shoo. Why are you still here?"

Malcolm sighed dramatically. "You're always putting me out."

"Your solve rate is up. I want it to stay that way." She fixed her penetrating, hard stare on Seong-Jae. "Keep an eye on him. You're his good luck. Ever since you showed up, his solve rate is through the roof."

Malcolm growled. "My solve rate was well above average before Seong-Jae."

"And now it's even more above average." She made an irritated sound. "Get out. *Go*. Solve cases. If you're sitting on your ass, that's another murderer finding a way to slip through the cracks." She was already turning away, her back retreating through the door, but she let go with one last parting shot: "And don't forget to see Ryusaki!"

Malcolm swore softly. "For fuck's sake."

Seong-Jae gave him one of those too-bland looks. "So am I your good luck now?"

"I don't need your mouth right now, Seong-Jae," Malcolm muttered—then flushed, a touch of heat creeping over his cheeks, down his throat, as he thought of Seong-Jae's ripe, soft mouth, hot and needy and— He bit off a few more curses in Persian, and glowered at Seong-Jae. "So that wasn't much help."

"No?"

"I was trying to clear her."

Seong-Jae's brow furrowed. "Why?"

"Because I don't think she did it, but I have to eliminate the most probable suspect before I can start looking at other possibilities. I was just…"

He made a helpless, frustrated sound. He didn't know how to explain himself. He felt *wrong* about everything right now, and he couldn't shake the feeling he was fucking botching this case, but he'd always followed his instincts before and he could only trust them now.

"She didn't do much to endear herself," he finished. "But she's out of our reach for now, so we'll move on."

"Ah."

"Just 'ah?'"

"I do not have anything conclusive at the moment."

[79]

"Seong-Jae?"

Seong-Jae had glanced away, but now he lifted his inscrutable gaze to Malcolm, black eyes seeming to see into him—to see every doubt, every question that was creeping up on Malcolm and making him second-guess his every decision.

"Yes, Malcolm?"

"If you get something, you'll tell me, yeah?"

Seong-Jae considered, then asked, "If I tell you, will you listen?"

"…I'll try."

"Then when I have something, I will tell you."

"Thanks." Fuck. That shouldn't have been so hard to say. He didn't know if he was having trouble trusting Seong-Jae, having trouble trusting himself, or both.

Maybe that visit to Ryusaki really was in order.

He was saved from finding something else to say by the buzz of his phone, still sitting on the table. He leaned over to snag it, while reaching up to pull the tie loose from his hair and rake it down, easing the stress headache pounding behind his temples. A new text popped up from Stenson:

you want to come do prelim before we cut garvey open

Be there in a few, he tapped with his thumb. *Thanks, Sten.*

i save all the best dead bodies for you

He grinned, chuckling under his breath, and pocketed his phone. "Morbid little fucker," he muttered, then slid off the table and tossed his head to Seong-Jae. "Come on. Let's go look at a body."

[5: ON A STAGE]

ONE PLACE SEONG-JAE HAD NOT yet visited since arriving at BPD was the coroner's office.

He had not even been certain if the coroner's office was in the building, or off-site. But Malcolm—with his aversion to elevators—led him downstairs to below the ground floor level, into dimmed, chilled hallways that made him think of an eerie, abandoned hospital in horror films. Only no abandoned hospital was this busy, forensics and medical personnel moving about everywhere, bustling glass-walled labs through every doorway they passed. Seong-Jae leaned in, watching curiously, but then hurried to catch up with Malcolm as Malcolm headed for a pair of double doors marked *Autopsy Room 4.*

The scents of chemicals, decaying flesh, and blood were nearly overpowering, but not unfamiliar. They stepped into a room of steel walls, including a wall of labeled drawers that Seong-Jae didn't have to be told were full of refrigerated bodies kept slotted away until the forensics team was ready to process them and perform an autopsy. Harsh lights fell down in spots over working areas, turning steel nearly white, while shadow enveloped other areas fully. At one workstation, surrounded by carts full of tools, Garvey's body rested on an autopsy table, waxy white and almost glowing beneath the light.

Stenson was barely recognizable at his side, shrouded in a blue hospital apron and cap that hid her blond hair, a splash guard over her face. She leaned over the body, prodding and palpitating, then glanced up at the click of Malcolm's shoes on the tile.

"Hey," she said. "Glove up. We held off on cutting him open until you had a chance to take a look at entry and exit wounds."

Seong-Jae already knew without asking that Malcolm had not yet returned to his desk to fetch his own vinyl gloves.

Sometimes, Seong-Jae thought Malcolm needed more looking after than the man would be comfortable admitting.

But he said nothing, as he simply retrieved two pairs of gloves from his pocket and offered one pair to Malcolm. He claimed the other for himself, and snapped them on before stepping forward and circling the table to stand opposite Stenson.

"May I?" he asked.

"By all means," Stenson said, gesturing for him to proceed.

Seong-Jae took a cursory look over Garvey's body— checking his eyes, his lips, his tongue. No signs of any other cause of death beyond the apparent. He had thought it unlikely, but preferred to rule out any other possibilities early on. A slash on the cheek; the lack of coagulation and the angle indicated likely part of the struggle. He studied the defensive wounds on the hands again, the thickness of the incisions. The depth and width indicated the same size blade as the one that had made the marks on the cheek. Quick, slashing movements. The attacker had not thought to stab him first; they had simply acted on impulse, he thought, and likely had very little experience with using a knife with deadly intent.

This was most certainly an act of passion, and not premeditated. Particularly considering that no attempt had been made to hide the body afterward. The killer had done the act on impulse, run, and then afterward...

Afterward, simply fallen into the pretense of innocence in the hopes that no one would trace the crime back to them.

That killer would have been someone with advance knowledge of the blank window of time on the recordings. The safe zone.

Which, Seong-Jae thought, left only Lillienne Wellington, Brixton, and every member of the security staff. Possibly her husband, if he had been more cognizant of the affair than Lillienne had thought. At the moment a member of the security staff made the most sense—perhaps someone obsessed with Lillienne Wellington. But trained security staff would have been more adept with a knife.

No. Scratch that. He had seen many of what people often dubbed rent-a-cops, and many weren't even allowed or licensed for a weapon, bladed or otherwise. Nor would they have had any training. It was possible, then, that a member of the security team had been the perpetrator. Perhaps not even those on duty last night; simply a staff member who knew about the arranged trysts.

"Seong-Jae?" Malcolm asked.

He blinked, and realized he had been simply staring at the body without truly examining it, lost in thought. He lifted his gaze to Malcolm. Slate blue eyes watched him in silent question below the thick crags of Malcolm's brows, that scar across his eye that made him look even more feral.

Feral. If anything the old wolf was beyond feral right now, on edge, ragged, on the verge of going rabid.

If you get something, you'll tell me, yeah? Malcolm had asked.

Yet for the moment, Seong-Jae chose to keep his train of thought to himself. He wasn't certain enough of his line of reasoning, and as erratic as Malcolm's behavior was lately, Seong-Jae didn't want to send him off in the wrong direction with such single-minded force that Malcolm couldn't be diverted.

"My apologies," was all he said, and transferred his gaze to Stenson. "Did you take blood alcohol content at time of death?"

"Yeah. He was at point-zero-six, so pretty close to legally over the line," she said.

"So alcohol-induced lack of coordination likely made

him easier to overpower, but also more unpredictable, resulting in multiple defensive wounds before the perpetrator was able to land a killing blow."

Seong-Jae prodded carefully at the entry wound, then caught Garvey's shoulder and lifted him. Malcolm circled around to the other side and caught the body's other shoulder, and together they gingerly lifted the stiff, unresponsive body enough to peer at the exit wound on his back.

"I believe your assessment was correct," Seong-Jae said. "The entry wound is far larger than the exit wound, approximately the width of the base of the blade suspected as the murder weapon."

"Not suspected anymore," Stenson said. "Blood came back a match. That's all we got off the knife, though. Someone wiped the handle. No prints."

"As you say." Seong-Jae nodded to Malcolm, and they lowered the body before Seong-Jae reached up to draw down one of the overhead magnifying lenses, maneuvering its arm until he could get a close view of the entry wound. The edges were clean, but… "Fibers in the wound indicate his clothing tore during the initial thrust. Momentum and friction deposited the fabric fibers in the wound as the blade plunged deeper."

He felt blindly for the cart close by, reaching for a pair of forceps and then using them to gingerly clip out a long fiber that looked like it matched the fiber of Garvey's suit, holding it up under the light and the magnifier for a closer look. Then he set it aside and carefully used the sides of the forceps to nudge the wound wider, peering in. "Malcolm. Look."

Malcolm rounded to Seong-Jae's side of the table, leaning in close. His broad shoulder pressed against Seong-Jae's arm; in the chill of the room he was almost too warm, that vibrant and radiant heat that made him seem like a man with a forge at his heart, a deep-burning thing too hot for most to endure, capable of tempering steel and melting stone.

Is he melting your stone, then, Seong-Jae?

He pushed the thought away fiercely and instead held the wound open for Malcolm, letting him see down to the raw exposed bone.

"What am I looking at?" Malcolm asked.

"Scrapes on the sternum." Seong-Jae turned his head to look at Malcolm. This close, Malcolm's beard brushed Seong-Jae's jaw, teased against his cheek and throat. "Deep scrapes."

Malcolm made a soft sound, rumbling low in his throat, deep enough for Seong-Jae to feel the vibrations. He pressed closer, his entire body against Seong-Jae's side, all heat and firmness and hard-sculpted granite. His hand covered Seong-Jae's without so much as an if-you-please, massive and enveloping him in warmth. Seong-Jae stiffened with an odd jolt in the pit of his stomach, jerking his head up, glaring at Malcolm, but the man didn't even notice. He was completely and utterly engrossed, and used Seong-Jae's hand and grip on the forceps to pry the wound wider, his gaze dark and searching.

"Look," he said, rising up on his toes, leaning even harder on Seong-Jae. "It looks like the knife slid, then severed the sternocostal joints and forced past into the heart."

Stenson snorted. "When did you start learning such big words, Mal?"

Malcolm flipped her off idly. "Shut it, Sten."

"Okay, but if I shut it then I can't tell you he died from blood in his lungs. The heart wound was only incidental. A nick. It would've killed him, but not as fast."

"Got it." When Malcolm sank down on his heels again, the pressure of his weight eased away from Seong-Jae; his hand loosened its grip, then fell back. "So we're looking at a knife plunged with a lot of force."

Seong-Jae shot Malcolm a dirty look, pulling away and easing the forceps out of the wound carefully. "Is it a possibility that Lillienne Wellington could have exerted that level of force?"

"It's possible with the right angle and arc of descent. Adrenaline could play a factor, as well." Malcolm started to scrub his fingers through his beard—then stopped, looked down at his blood-smeared fingertips, and snapped his gloves off. "But I'm thinking it's more likely an adult male. One shorter than Garvey, from the angle of the wound. Under six feet." He frowned, idly stretching the inverted gloves between thick fingers, gaze locked on the body. "It's likely the perpetrator came in with an overhead downward plunge, but Garvey's chest would have been on eye level, from the angle of the cut."

Seong-Jae circled down to the foot of the table, visually calculating angles and arcs of descent, picturing in his mind's eye and tracing the trajectory back to estimate. "So an adult male of approximately...five foot eight?"

Approximately Brixton's height, then.

But did Brixton have it in him to murder, when the crime scene had left him so distressed?

Had his distress not been shock at the sight of a body, but remorse at his crime?

Where was the *motive*, then?

Malcolm frowned. "I'd say that's a good estimate. It would have taken more strength to sever the ribs at the cartilage and stab through to the lungs, at that angle."

"Again, adrenaline is a factor," Seong-Jae pointed out. "And Lillienne Wellington is approximately the appropriate height."

And again, he kept his thoughts on Brixton and other suspects to himself.

Did he trust Malcolm so little, right now?

Or had he never trusted Malcolm—or anyone else—from the start?

He pulled himself out of his increasingly brooding thoughts as Malcolm spoke again. "I'm not feeling her for this, though."

"You and your 'feelings,' once again."

"I trust my gut," Malcolm rumbled. "I don't see her for

motive, that's the problem."

"Guilt, perhaps. Over the affair. Guilt can drive persons to do strange things." Seong-Jae peeled out of his gloves. "Perhaps Garvey proposed, and she snapped and stabbed him."

"The ring box was still in his pocket. I doubt she even saw it," Malcolm countered. "If he'd proposed before the murder, the ring would've been in the debris. Dropped on the floor, on the cart, somewhere."

Seong-Jae inclined his head. "That is a fair point."

"So we're casting a wider net. She was the easy suspect." Malcolm groaned and dragged his hand over his face. "We still need to look at everyone connected to her."

"Husband?"

"Husband," Malcolm confirmed. "But we'll try a few other avenues first. Just so we can say we tried before we have to face a pissed off District Attorney chewing our asses for casing the daughter of his golfing buddy."

THEY STAYED LONG ENOUGH TO witness the autopsy.

Or rather, Seong-Jae witnessed while Malcolm was busy

on his phone, texting with someone. Seong-Jae kept his eyes studiously averted, focusing instead on watching Stenson crack the body open and take photographs of the stab wounds on the lungs, the evidence that the victim had essentially drowned in his own blood-filled air sacs.

If whatever Malcolm was texting about was important to the case, he would tell Seong-Jae.

...Seong-Jae hoped.

And if it was about his personal life, Seong-Jae had no right to know. He didn't *want* to know. It wasn't his business.

At all.

Once Stenson was done cleaning up and had shut off the recorder for her autopsy notes, though, Malcolm glanced up from his phone. He'd propped himself against the wall, casual and almost elegant with one hand in the pocket of his slacks, one foot braced against the wall. "Witness?" he asked, slate blue eyes sliding toward Seong-Jae.

"It does seem the simplest course of action."

"I bullied her contact info out of Brixton before we left." Malcolm pushed off the wall in an easy flexion of powerful sinew. "So let's go."

Seong-Jae chose to let that bullying comment slide, even if it had been rather clearly pointed. He sighed, glancing at Stenson. Stenson only shrugged, as if asking *What do you expect me to say?*

Seong-Jae briefly pinched the bridge of his nose, then turned and followed Malcolm out to the parking garage.

He was accustomed to their silences, on long drives. It had almost become comfortable, but there was nothing comfortable about the prickling, bristling tension radiating from Malcolm. Seong-Jae didn't even think Malcolm was aware of it, perhaps even thought he was behaving absolutely normally and it was everyone else who was being unreasonable. It was not uncommon in situations of emotional trauma and denial.

As if Seong-Jae had any room to talk, when for all he knew his irritation with Malcolm was his own trauma reaction filtering how he viewed the other man's behavior.

His own trauma reaction, and not concern over Malcolm's well-being.

Nonsense.

He didn't even *like* Malcolm.

The man was an annoying bundle of contradictions, and Seong-Jae would like it very much if he would settle on one mode of behavior, one psychological archetype, rather than continuously contrasting himself and redefining himself with each new thing Seong-Jae learned.

Nonetheless.

Even if Seong-Jae could not say that he particularly liked Malcolm...

He liked this erratic, tense, forcefully intimidating version of Malcolm even less.

And he did not think he was being presumptuous in thinking that were Malcolm himself, he would be unsettled by his own behavior. For all his gruffness, Malcolm was a kind man. Tired, worn, a complete and utter ass…but kind.

Not this hard-edged and unyielding thing.

Malcolm said nothing to Seong-Jae, as they traveled through Baltimore's streets to a bank of high-rise apartment complexes in a rather nice neighborhood. The address scribbled in Malcolm's notebook took them to a building that took up an entire block on its own, lined in glassy, sleek balconies that looked out over the harbor. Seong-Jae tried not to think of the silence between them as strained, as they parked and stepped into the building's lobby.

But he felt like Malcolm was pretending he wasn't there, avoiding eye contact, avoiding even looking in his direction.

That shouldn't sting.

And it didn't, he told himself.

It *didn't*.

The moment they were inside, Malcolm made a beeline for the stairs—but Seong-Jae stalled. "Malcolm. Her apartment is on the fifteenth floor."

Malcolm stopped short, back to Seong-Jae.

Then turned and strode toward the elevator without a word, without making eye contact.

And in the elevator, Malcolm leaned against the wall as far from Seong-Jae as he could get, tapping his pocket notebook against his arm restlessly and fixing his gaze on the numbers.

This had to stop.

[93]

But now was not the time, and Seong-Jae held his tongue as he followed Malcolm to the apartment number noted. Malcolm knocked on the door, while Seong-Jae hung back.

Again.

After a few moments the door lock unlatched slowly, uncertainly. The door cracked open just as far as a chain lock would allow, and below the arch of the chain a large, soft-lashed brown eye peered out. "…yes?"

"Kiara Jacobs?" Malcolm asked.

"Yes, that's me."

Malcolm flipped his badge up with a practiced flick of his wrist. "BPD. Could we speak to you for a bit, ma'am?"

The door closed, then opened again after a rattle of the chain. The woman who greeted them was short, middle-aged, tired, wearing a pair of yoga pants and a pink zip-up hoodie—but her smile was warm enough, colored even warmer by the deep rich hue of her dark brown skin. She tucked back a lock of hair that had escaped her clip; she looked relieved to see them, and she stepped back to make room.

"Please," she said. "Come in."

They followed her into a spacious apartment decorated in tasteful glass and white leather, accents of color in the delicate potted plants here and there. She guided them to the living room, then sank down on one side of the long, low leather couch, wrapping her arms across her stomach and giving them both hopeful looks.

"Have you caught who did it?"

"No, ma'am." Malcolm settled down on the other end of the couch, watching her thoughtfully but not unkindly—the harsh glare of glacial eyes softening, something of that protective kindness that made Seong-Jae think of him as *old wolf* emerging once more. "We're hoping you can point us to a few leads."

Kiara shook her head. "I didn't see anything but the body. I'm sorry." She pressed her lips together, face crumpling slightly. "I...I've never seen a dead body before. And I keep thinking 'what if the killer saw me? What if I'm next?'"

Seong-Jae glanced about for somewhere to sit that would not violate the unspoken rules of space already established by Malcolm's and Kiara's positions on the sofa, then settled on a leather-upholstered white U-shaped chair. When he sank down in it, his knees folded awkwardly; the chair was not made for someone of his height, and he fidgeted uncomfortably for a moment before settling on stretching out his legs slightly, even if he did not like the informal posture when he was a *guest.*

"It is very likely," he pointed out, "that by the time you found the body, the killer had been away from the crime scene for hours. It is doubtful they were ever aware of your presence."

"Typical. The maid's always invisible." Her laugh was strained and tight. "For once I'm glad."

Seong-Jae cocked his head. "Miss Jacobs? Can you think

of anything out of the ordinary this morning?"

She hesitated, then shook her head. "No. Nothing. The rounds were pretty ordinary. Brixton hadn't been up to do his inspections yet, so I was rushing. They only let senior maids onto the upper floors, you know? We've been with the hotel longer and we do the best work, but I was running behind and trying not to be sloppy, so I had my head down. Completely focused. In the zone. Brixton said the big guy—the owner, you know, Wellington?—was gonna come walk the floors today on a random quality check, so it had to be perfect."

"So you didn't see anyone else while you were up there," Malcolm clarified.

"Only Alina. The other fourteenth floor maid. She didn't see the body. Only me."

Malcolm fixed her with a searching look. "Kiara."

She stared at him with her eyes wide, leaning away subtly, as if afraid of what he would say. "...yeah?"

Malcolm held himself perfectly still. Seong-Jae couldn't help but observe him; Malcolm's stillnesses were a thing of their own, of body language and quiet things, and right now his stillness said that he wasn't going to hurt her, that he wouldn't make a single threatening move, she didn't have to be afraid.

And when he spoke his voice was gentle as he asked, "You doing okay?"

That one question seemed to break something inside Kiara. Her eyes widened, welled; her mouth trembled softly.

"No," she said, gulping, then sniffled and rubbed at her nose, looking away. "I tried to sleep this afternoon just to make it go away, but I keep seeing all that *blood*..."

"I know. I know," Malcolm soothed. "If you've never seen it before, it can be a lot to take in. I'm sorry you had to deal with that."

She scrubbed her knuckles against one gleaming eye. "Mr. Brixton was real nice. He let me go home, but I just feel scared here all alone."

Malcolm leaned a touch closer. "Is there someone you can call to come over and stay with you?"

"My sister...?" Kiara fidgeted, then looked down. "I didn't want to bother her, but..."

"Bother her. She's your sister. She'll care that you're okay." Malcolm smiled. "Detective Yoon and I are going to stay with you until your sister gets here. Go and give her a call."

"Really?" Kiara brightened, a smile creeping across her lips as she stood. "Okay. Okay. Thank you."

She bustled off, already flipping her phone from her pocket. Seong-Jae's gaze trailed her, before returning to Malcolm. Malcolm stood, watching the woman as she rounded the wall into the kitchen; Seong-Jae stood as well, drifting closer, and pitching his voice low so as not to be heard over the sound of Kiara speaking into her cell.

"Do we have time to remain here until then?"

"We'll make time," Malcolm said, his jaw tight. "I need

to think anyway. And the next people we're going to see don't operate by daylight."

Seong-Jae studied him closely. No matter the façade he'd put on for Kiara, Malcolm was still tense and on the verge of snapping; it wasn't hard to see, and Seong-Jae wondered at the wisdom of venturing into less than desirable environs when Malcolm was in his current state.

But if he said anything, Malcolm would only bristle with irritation and pride. So Seong-Jae only sighed and asked, "Where do you intend to go next?"

"Nowhere I really want to." Malcolm's gaze still tracked Kiara, as if afraid she would disappear if he took his eyes off her. "Baltimore's quieter about it than L.A., but it's not exactly the cleanest city."

"Then you intend to interrogate Garvey's criminal associates."

"I don't know if 'interrogate' is the right word. It's more that we have a sort of collective bargaining agreement," Malcolm answered dryly.

"This should be quite interesting to observe."

"Normally these people wouldn't be our problem. They're more for the folks in narcotics, vice, sometimes major crimes." Malcolm shrugged. "But, well, sometimes people turn up dea—"

Kiara returned, ending the conversation. "Detective?"

Malcolm smiled slightly. "Yeah?"

"My sister said she'll be here in half an hour." She

looked between them. "Thank you for staying. Can I get you something to drink? Lemonade?"

With a nod, Malcolm said, "I'd love some. Thank you."

Seong-Jae wrinkled his nose. "I do not like—"

Malcolm's elbow bit into his side. Seong-Jae closed his eyes, biting back a curse, clenching his jaw, then opened his eyes and forced out,

"I would appreciate a glass as well."

Kiara smiled warmly, then turned and disappeared into the kitchen again. Seong-Jae shot Malcolm a look, edging out of elbowing range.

"You *are* a bully."

"You intimidate people, Seong-Jae," Malcolm said. "She's scared. She doesn't need to be intimidated by the people who're here to protect her."

Seong-Jae tensed. "I am not attempting to be deliberately intimidating."

"You don't have to attempt. You *loom*. Your presence is imposing."

For a moment, Seong-Jae couldn't breathe. Just a fleeting second, an instant when he felt as if the breath had been knocked from him, replaced by a tight knot of pain in his lungs. It was an old pain, one dull about the edges, blunted enough by time that it shouldn't be able to cut him anymore—especially with such a meaningless, offhand comment.

But it still stung.

And he kept his gaze fixed straight forward, following

Kiara's movements without really seeing them, as he murmured a neutral, "Ah."

He felt Malcolm's gaze on him, but didn't meet it—those storm-colored eyes suddenly skewering. Where Malcolm had practically pretended he didn't exist before, now he had the other man's full attention, precisely when he didn't want it.

"You're offended," Malcolm murmured.

"No," Seong-Jae retorted. "Not offended."

Let it go.

But Malcolm only continued to watch him, gaze searching, heavy, dark.

"...wounded," he corrected thoughtfully, and Seong-Jae nearly flinched.

"*No,*" he bit off.

He was saved by Kiara returning with tall, condensation-frosted glasses of lemonade, offering them with that same bright, relieved smile that said somehow, in some way, they were something good to her when they were nothing but bad for each other.

"Detectives?" She pressed the glasses into their hands. "Here you go." Stepping back, she wiped her condensation-dewed hands on her yoga pants. "Can I fix you something to eat?"

"We're fine, thanks," Malcolm said with a reassuring smile.

Seong-Jae said nothing.

He only turned away, pressing his mouth to the glass of

lemonade and forcing himself to take a sip of the vile, cloyingly sweet-sour brew.

It still tasted better than the hollow feeling in the pit of his stomach.

Or the bitter annoyance that he even gave half a damn about Malcolm Khalaji and his irritating observations.

[6: WORDS ON A PAGE]

MALCOLM MIGHT HAVE ALMOST ENJOYED the quiet stop at Kiara Jones' apartment.

If he hadn't thought Seong-Jae would spontaneously combust over being forced to drink one little glass of lemonade.

By the time Kiara's sister had shown up to take her in tow with fussing and warm embraces and concerned questions, Seong-Jae had managed to drink almost exactly one quarter of the glass, as if he'd been measuring precisely how little he could get away with drinking without offending their host.

The trip had been worth it almost for that, especially with the face Seong-Jae made after every sip.

True, talking to the witness hadn't really yielded any information of use. But now and then it was nice to be able to make people feel safer, instead of making them feel threatened. Malcolm was so used to being the enemy. To understanding exactly *why* he was the enemy, when people had more reason to hate the Baltimore police than they did to trust them.

That didn't mean it didn't leave him tired.

And now and then it was nice to have someone look at him as if they thought he could actually protect them.

Who do you think you could protect?

You couldn't protect Gabrielle.

And now she wants to move back here.

How's that going to feel, seeing her again?

He pushed the thoughts away violently, fixing his attention on Seong-Jae instead as they stepped out of the elevator and into the apartment building lobby. Seong-Jae's shoulders were still tense, his gaze slitted and focused outward. Malcolm sighed and bumped Seong-Jae's arm with his elbow.

"Come on," he said. "We're going for coffee and fries."

Seong-Jae immediately jerked away from him with a cutting look. "Why do you insist on taking me to that vile place every chance you get?"

"Because I like going to that vile place every chance I get, you're my partner, we stick together, and I already said you don't hate it as much as you pretend to."

"I find this unamusing."

"We need to talk, Seong-Jae. And I'd rather do it somewhere outside of work."

A muscle in Seong-Jae's throat jumped. He averted his eyes. "What do we need to talk about?"

Malcolm just stared at him for long moments, then dragged a hand through his hair and pushed through the lobby doors out to the street. "Let's just go."

THERE WAS NO SUCH THING as a lunch rush at Swabbie's.

Swabbie's made all their money between last call and dawn. The beer wasn't good enough for it to be a night spot, the food a questionable enough prospect to those who weren't in the know, so when they settled in their usual spots at the bar the joint was just as empty as always. A few of the day drinkers were already propping up their stools, completely absorbed in their phones or the game on TV or just staring at their own haggard reflections tinted beer-brown or whiskey-gold. A couple of college kids snuggled in a corner booth, pretending to do homework. Otherwise, Malcolm and Seong-Jae had the place mostly to themselves.

Exactly how Malcolm liked it.

George stabbed a finger at him before he could even open his mouth. "Don't even fucking ask me for a kosher menu."

Malcolm held both hands up. "I didn't say a word."

"Uh-huh." Rolling his toothpick from one side of his mouth to the other, the squat, bald bartender wiped his hands on the edge of his stained apron, before George squinted one eye. "Usual for both of you?"

"I'm good with that," Malcolm said.

"Marginally acceptable," Seong-Jae added.

"Marginally acce—" George broke off, glowering at Seong-Jae. "One of these days I'm going to poison your food."

"You say this as if said food is not an invitation to food poisoning at the onset."

George went purple and glared at Malcolm. "Stop bringing him here," he bit off, then stalked back to the kitchen, muttering "marginally acceptable, my left nut" and a few other choice things under his breath. Malcolm held back his laugh, shoulders shaking with the effort to silence his chuckles.

"For hell's sake, Seong-Jae. If you keep antagonizing him he just might actually poison our food."

"Please explain the difference."

"If you hate it so much, you really don't have to eat it."

Seong-Jae shrugged stiffly. "It seems to have significance to you."

That caught Malcolm up short, and he watched Seong-Jae in silence for several moments. The man looked fixedly down at the bar-top, but there was that tension in his shoulders again, different from his usual stiff, self-isolating withdrawal. He really didn't make sense, sometimes. Cold, closed off, downright menacing half the time...but he'd sit here and eat food that apparently disgusted him simply because it meant something to Malcolm?

It really was about the small things with Seong-Jae, sometimes.

George cut off his train of thought, returning with their coffee mugs plus a large carafe of creamer and a mountain of sugar packets for Seong-Jae. The burly man swept them both with hard-edged side-eye.

"I'll let you decide for yourselves if the cook pissed in your coffee," he said, and vanished huffily into the kitchen again.

Seong-Jae's eyes widened. He stared at his mug in dismay. "Pardon?"

"The cook didn't do anything," Malcolm said, leaning over and stealing one of Seong-Jae's sugar packets to shake into his own coffee. "George doesn't want a health code violation. He's not going to mess with our food."

Nonetheless, Seong-Jae seemed skeptical, eyeing his coffee—which, despite his complaints, George had pointedly and courteously filled only two thirds of the way. Leaving room for the approximate half-gallon of creamer Seong-Jae upended into the mug, pouring it to the brim until the coffee was barely a watered-down shade of tan. Tan that quickly swirled with white sprinkles, as Seong-Jae began methodically shaking, ripping, and dumping in sugar packets to make the coffee palatable to his apparently rather picky tastes.

Malcolm hid his smile behind his mug.

Cold, closed off, downright menacing.

And fussy as hell about his coffee.

Malcolm might be getting used to it, but that didn't mean it didn't make him smile every time.

Especially when Seong-Jae took such a careful, ginger sip of his coffee, as if he could taste *anything* mixed into it under all that cloying, creamy sweetness.

"So," Malcolm said, "we should talk."

Seong-Jae choked mid-sip, setting the mug down quickly and covering his mouth with the back of his hand. He coughed sharply, then reached for a napkin and wiped his lips, fixing Malcolm with a dire look, as if he'd done that on purpose. "About what?"

Malcolm considered his words, then decided out with it. Even if Seong-Jae came at things sideways and with subtleties, this didn't seem like something to dance around.

"I upset you back there," he said. "You're good at hiding it, but I'm getting better at reading it." Malcolm paused. "I think."

Seong-Jae's glower melted away into cool indifference. Again. That black-eyed mask was fucking infuriating, smooth and perfect without the slightest crack. "You did not upset me. Not specifically."

"Then what was it?"

Nothing. Seong-Jae was silent, only taking another sip of his coffee, gaze idly focused on the thin window leading back into the kitchen, as if entirely interested in the glimpses of movement beyond.

"Seong-Jae." Malcolm sighed. "I need you to tell me these things."

Still nothing. Malcolm closed his eyes, swearing under his breath, then forced down the knot of his pride swelling in his throat.

"...so I don't *hurt* you with them," he added.

He thought Seong-Jae wouldn't answer. Because Seong-Jae hardly ever answered with anything other than superficial details. Facts, such as the existence of his younger sister or his former job with the FBI's Behavioral Analysis Unit.

Actually talking about how he felt about anything?

Maybe he might with someone else.

But not with Malcolm.

And Malcolm shouldn't let that bother him so much, when he'd hardly known the man for two weeks and they were coworkers.

Nothing else.

Seong-Jae set his coffee mug down slowly, methodically, as if trying to place the base in the exact same spot it had been in before, not even a micron off. "I..."

Then silence. A thinning of his lips, a darkening of his eyes, gaze fixed rigidly on the coffee in the mug. His breaths were even, slow, almost too measured—as if he were pacing them, counting them. Four times, in and out in long, slow draws. Five. Then, coolly:

"I am aware that here in America, men of height and imposing stature are considered attractive and somehow more masculine." He recited the information as if reading it out of a handbook, but his stillness in and of itself was a giveaway. Stillness and a single restless motion, his long, elegantly crafted finger tracing the edge of the coffee mug in a slow circle, his gaze tracking that rather than looking at Malcolm. "In my culture, I am oversized, awkward, and uncomfortable. I take up too much space. I am too obtrusive, to the point of being vulgar with my very presence. Were I to return to North Korea or visit South Korea, I would not even be able to find clothing to fit me."

Malcolm understood, then. More than he thought Seong-Jae wanted him to, when Seong-Jae spoke as if the information imparted belonged to someone else, as clinical and dispassionate a description as if outlining a crime scene. For all that he moved with such lethal grace and composure...

Seong-Jae was uncomfortable with his own body.

That compact, efficient body language and those tight, controlled movements weren't born of combat training or even some internal mental discipline.

They were a reflection of a quiet, deep-seated insecurity that had probably lived in Seong-Jae since childhood, driving him to an economy of movement that was as unobtrusive as possible.

And Malcolm had prodded at that insecurity thoughtlessly.

Because as usual, he was a fucking asshole.

He might understand criminal psychology down to the most minute behavioral pattern, but sometimes ordinary human psychology left him stumped.

"I'm sorry," he said. Sometimes those words choked him, but sometimes they were the first thing that needed to be said. "For what I said. Is that why you always seem to melt into the background?"

Seong-Jae blinked. For a moment a startled, unguarded look flew toward Malcolm, before shuttering over and fixing on the coffee again. "I was not aware that I did."

"You hang back, even when you have every right to take the lead."

"I am new to Baltimore, and lack the familiarity to take point on a number of matters."

"There is that." And Malcolm let it go. He'd dug at Seong-Jae enough. He applied himself to his own coffee instead, taking a sip of the bitter brew, lingering over it. But after a moment he added, "For what it's worth, I don't find you oversized, awkward, uncomfortable, obtrusive, or vulgar."

"But I do take up too much space," Seong-Jae observed.

Malcolm sighed. He wasn't going to lie, but that was a wholly different matter and Seong-Jae couldn't be that damned oblivious. But George elbowed out of the kitchen with their food, saving him for a least a few moments until he'd deposited Malcolm's sandwich and fries in front of him, a tray with just the crispy, seaweed-flecked, goat-cheese-drizzled fries in front of Seong-Jae.

Only when George had vanished into the back again did Malcolm say, "A toddler would take up too much space, if they were my partner."

"Ah. So we are back to that."

"We're back to that," Malcolm growled against the rim of his mug. "Drink your coffee. I don't want to talk about it."

A needling look cut into him. "So you pry my insecurities from me, and then become close-mouthed yourself immediately after?"

"Unfair as fuck, isn't it?" Malcolm caught up a few fries and bit the ends off the entire cluster, mouthing around them, "Can't talk. Mouth full."

Seong-Jae made a disgusted sound—Malcolm wasn't sure if it was at him, or at the food. But he picked up a French fry, studying it intently, before biting the tip off a bit harder than Malcolm thought was entirely necessary.

"...Malcolm."

"Mm?" Malcolm murmured around another bite.

"You are impossible. Are you aware of that?"

"Entirely." Malcolm swallowed and reached for his sandwich with a grin. "Eat your fries. We've got a little time to kill."

PERHAPS SEONG-JAE WAS GROWING ACCUSTOMED to the questionable cuisine at Swabbie's.

That still did not mean he understood why Malcolm was so content to just *stay* here, idling away and saying not a single word that was not necessary. Malcolm spent the majority of the afternoon writing in his leather-bound pocket journal, speaking to Seong-Jae only to ask a question about the crime scene or about his observations of Lillienne Wellington's behavior.

Seong-Jae answered truthfully, but still kept his alternative theories to himself. He was still bothered by something about Brixton, and yet if he mentioned that to Malcolm it might end up subjecting an innocent and already traumatized man to an unnecessary and potentially hostile interrogation.

Do you really think Malcolm would do such a thing?

Perhaps not the Malcolm he had initially met on the Darian Park case.

But Malcolm had been straying farther and farther away from that man by the day, and Seong-Jae could sense something building to a potentially violent head.

In a room full of dynamite, one would have to be suicidal to light a match.

As the sun began to set, its brightness replaced by the tail lights of evening traffic, however, Malcolm finally rose from his stool and beckoned to Seong-Jae. "It's a little early, but we'd better get moving."

Seong-Jae arched a brow, sliding off his stool and leaving a tip pinned under his empty coffee cup—the sixth of the afternoon. "A little early for what?"

"For anyone to be awake and doing business."

Seong-Jae wrinkled his brows, but said nothing and only followed Malcolm out to the car.

The rushing river of traffic took them through busy, crowded downtown streets and west, where the traffic slowly tapered off until there were only a few cars before and behind them. Well-tended townhouses faded into old, cracked brick storefronts, lining the main avenue the Camaro cruised through—while run-down apartment tenements and small, ramshackle houses trailing along the cross-streets behind them.

The storefronts were graffiti-marked in urban arcana, casting a spell over the neighborhood that seemed to whisper the tatters of forgotten hopes in the bits of plaster-paper signage clinging to the sides of buildings, promise the sprouting of buried dreams reaching up between the cracks in the pavement. Groups of children pushed and shoved down the sidewalks, loud and laughing, bringing brightness and color to dingy and faded avenues, as if they were the glue holding the crevices of this place together.

He saw elders on their porches, seeming to prop up the eaves with their bony stick knees. He saw old men and old women parked in front of storefronts in folding chairs, pushing checkers across boards and laughing at each other, slapping their thighs. This didn't look like a neighborhood where anyone would come to find Baltimore's criminal elements.

It simply looked like a place where people came to find home, and *make* home in whatever way they could.

But Malcolm took them down a side street between two buildings, easing into a darkened lane where the street lamps had been broken out and the night was near-black save for dim squares of gold falling out of the windows overhead to shatter on the street below. The back of one of the larger shop buildings opened out onto an even narrower street, too wide for even a single car, intersecting the cross-street that passed it and dead-ending at the rear of another building. A large garage-style door had been opened in the back of the building, and several men offloaded unmarked wooden crates into what looked to be a large, neatly-organized storage area.

Malcolm parked the Camaro with the headlights nosing just past the curb of the corner, then tossed his head to Seong-Jae. "Come on. Hang back if you want to. Technically we're not here on official police business, so keep a low profile. Don't do anything to make anyone think we want trouble."

"Do we?" Seong-Jae asked as he slid out of the car.

"Do we what?"

"Want trouble."

"Not if we can help it," Malcolm said grimly, and strode up the sidewalk, lifting his hand to the men unloading the truck.

There were four in total, and they all paused, setting down the crates they were handing off, straightening slowly and watching both Malcolm and Seong-Jae with hard, wary eyes. Seong-Jae held eye contact with each of them for a moment, then looked away. He was not certain what situation they were entering, but perhaps it was best to appear neither hostile nor overly interested.

Nonetheless, he was painfully aware of the weight of his Glock holstered underneath his arm.

In the silence, their footsteps were the only sound. Until, as they rounded the edge of the loading zone's door, a faint whistle of air zipped toward them, a buzzing edge underneath like a darting hornet. Seong-Jae caught a glint of metal, flung himself to one side—but Malcolm was faster.

"Seong-Jae!"

Malcolm's bulk slammed into him, crushing him back against the brick of the store, thick arms snapping around Seong-Jae and clasping him close. A slim knife—no more than two inches long in the blade, the hilt an inch-wide finger ring—zipped past, narrowly missing grazing Malcolm's shoulder, and embedded in the slats of one wooden crate propped on the loading ramp. Breathing shallowly, gut tight as a clenched fist, Seong-Jae stared after it. Had Malcolm not shoved him, that blade could have buried in his throat.

He could feel Malcolm's heart beating through his chest as if trying to slam into Seong-Jae's body—and Malcolm still had a tight hold on him, pinning his arms to his sides, trapping him between the wall's gritty, scraping brick and Malcolm's heavy-set, densely muscled body, Malcolm's face half-buried against Seong-Jae's shoulder. Seong-Jae took in a ragged breath.

"Thank you," he murmured.

Malcolm lifted his head, searching him, slate blue eyes flicking back and forth, so close they filled Seong-Jae's vision. Malcolm's breaths stirred his hair and brushed his cheeks as he growled, "You all right?"

"I am unharmed."

Slow, mocking applause echoed over the night. "You still got good reflexes, Khalaji," a coarse, laughing British accent called. "Who's the new bloke?"

Malcolm slumped against Seong-Jae for a moment, before giving him a weary look, mouthing something that looked like *just roll with it*, and pushing away, leaving Seong-Jae feeling almost cold in the wake of that heated body pressed against him, his senses high on adrenaline. He took another ragged breath, then straightened and pulled away from the wall, following Malcolm under the overhang of the loading area. The men on the ramp were grinning, now.

So was the man who strode toward them, still clapping in slow, exaggerated motions, his teeth bared white in a broad, mocking smile. He watched them with dark, intelligent eyes, the faint overhead lights glinting off the sharp lines of high cheekbones and turning dusky skin to gold in every angle and hollow.

Malcolm growled. "Not target practice," he said. "Fuck me, Vasquez. Could you not pull that kind of shit?"

"Keeps the hounds off my feet," Vasquez said without the slightest hint of chagrin, shrugging. He was an unassuming man of average height, plain in jeans and a checkered shirt, his black hair neatly combed back. He glanced at Seong-Jae with an assessing gaze, then returned his attention to Malcolm. "Got something you want me for today, or you here for someone else?"

"Someone else," Malcolm said. He looked over his shoulder at the men on the ramp, then dropped his voice. "Marion Garvey went and got himself dead."

Vasquez shrugged again, clasping his hands together nonchalantly. "Can't say I didn't see it coming. That man was an obnoxious cuck even when he wasn't slipping his fingers where they didn't belong."

"Where they didn't belong?" Malcolm pressed. "As in someone else's business?"

"As in someone else's wife, my man." Vasquez snorted. "But he'd been sniffing around the back docks, too. You know. The ten-key boys."

Malcolm swore. Seong-Jae frowned, glancing at Malcolm, then at Vasquez.

"Ten-key boys?" he repeated.

"The local cocaine racket," Malcolm clarified grimly. "We've got a few importers here, though they always manage to slip the noose."

Vasquez cocked a brow. "How rookie not know about the ten-key boys?"

"Transfer," Malcolm said. "He's actually my boss."

"Yeah?" Vasquez swept Seong-Jae with a slow once-over, then whistled low. "I wouldn't mind being bossed around by someone that pretty, eh?"

Seong-Jae recoiled. "Excuse me?"

Malcolm dragged a hand over his face. "He's straight and just trying to fuck with you. Don't give him the attention he wants."

"I'm hurt, Khalaji," Vasquez retorted with a smirk.

Seong-Jae eyed Malcolm. He felt as though there was some byplay taking place that he wasn't quite catching on to, some reason that Malcolm had felt the need to inform Vasquez of Seong-Jae's rank.

"I am not your 'boss,'" he corrected. "Not by the technical definition."

Malcolm spread his hands. "Everyone's disagreeing with me today. I can't catch a break." Then he sobered, that flinty, hard edge emerging, the wolf on alert. "So give me a break, Vasquez. You think someone down dockside had something to do with Garvey's murder?"

Vasquez tensed. So, too, did the men on the ramp. Seong-Jae kept one eye on them, one on Vasquez, his fingers relaxed at his side but itching for the hilt of his pistol.

"I'm no snitch," Vasquez said carefully. "You know that."

"What do you want?" Malcolm asked bluntly.

"My baby cousin got picked up last week on a holding charge."

Malcolm shook his head. "I can't get him out. You know that."

"Nah. I know. You ain't that dirty, no matter how hard I try." Vasquez chuckled. "I get you a care package, you get it in to him?"

"Depends on what's in the package."

"Black beans, cabbage, and chocolate." Vasquez flashed a disarming smile. "Baby boy's gotta eat. Prison food's no thing, now is it?"

"Black beans, cabbage, and chocolate," Malcolm repeated skeptically, before his shoulders drooped in a sigh. "You have it delivered, I'll get the dogs to work it over and send it in."

With an exaggerated pout, Vasquez said, "You'd almost think you don't trust me."

"I've seen your rap sheet," Malcolm retorted. "Details?"

Vasquez paused, looking at his men, then stepped closer to Seong-Jae and Malcolm, glancing between them and lowering his voice. "Talk to Huang," he said. "Anybody had Garvey cut down, Huang knows. If Huang don't know, then it wasn't one of us."

Malcolm's brows drew together. "You think Huang's going to talk to me? Huang fucking hates me."

Vasquez quirked his brows at Seong-Jae. "Maybe talk to him."

Seong-Jae closed his eyes and counted to five. Just long enough to keep his patience. Just long enough to keep from snapping and maintain a neutral tone when he ground out, "Huang is a Chinese name. I am Korean. We are not overly fond of each other as a people. He is more likely to be more hostile to me than to Malcolm."

"Thanks for the lesson on Asian history," Vasquez said sardonically, then dusted his hands together as if wiping them clean of the whole thing. "Good luck with that, then."

"Thanks, V," Malcolm said, then took Seong-Jae's arm lightly. "Come on."

Seong-Jae pulled his arm free from Malcolm's grip, but held his silence until they had rounded the corner of the building once more and escaped the watchful eyes of Vasquez and his workers. He glanced back over his shoulder, then stared at Malcolm.

"That is it?"

"That's it," Malcolm said, fishing his keys from his pocket. "We follow the threads. We trace the web back to the spider at its heart." He shook his head. "But I think we're chasing a dead end, right now. I just don't feel this for a hit job."

"Do you regularly consort with criminals to gain information on other criminals?"

"When it's necessary," Malcolm replied, an edge to his voice, and he flung Seong-Jae a sharp look. "Don't. Don't start. I have my way of doing things, and it works."

"And you allow that man to go free and possibly harm others for the sake of your own convenience?"

Malcolm pushed away from the wall and stalked around to the driver's side of the car. The alarm's beep followed. "You're assuming he's some kind of mass murderer, or a drug-dealing gangster. You have no idea what his rap sheet is."

Seong-Jae held his ground. This—he—he was not sure if he could accept this, if he could even get in the car with Malcolm. By all rights Vasquez should be under arrest for the simple crime of attempting to assault an officer alone, and the contents of those crates thoroughly inspected.

"But you do," he pointed out, "and you decide what is an acceptable level of criminal activity to turn a blind eye to in order to accomplish your own ends."

"If that's what you want to think." Malcolm yanked the car's door open. "I'm not defending myself to you."

And then he slammed the door. The Camaro's engine came to life with a growl, the headlights flashing on.

Seong-Jae bit back a growl. Why that stubborn, mulish,

obstinate jot—

He yanked the passenger's side door open and leaned in, glowering. "What if I choose to hold you accountable as your direct superior?"

"Then *do* that," Malcolm snapped, twisting in the driver's seat and scowling at him, blue eyes a crackling, lashing storm. "*Do* it, and stop waffling around with thinly-veiled disapproval. Report me. Get me fired. But either shit or get off the pot, instead of just making faces at me and starting arguments over me trying to do my *job*."

Seong-Jae opened his mouth—then swallowed back the furious retort on his lips, forcing down the snarl that wanted to rise. Calm. Control. He was not going to lose his temper.

Especially not standing out here in the street where Vasquez and his men could overhear them bickering like a married couple.

He growled under his breath, then blanked it out, breathing in slow and making himself move, sliding into the car, yanking the door shut and staring fixedly out the passenger's side window.

"I will consider it," he bit off.

"You do that," Malcolm growled right back, and sent the car jouncing forward into the street.

Seong-Jae held his silence, working his jaw, slowly talking himself down as the street lights fell over them and guided them like bread crumbs through the city, down winding avenues and onto the overpass leading down to the harbor. He didn't lose his temper like this. Not now. Not ever. Never again. He couldn't let Malcolm goad him into forgetting himself.

But the silence between them bristled; irritation simmered deep in the pit of his stomach, hot and acidic.

And he didn't know what to *do* about it. By all reason he should be reporting Malcolm, but he didn't have any evidence of anything other than Malcolm talking to a man who had the audacity to throw a knife at Seong-Jae's head.

Some quiet, bitter part of Seong-Jae rebelled, too. Rebelled at the idea of reporting Malcolm. That would be a betrayal, and he had done enough of that in his lifetime. Nevermind that he had no loyalty to Malcolm. They'd only been partners for less than two weeks, and they'd spent more time jabbing each other with their thorns than working together. He just…

Fuck.

He closed his eyes, tilting his head back against the seat, swearing softly under his breath before he made himself speak. "Malcolm?"

"What." Flat. Forbidding. Clearly still angry.

Fine. Whatever.

"What was Vasquez's crime?"

"Illegal imports," Malcolm replied. Clipped, toneless delivery of information. "Mostly novelty products for children. Fireworks. They wouldn't even be illegal if he'd go through official channels, but he avoids customs fees and maximizes his profits."

Seong-Jae lifted his head, opening his eyes and staring at Malcolm incredulously—at the hard, cragged line of his profile, the tense set of his jaw. "Fireworks. Children's toys. Then why did he throw a knife at me?"

"Because he's a sadistic bastard. And there's a lot of profit in duty-free merchandise. People try to steal things from him." Malcolm shot him a simmering look. "Are you satisfied with that answer? Does that meet your lofty standards?"

A spark of irritation tried to rise. Seong-Jae smothered it firmly and looked out the window once more. "I have no comment."

"Of course you don't," Malcolm said.

Seong-Jae chose not to dignify that with a response.

[7: HEAVY IN YOUR ARMS]

THE TENSION BETWEEN THEM STILL had not dissipated after nearly twenty minutes in smooth, quiet traffic. Minutes in which Seong-Jae withdrew into himself, cutting himself off as much as possible. From Malcolm. From himself.

He could not allow his emotions to get in the way of his work, whether it came to dealing with a criminal informant or came to dealing with infractions on the part of his newly-assigned partner.

Besides, some part of him thought bitterly, Malcolm seemed to prefer him silent and hovering in the background, offering only enough of a presence to counterpoint Malcolm's own thoughts.

Very well.

For now, he would be silent.

No matter the friction between them, if they were to be negotiating with cocaine importers Seong-Jae would prefer to present a united front and keep their private difficulties just that:

Private.

The overpass took them down onto the curving roads leading to the harbor's industrial freight docks; from a distance they were unimpressive, but up close the clusters of towering buildings and massive cranes and stacks and stacks of freight cars made for a rather imposing sight. Malcolm parked far back from the security gate, leaving the Camaro curbside, and together they slipped out of the car. Malcolm's gaze fixed on Seong-Jae, lingering, before he seemed to come to some sort of decision, likely the same that motivated Seong-Jae's silence.

"Stay close," he said quietly. "And follow my lead."

Seong-Jae inclined his head. "As you say."

Malcolm led him across a night-shaded street to a gate guarded by a dimmed security booth. The guard inside looked half-asleep, though there was a tension to his shoulders that said he might well be pretending. Seong-Jae could imagine why.

If he was asleep on duty, he could conveniently not see any illegal activities he had been paid to ignore.

Seong-Jae creased his lips, but forced himself to look away as Malcolm rapped the window, held up his badge, and exchanged a few quiet murmurs before the chain-link gate buzzed, the light flashing green over the automatic security lock at the top and the gate seeming to pop loose. In some strange nightside echo of the earlier scene at the Wellingtons', Malcolm and Seong-Jae slipped through the gate.

Malcolm seemed to know where he was going; the docks

were a cluster of warehouses and cargo containers, but Malcolm threaded his way unerringly through and toward a more poorly-lit area. Seong-Jae glanced up, tracking the security cameras mounted at intervals along the light posts. Every last one was turned in the direction from whence they came, not one pointing toward this far corner where activity rustled and moved in quiet, furtive darts. Malcolm's stride slowed as he drew close. Over two dozen men and women worked to offload paper-wrapped parcels from a cargo container onto wooden pallets on forklifts—but as Malcolm stepped around a wall of containers, every last one froze.

"Scatter!" someone snapped—and more than half the workers disappeared into a warehouse, while the rest drew firearms, pointed at Malcolm and Seong-Jae defensively as the cluster of workers retreated back one step at a time.

Malcolm stopped, raising both hands, and hissed to Seong-Jae. "Hands up."

Seong-Jae sighed but complied, lifting his hands.

Malcolm pitched his voice forward. "Not here on official business. Just came to see Huang. In, out, we were never here."

The workers eyed them suspiciously, before one man took the lead, stepping forward and nodding to another. "Search them."

The other man nodded tightly, holstering his gun and approaching, crossing the distance quickly. He patted Malcolm down, pulling his service pistol from his shoulder holster and another Beretta from an ankle holster, then approached Seong-Jae. Seong-Jae flinched back, but Malcolm made a low warning sound in the back of his throat, catching his eye and raising a brow significantly.

Seong-Jae clenched his teeth, but made himself hold still while the strange man patted over him. Glock first, then the second Glock against his spine, then the Colt at his hip, the dagger against his calf, the second dagger up his left sleeve, the brass knuckles in his coat pocket—until the man was having trouble juggling everything.

"What the fuck, Seong-Jae," Malcolm said.

Seong-Jae arched a brow. "I like to be prepared."

The man snorted with a sour-sounding laugh. "This ain't prepared, it's paranoid."

"I do not particularly find any sort of difference."

The man only shook his head and called back, "They're clear." Then he jerked his chin at them. "You can put your arms down."

Seong-Jae let his arms fall and followed Malcolm across the loading area. He felt naked without his weapons, and glanced back at the man trailing in their wake with his arms full. "Malcolm."

"We'll get them back when we leave," Malcolm muttered from the side of his mouth. "Armed, we're not getting in. Or walking out without a few extra holes in us."

The warehouse was open, its entrance a dark mouth swallowing people and pallets into its gullet. The flurry of activity had stopped short, the dozens of workers disappeared. Only one man remained, standing at the far end of the warehouse flanked by tall pallets stacked with paper parcels. He was large, larger than Seong-Jae had expected, with thick barrel shoulders and meaty arms. His black hair hung lank around his seamed, weathered face, brushing against his shoulders and catching on a black T-shirt that strained at the seams.

"Detective Khalaji," the man said with a smirk. "You're either here to try to arrest me, or you're looking for a good ass-kicking."

Malcolm chuckled. "Neither. And you know better than to try it."

"Still practicing?"

"When I have time."

Seong-Jae inclined his head toward Malcolm without taking his gaze from the massive man—one of few Seong-Jae ever had to meet on eye level, rather than looking down. "Practicing?"

"Krav Maga," Malcolm answered almost subvocally.

"Ah."

The man, whom Seong-Jae could only presume was Huang, watched them in silence from across the warehouse, arms folded over his chest, before he let them drop and prowled toward them on a confident, easy stride. He inclined his head toward Malcolm, then locked dark eyes on Seong-Jae, taking him in assessingly. Seong-Jae met that gaze

[129]

frankly, waiting. He was accustomed to being sized up by criminals, and had little patience for the posturing games that went into these displays of masculinity, arms proficiency, or whatever other game this man wished to play to establish dominance on his turf.

And so he only waited, until Huang asked, "You fight?"

Seong-Jae considered his answer, then chose simple honesty. "Kickboxing."

"Nice," Huang said, then snorted. "Either you're a lightweight hobbyist, or damned good."

"Why do you make that assessment?" Seong-Jae asked.

"Not a single scar."

"Where you can see," Seong-Jae pointed out.

"Fair point." Huang offered one massive, brutish hand lined with several scars of his own. "Jason Huang."

Seong-Jae considered that hand, and the wisdom of shaking hands with a stranger who had already been identified to him as a cocaine dealer. A handshake might, perhaps, indicate his approval of this clandestine meeting, when the hairs on the back of his neck were standing up and he was painfully aware of movement beyond the walls, the sense of being observed, the tension in this seemingly easy meeting that could turn it sour at any moment.

But it was that tension that made his decision for him, when unarmed he was at a disadvantage—and he had Malcolm to consider. And so he gripped Huang's hand, nodding briefly.

"Detective Seong-Jae Yoon."

Rather than play at posturing, Huang's handshake was brisk, to the point, a friendly squeeze before letting go. He cocked his head, looking at Seong-Jae, before a wry grin curved his lips.

"You look a little surprised, Detective Yoon."

"I had not expected you to be congenial. Our conversation with our last informant indicated that you are not overly fond of Detective Khalaji."

"I think Detective Khalaji's a nosy piece of shit, and I haven't forgiven him for the fuckery he pulled before he got pulled off narcotics into homicide." Huang's voice hardened briefly, before smoothing into affable pleasantry. "But being hostile gets you in shit. Nobody in my line of work wants to get caught, or wants to die. So we play nice, and do our ugly behind closed doors. Guessing they do it a bit different where you're from."

Seong-Jae arched a brow. "What makes you think I am not from here?"

Huang's response was a scoffing sound, a wide-creased grin. "You don't talk East Coast. We don't like all that formal nonsense here. We talk business and get straight to the point. So this is the part where you don't ask me what my line of business is, and tell me what you came for."

Malcolm interjected smoothly, diverting Huang's curious regard from Seong-Jae. "Trying to finger someone for the murder of Marion Garvey."

Huang's smile faded. "Garvey's dead? Fuck." His face set in grim lines, thoughtful, introspective. "That's going to fuck up a large part of my network."

Malcolm's brows drew together. "So he *was* dealing out of his club."

"You know I can't answer that without incriminating myself."

"But you just gave me the sideways answer I needed anyway." Malcolm stroked his beard. "So you don't know anyone who put a hit out on Garvey."

"Nah. He was a prick, but he wasn't worth killing. No value in it. He was at least kind of useful alive." Huang rolled broad shoulders, his neck cracking. "You don't kill someone just for being a smarmy asshole."

Malcolm pursed his lips. "I've been tempted a time or two."

"Is it possible he was the victim of a deal that played out poorly?" Seong-Jae asked.

"It's possible," Huang said. "I can keep my ear to the ground. Junkies aren't exactly good at keeping things secret. And if one killed his dealer, he's going to be sniffing for someone new pretty soon, once the jitters set in."

Seong-Jae bit back a retort. It sat sick in the pit of his stomach, how casually Huang spoke of people with addiction problems, the pain they faced, that clawing emptiness, that desperation like worms in the blood. But he couldn't take his gaze from the man—and Huang slowly swung his gaze back to Seong-Jae, cold eyes staring into him as if he knew his every thought. Every bitter drop of loathing, melting on his tongue. Every ounce of force exerted to restrain himself, unarmed and outnumbered or not.

They stared at each other in silence for long moments— before Malcolm was there, his hand on Seong-Jae's arm, his body injected between the two of them and breaking their line of sight, his voice splitting the silence.

"Thanks, Huang," he said. "We'll get out of your hair."

Seong-Jae moved stiffly; he didn't want to turn his back on Huang, but Malcolm gave him little choice, almost herding him with his body, guiding him back toward the mouth of the warehouse. After a few steps, though, Huang's voice drifted after them.

"You didn't think we had him done to start with, did you?"

"No," Malcolm tossed back. "Just chasing loose ends before I have to go put my badge on the line pissing off some very rich people." Then, more firmly: "Let's *go*, Seong-Jae."

"Nice meeting you, Yoon," drifted after them mockingly. "Drop by any time."

"I think not," Seong-Jae hissed—only for Malcolm to elbow him with a dire sidelong look, silencing him.

Seong-Jae held his tongue, but his tension felt like it would snap him in half as they retrieved their weapons from the man who'd taken them. He didn't feel right again until he'd holstered his pistols and slid his daggers back into their sheaths, brass knuckles a comfortable weight in his pocket. But he couldn't start to relax until they were across the broad concrete expanse and almost to the fence, only his pride and absolute refusal to show weakness stopping him from looking over his shoulder to keep a close eye on Huang and his people.

But as they stopped to wait for the gate to open, he glanced back, watching the busy flurry of activity that had resumed as if they'd never interrupted—even if he could feel the weight of multiple watchful gazes keeping a close eye on them. They'd just walked unarmed into hostile territory, and walked out unscathed.

It seemed a little too simple to get away that easily.

"You believe him?" he asked Malcolm as they slipped through the gate.

"He's got no reason to lie." Malcolm straightened his suit coat. "If he lies, if I get the slightest hint of anything fishy, I'll haul him in—and he knows it. He wants to stay a free man, he tells me the truth when I ask."

Seong-Jae stared at him. "You cannot dismiss his crimes as easily as an importer of children's novelties. Not if he is involved in cocaine trade."

He expected a snarl, a dismissive response that this was simply *how things were done* in Baltimore. Instead Malcolm stopped cold. He stood silently beneath the golden disc of a street lamp, the light falling over him and casting him in sepia shades, softening the hard edges of his tense body, smoothing at the lines of him as if the light could ease away the sudden weary weight that seemed to crush him down until his heavy bulk was somehow *smaller*, taking up less space than that forceful presence normally occupied.

"No. I can't," Malcolm said softly. His jaw worked from side to side, before he continued, "And I don't like it. But I can't pin him for anything concretely. Huang's good at what he does. He's slipped through my fingers and the fingers of every other narcotics beat that's gone after him." He turned his head, one exhausted, darkened eye lingering on Seong-Jae over his shoulder. "That doesn't mean we haven't dragged him in a dozen times, and will do it a dozen more times until it sticks. Puts a hiccup in his dealings, at least. He loses money, and he's more cautious. More caution means more careful sales, and fewer buyers. It's only a small victory, but he'll dig himself into a hole he can't wiggle out of one day. And we'll be there." He exhaled slowly, shaking his head. "Until then, we use him for what we can."

Seong-Jae studied Malcolm, and wondered if in ten more years he, too, would be this bitter, this tired from walking the tightrope between fierce determination and inevitable crushing defeat, worn down again and again by trying to stand against a battering tide. Malcolm, he thought, was a stone shore that waves slammed against again and again.

He might seem endless and immovable, but time and time again each dash of waves against rock eroded more and more of him away.

[135]

Seong-Jae looked away. He couldn't condone it. But he could tactfully avoid challenging it, and the only thing he said was, "Practical."

"So you actually approve?" Malcolm shot back sardonically.

"I did not say that."

"I swear to all hell…" Malcolm clenched his fists, then growled and moved forward, toward the car. "Nothing. Nevermind. *Nevermind*. It's late. Let's call it for the night, go home, and annoy the Wellingtons bright and early. I think I'd like to meet Lillienne's husband."

"As you say," Seong-Jae said, quickening his stride to catch up.

"As I say," Malcolm repeated, an annoyed edge in his voice. "And Seong-Jae?"

Seong-Jae paused, hand curled against the cool metal of the car door handle. "Yes?"

"Later, we are going to have a *talk* about those non-regulation issue weapons."

"Of course we will," Seong-Jae said. "The moment we have a talk about your non-regulation issue informants."

Malcolm only gave him a flat, needling look.

Then shut himself into the car without a word.

MALCOLM LET SEONG-JAE OFF AT the station's parking garage.

I can drop you off at home, he'd offered, as he did almost every day.

And *no thank you,* Seong-Jae had said, once again as he did almost every day. Malcolm didn't even know how he got to and from the office—if he had his own car, if he took the train, if he took a cab.

But it was bothering him more and more, for some reason.

That Seong-Jae trusted him so little.

Then again, had he really given the other man reason to? If Seong-Jae was closed, so was Malcolm—and it wasn't hard to see that Seong-Jae disapproved of Malcolm's methods.

Fuck, Malcolm was so used to his own way of doing things that it was hard to actually step back and look at his habits through an outsider's eyes. He'd thought, working homicide in L.A., that Seong-Jae would understand that sometimes you bent to keep from breaking.

But maybe Seong-Jae wasn't the one who had the wrong of things, here.

Malcolm lingered a moment, the Camaro idling, as he watched Seong-Jae's shadowed shape disappear into the parking garage, melting into the darkness between irregularly spaced lights. The grace in his movements was captivating; Malcolm had never seen anyone he liked to simply watch *walk*, but watching Seong-Jae move was like watching an elegant, slim blade in motion, wielded by a practiced hand. No one Malcolm had ever met married fey, foxlike beauty with cold-edged, killing strength with such smooth simplicity, and—

And if he wasn't careful, he was going to end up fucked up over a partner he didn't want or even *like*.

Goddammit.

He tore his gaze from Seong-Jae, staring down the street at the sluggish molasses flow of traffic. There was a restlessness in him, a raw and jagged ache that sat deep down in his lungs and dug its teeth in on every inhaled breath. If he tried to go home and relax right now, he'd burst out of his skin. He got like this mid-case if he couldn't get close to a solve within twenty-four hours, but it usually wasn't this bad. Just right now, everything was...

Everything was too much.

Seong-Jae. Gabrielle. A painful, horrible ache that wanted to check on Nathan McAllister even though it wasn't his business and wasn't his *place*, and he had to keep his distance. He was the last person that kid would want to see, when he'd be haunted for the rest of his life by the faces of dead boys Malcolm hadn't been able to save.

It's not your job to save them.

That wasn't his voice. That was Ryusaki's. She'd told him that, time and time again—not to be cruel, no, but to give him perspective. In homicide...no. No, it wasn't his job to save them.

He'd made that his mantra, but right now it wasn't that easy to remember.

You need to see Ryusaki. You need to get this out of you, before it poisons you.

But Ryusaki would have left the office, by now. He wouldn't violate the sanctity of her private time by calling her at home, even if more than once she'd told him the invitation was open.

Tomorrow. He'd go first thing tomorrow.

He just had to figure out what to do with himself tonight.

He pressed down on the gas, easing the Camaro away from the curb and into traffic. Home, he thought—but home wasn't where his path took him, as he navigated Baltimore's narrow streets. He drove past home without a second thought, his apartment building waiting with its soft quiet music and every bit of furniture chosen to make him feel completely shut off from the world in an environment of his choosing. It was where he needed to be, but it wasn't where he *wanted* to be.

He wanted to be around other people, even if he held himself apart.

He needed some kind of human connection with the

living, to remind him why he fought so hard for the dead.

His heart was sick and heavy, by the time he pulled into a parking spot in Little Italy, outside *Blue*. The exterior of the bar was small and unassuming, just a gray-painted corner brick building bumped up adjacent to a small, cozy bakery that was still shutting down for the night, the scents of pastries drifting across the sidewalk and bringing with them the sounds of laughter, quiet conversation, a neighborhood settling for the evening and shrugging the day off its shoulders.

Inside, *Blue* was all warm wood tones, intimate shadows, the soft golden glow of bulb lights hanging in tiered strings from the ceiling. Mirrored glass, a polished wooden bar, floor carpeted in rich sound-absorbing pile in deep, welcoming burgundy. The entire room was subtly designed to improve acoustics, from the placement of the seating arrangements to the lightly textured sound panels spaced between glossy wooden framing on the walls, the dark black patterning adding a strange elegance to the atmosphere.

Malcolm may not have been to temple in weeks, but places such as this bar were his houses of worship; the stillness, the quiet, was one of reverence, patrons who came more for the experience than the liquor. In places like this, other people were incidental. Their oneness came in the quiet communion of experiencing the music together, appreciating it in silence, sharing without words the bliss of a perfect performance captured in this place like a hidden pearl within an oyster, secreted away only for the eyes of a small few.

This close to dinner, only a few people had drifted in to enjoy the early performances. There was no stage, not really; only a raised dais at the far end of the room, where a baby Grand sat waiting to be caressed, loved. A young man sat at the bench, cracking and working his knuckles, massaging his hands, preparing to warm up. He was slim and pale with a certain sharp-edged beauty that rung hauntingly familiar, his shag of black hair falling to frame his face and catch on the collar of his button-down shirt. His hands were long and elegant, his knuckles stark, the craftsmanship of his fingers promising deft motion across the keys and strong bridging movements, complex chords.

He glanced up as if he could feel Malcolm's gaze on him. Malcolm hovered near the door, tucked to one side and making himself unobtrusive. He wasn't quite ready to step into the stillness of his house of worship yet, where the hymnals were counted out by the tinkle of ice against tumblers and the trill of piano keys. He suddenly felt too brutish to be here, too bloodied, as the pianist—God, young, so young, he had to be in his mid-twenties at the most—watched him with translucently clear, pale blue eyes, before a blush stained his pale skin and a shy smile tugged his lips as he lowered his gaze to the keys and his hands.

Then peeked back again from the corner of his eye, biting his lip, lingering on Malcolm while Malcolm wondered if he could even touch all that fair, pale skin without getting it so dirty the young man would never be clean again.

But that restless ache was back in his gut, that pull, that

yearning, and it roused with a hungry growl at those curious, questioning hints of interest. He lingered on the pianist, wondering, then pushed himself away from the door and headed for the bar.

He knew the bartender by sight, not by name, and the woman—in her crisp white shirt and glossy black waistcoat—knew him by his order of Johnny Walker Blue, neat. He shed his suit coat and folded it over the seat next to him, loosened his tie, and settled to take his first slow, soothing sip, the burn a raw thing that heated his mouth and scorched all the way down, cleansing fire washing away his sins from the inside out.

The first practice scales rippled over the bar like glissandos of rain. The pianist was deft—Malcolm could tell that even in scales, with how fluidly the notes blended into each other with hardly a pause as his fingers pattered across the keys. Malcolm leaned against the bar, watching the young pianist warm up, watching how he lost himself in such utter concentration as he sank into the music. That was one reason why Malcolm loved this; there was something pure and sweet about watching someone so absorbed in creating art and passion that lifted others on the rising tide of their emotions, *giving* so much to others through their creativity when Malcolm was constantly surrounded by how cruel people could be when all they ever did was take and take and *take*.

But the young man behind the piano, settled with his shoulders so straight and upright, was more than giving right now. As the lights dimmed, as a hush settled and a stillness took the few people dotted around the bar and bowed over their own conversations at isolated, intimate little table settings…he *poured* himself into pulling soft, heartfelt notes from the keys, making them sing and cry with aching poignancy. Malcolm didn't recognize the composition, thought it might be original—but it made him think of the slow sweet fall of water dripping from new spring leaves after a lashing, violent thunderstorm.

He sipped his whiskey and let himself be caught—by the notes, by the entranced, rapt expression of ferocious concentration on the pianist's face, his red soft lips parted as if he would sing forth notes to match the low sweet melody he coaxed from the piano. He played with his entire body; it was bad form to be so mobile, Malcolm knew, and yet the rhythm and sway and flow of him were all a part of this, in the way he threw his entire body into building crescendos and nearly stretched himself along the width of the piano to bring alternating chords together.

Lovely, Malcolm thought as the droplets of music melted into his blood and the warm burn of whiskey simmered low in the pit of his stomach.

Simply lovely.

He wasn't sure how long the pianist played; Malcolm measured time not in seconds or in minutes but in fingers of whiskey, and he was one and a half down out of two by the time those notes hit a bursting peak, broke, and seemed to collapse apart in showers of soft sound like falling colored glass.

As the last note trailed off, stillness fell, ringing and brimming with tension—before a smattering of soft applause followed, too quiet to break the reverie. The pianist was flushed, his neck glistening with a touch of sweat that Malcolm lingered on; beaded droplets begged to be licked from the pounding throb of his pulse against pale, fragile skin. Malcolm followed a single trailing droplet down until it vanished into the man's collar, then tore his gaze away and fixed on his drink.

Fuck, he was a mess. His mind should be on the case right now with complete and obsessive focus, but instead it was anywhere but.

When he looked back, the pianist was gone—replaced by a middle-aged woman in a slim cocktail dress, rolling her wrists with the practiced movements of someone with decades of experience behind the keys. Malcolm studied her for long moments, idly wondering what kind of notes lived inside her hands, before turning back to the bar and signaling for another drink, then tossing back the last skim of whiskey left in his tumbler and letting it scour through him.

He shouldn't be here tonight. The wrongness of it sat heavy on him. These moments of benediction in whiskey and rippling notes were for when he finished a case. But he'd never bothered, after the McAllister case—because that case had never felt finished. Not even with Sarah Sutterly behind bars, awaiting a competency hearing and, the last he heard, in the process of being transferred to a psych ward for counseling prior to standing trial.

There was nothing else he could do.

There was nothing else he could have *done*.

And he should be at home building out a suspect list, instead of sitting here drinking and wondering what Seong-Jae was doing right now. Where he took himself, when he walked away from Malcolm without looking back.

What kind of private life did a man like that have?

For all Malcolm knew, Seong-Jae went home to a loving husband every night, and dropped his cold façade with a laugh while they tucked together on the sofa, leaned in close, read books in completely different genres, and teased each other for their tastes…only to mock-bicker over whose night it was to make dinner and whose night it was to do dishes. They probably had a *cat*. They wanted two, but neither had the time to keep their furniture spotless and fur-free with two. The mental image, painted warm in golden lamplight, made Malcolm smile—when it really wasn't any of his goddamn business.

Nor was it his business to wonder what kind of man Seong-Jae would go home to.

Or to wonder any goddamn thing about Seong-Jae at all.

Maybe another tumbler of JW Blue had been a bad idea.

"This seat taken?" a soft, slightly breathy voice asked, masculine tenor underscored by a certain shy sweetness.

Malcolm glanced up. The pianist leaned over the barstool

occupied by Malcolm's coat, resting his elbow on the bar and watching him with uncertain interest glimmering in luminous eyes. He was *arresting*, Malcolm thought, a certain kind of soft entreaty in his gaze that could make it far too easy to fall into those eyes and forget how to climb back out.

He considered, then snagged his coat and transferred it to lie across his lap. "It's not now."

The pianist grinned, pulling his long, lanky frame up onto the barstool, folding himself with a certain consummate grace. He flicked his fingers to the bartender, catching her attention, and mouthed something—before turning his attention to Malcolm. He propped his cheek against his palm, watching him without a word, before suddenly grinning.

"You were actually paying attention."

Malcolm shrugged. "You're good."

"I'm the warm-up act," the pianist said with a self-deprecating laugh. There was a quiet intimacy in the way he spoke, but then the bar lent itself to that; every conversation was a secret whispered from one to the other to keep from disrupting the performance. He trailed off as the bartender returned with Malcolm's fresh whiskey and a vodka and soda for the pianist. The pretty young man took a testing sip, then a longer one, before flashing Malcolm a wry smile. "I'm just someone to keep the noise on until the heavy hitters come in for cocktail hour. You know. Jerome Wilson, Jan Newsome. Those types."

Malcolm inclined his head, pressing his mouth to the rim

of his glass but not drinking yet. He only watched the pianist, taking in the slightly overeager breathlessness, the way he'd opened the collar of his shirt to breathe and bared the fine, articulated line of his collarbones, the way he flushed the longer Malcolm lingered on him, ducking his head and making eye contact, only to look away, then back, as if he didn't know where to look when Malcolm was only watching him. Inexperienced, Malcolm thought, but not too inexperienced. Shy, but not lacking in confidence. Looking to fall in love, but not tonight.

No, tonight…

Tonight, a man like that just wanted to feel loved.

Just an illusion in vodka kisses and grasping hands, so flimsy it would burst apart with the light of day.

Those kinds of illusions, Malcolm dealt in all too easily.

He turned his gaze away from the pianist, before he might end up making him uncomfortable with his unsmiling scrutiny. "I was here for one of Jan's performances last week," he said neutrally. "She was good."

"You left in the middle, though."

Malcolm blinked, startled from his neutral withdrawal, gaze flying back to the pretty young man. "You saw me?"

"I remembered you." A boyish grin. "You came in after my set was over. They give free drinks to performers, so I tend to stay after my set and watch." Pale blue eyes flicked over Malcolm, dipped to his lips. "You left with a man," he ventured softly.

Malcolm tilted his head. "I did."

"He's not here tonight."

Malcolm almost, *almost* smiled. "Are you trying to ask me something?"

A soft sweep of dark hair fell across the young man's face as he ducked his head, running one long, agile fingertip along the rim of his glass—and for a moment Malcolm saw a raven's wing of messy hair falling across black eyes, a sullen red strawberry of a mouth...

He pushed the thought forcefully away. "Or are you just guessing at things?"

Slim shoulders shrugged. "Just wondering if he's your boyfriend."

"I don't even know his name."

One pale eye caught Malcolm from beneath that loose tumble of hair. "...do you have a boyfriend, then?"

"I don't do long-term." Malcolm set his tumbler down and rested his elbow on the bar, leaning on it—leaning closer, letting himself drift close enough to feel the faint prickle of overheated exertion rising off the pianist like steam, close enough to smell the subtle hint of sweat cooling on his skin and something lighter, airier, likely shampoo or soap or just the light clean scent of him. Malcolm let his gaze dip down to the hollow of his throat, the tempting dip of pale bare skin vanishing past the open collar. "Why don't you ask me what you really want to ask me?"

"What I really want to ask you..." The pianist lifted his

head, his eyes a little too wide, a little too guileless, as he met Malcolm's eyes. His tongue darted, soft and pink, over his lips, leaving behind a sweet sheen. "Am I wrong about you?"

"You're not," Malcolm growled.

The pianist flushed, leaning in closer, eating inches of the space between them until body heat met body heat in warring clouds. "So were you watching me for the performance, or because you're attracted to me?"

"What if the performance is what attracted me?"

"I'll take it." The pianist laughed, then, husky and low, and the soft throaty burr of desire edging his voice made heat clench in Malcolm's gut, turning the whiskey burn into something deeper, hungrier. He watched the part and glisten of the pianist's lips as he took another sip of his vodka and soda, wetting his mouth until it was luscious and nearly dripping and begging to be licked. And those lips had Malcolm's utter attention, as the pianist murmured, "...we could get out of here."

"It's a thought."

That shy smile turned sly. "My place or yours?"

Malcolm tossed down his second tumbler of Johnny Walker, letting the rush hit him hard this time: embers and ash in his blood, desire a slow liquid thing that flowed down, down, ever down to pool in the base of his cock. Dropping the tumbler on the bar, he slid to his feet, shrugged his coat on, and plucked his wallet from the inner pocket to leave a few bills pinned underneath the empty tumbler. The entire time the pianist watched him curiously, but slid to his feet as Malcolm tucked his wallet away—only to let out a soft, startled gasp as Malcolm hooked an arm around his waist, closing the last gap between them to bring body to body and breath to breath, their chests pressed close.

"Mine," he growled, and savored the feeling of the pianist's shiver rolling through him as the man rested his hands lightly to Malcolm's chest.

Pale eyes lidded, and slim hands curled in the lapels of Malcolm's suit. "So you like to keep control," the pianist said, tilting his head up until his lips were insolent things mocking Malcolm with their closeness, their temptation, as he whispered, "Good." He leaned harder into Malcolm, until there was no mistaking the need pressing between his thighs, the hardness caught against his slacks. "Tomorrow, will I be someone whose name you don't remember, too?"

"I can't remember something I never knew." When the pianist's lips parted, Malcolm stilled them with a touch of his fingertips—and nearly groaned. His mouth was so fucking *soft*, and Malcolm wanted to do terrible things to those plush and yielding lips. He was developing an obsession with red, overripe mouths, and he didn't want to think about why. "Don't tell me. I like it better that way."

He traced his fingertips along the pianist's mouth, absorbing the texture of his lips, the way they trembled…then pulled back, letting his arm fall from around his waist.

"Now," he said. "I'm going to give you my keys, and my

address. We're going to walk out to my car. You're going to kiss me. And then you're going to drive us home."

Coy amusement glittered in the pianist's eyes. "What's going to happen there?"

"Do I need to tell you?"

"No." The pianist fingered Malcolm's lapel, then let his hand slide away, drifting down Malcolm's chest to stop teasingly short at the waist of his slacks before drawing back, leaving Malcolm's cock throbbing in anticipation of a touch that never happened. The pianist smirked. "I should make you ask me. I don't like being told what to do."

Then he brushed past Malcolm, his entire body sliding against him, electric friction that scorched the breath from his lungs, every inch of him yearning after that promise of the pressure of flesh to flesh, the slide of skin to skin, breaths and lips mated and melding, enticement in every lazy stride, in the glance the pianist threw over his shoulder.

"But I'll make an exception for you," he murmured, then slipped through the door and outside.

Malcolm lingered long enough to let the door nearly close. Long enough to take a deep, slow breath and pull himself under control. He straightened his coat.

Then closed the distance in three long, swift strides, catching the door just before it shut. The pianist was waiting just outside as if he *knew*, as if he'd been tugging Malcolm's goddamned leash, and Malcolm was ready to let himself be tugged. Ready to be pulled in, giving in to the gravity of

COLE MCCADE

desire as he dragged that teasing, shy, pretty thing into his arms, crushed him back against the outside wall, and leaned down to capture and taste his mouth.

He tasted like vodka and something sweet, and gave in to Malcolm the same way he'd given in with his music: wholly and utterly, with rushing sighs and gasping inhalations and his lips parted and open for the taking. Where Malcolm was all teeth and hard edges, the pianist was all flow and softness, melding and yielding and meeting Malcolm's every demand with *more*: more of the slow, shy caresses of his mouth, more testing, feinting flicks of his tongue, more teasing caresses of grazing teeth and grasping hands and a warm, taut body that trembled as Malcolm raked his hands up his back. He was tight as a quivering bowstring under Malcolm's touch, and Malcolm groaned with pleasure as he nipped at the pianist's upper lip and *felt* his response in the shudders tightening sleek musculature under Malcolm's palms, in the rough heady throb of his cock against Malcolm's hips.

Malcolm hardly remembered breaking away. Hardly remembered the fumble for his keys, the delicious way the pianist shivered when Malcolm growled his address into his ear. Hardly remembered the blessedly short drive to his building, lips locked and breathlessly tangled at stoplights, the pianist's hand on his thigh at intersections, fingers drifting higher and higher until the backs of his knuckles brushed the seam of Malcolm's slacks and his cock jerked against the thin fabric with nothing between him and that warm skin except a single layer.

[152]

The pianist flashed him a sidelong look, pale eyes heated until they smoldered, pupils dilated, smoky. "No underwear?"

"I don't like it."

Malcolm could barely get the words out when that long, deft hand curled over him, cupping between his thighs and playing him like he was the most delicate of chords, agile fingers working over his cock and scorching him with brushes of dragging, hungry sensation. He let his eyes flutter half-shut, tilting his head back against the seat, lifting his hips into that warm, kneading palm that felt as though it molded his desire into any form the pretty young man wanted, shaping that molten feeling in the pit of his stomach until it was a tight-knotted, condensed ball of heat ready to burst through him.

"Here," he rumbled, breaths coming shallow. "Park here."

That tormenting hand eased away; the Camaro slid smoothly into its parking spot.

"Tell me you're on the first floor," the pianist whispered.

"Top floor."

"Fuck."

"That's the plan." Malcolm managed a smirk, sliding out of the passenger's seat and slamming the door shut. He rounded the hood of the car, dragged the pianist close once more, and stole a single heated, feverish kiss, hard pressure and hunger and a strange and desperate need to mark that soft mouth until the pretty young man would feel it for days after, only to pull away and draw him—flushed, dazed, gasping, utterly pliant in Malcolm's grip—toward the door to the building. "Come on."

Inside. Nearly chasing each other up the stairs, taking them two at a time. Keys in the lock, door flung open, and then Malcolm had the pianist up against the wall in the entryway, stealing his mouth again and this time tasting the lingering hints of his own drink branded in possessive whiskey aftertaste on his skin. Malcolm skimmed his hands up the lovely thing's sides and, when the pianist lifted his arms in response, caught him by the forearms and pinned him there with one hand, slender arms trapped over his head and his body arching against Malcolm as if he didn't have the will to struggle as Malcolm raked his free hand down his body, dragging the buttons of his shirt open, baring smooth skin to his touch.

For a single breathless moment Malcolm lingered, tearing from the kiss to watch his hand move over the pale skin of the pianist's chest. He was flawless as if he'd been newly minted yesterday, his skin so smooth that Malcolm felt as though he would sand him raw with his own rough touch, with how the calluses of his fingertips skated against him, with how darkly the tan of Malcolm's skin burned against pale flesh.

He traced the fine ridges of his stomach, walked his fingers upward until he slid them through the groove of his pectorals, flattened his palm, spread his fingers until thumb and pinky both grazed small, tightly puckered pink nipples. The pianist's stomach sucked in on a gasp, hazed eyes locked on Malcolm, pleading without words—only for his lashes to slam downward, head tossing back, as Malcolm raked his touch downward to cup him through his slacks.

The entire time Malcolm said nothing. But the pianist was more than vocal enough for both of them, crying out in short, harsh, needy sounds as Malcolm worked his cock against his palm, deliberately using the fabric of his slacks and boxers to tease him with dragging caresses—but every breaking cry nearly shredded his control, until he wanted the touch of unfettered flesh. Wanted the lovely man on the verge of breaking, and he caught the button of the pianist's slacks, ripped it open, then slid his palm skin to skin down the front of his boxers.

The moment he touched hot flesh, the pianist jerked roughly, straining against the grip pinning his arms to the wall. "Fuck—" the man cried, only to strangle off in a breathless, gasping sound as Malcolm wrapped his fingers around the full length of him.

One inch at a time he explored him: gripping his shaft against his palm, working his fingers over his length, tracing each vein and ridge and tapered circumference as if he could see him with touch, know him with the sensation of heat and slick skin against his fingertips. The pianist told him where he was sensitive by how his hips jerked when Malcolm circled just beneath his cock head, by how he curled forward with a whimper when Malcolm traced his thumb through the wet-dewed slit at the tip, by how he completely stopped breathing for one choked moment when Malcolm circled his fingertips just underneath the base of his cock, stroking the sensitive place where his cock joined his balls.

"Ah, *fuck*," the pianist gasped, trembling, hanging weak and boneless in Malcolm's grasp, his cheeks flushed, his lips parted on gasping, panting breaths. "Fuck, that's...oh God, right there, right *there*..."

Malcolm stopped—cupping his shaft against his palm, squeezing just tight enough to give pleasure without relief, and lingered on that beautifully disheveled face. "You gonna come already?"

The pianist made a soft, needy sound, only to catch it with his teeth cutting into his lower lip, ripening it further. "Cruel," he whispered, pale eyes slipping open, begging.

"I can be." Malcolm gently eased his grip on the pianist's arms, freeing him, just as he began working his cock once more, teasing him in slow, coaxing strokes, drinking in how his eyes went soft and his lips went lax. Lax enough to give utterly against Malcolm's as Malcolm gently tilted his face up, catching his mouth in a soft, slow kiss, murmuring, "If you want me to be nicer...I can be that, too."

Slim arms wrapped around his shoulders, clinging to him. "Do you like making your lovers suffer?" the pianist whispered against his lips.

"Only when they like it."

A slow smile curved against his mouth, only to trail into a shuddering gasp as he once more stroked the pianist's cock from root to tip. Damp, slick lips trailed against his cheek, grazed against his ear.

"I like it," the other man breathed.

That was all the invitation Malcolm needed.

He turned his head, seized that teasing mouth, made it *his*. He bit and suckled and toyed and licked until the pianist went weak against him, only to gasp out as Malcolm caught him under his thighs and lifted him bodily. Long legs wrapped around his waist. Their hips ground together in rough sparks of friction, rhythm matching the hard swift drumbeat of Malcolm's heart, the timpani of his strides as he crossed the massive single-room space to his bed. They struck hard enough that the mattress squealed in protest, the headboard thumping against the wall.

For half a second he tore away—just long enough to fling his coat to the floor, his tie and shirt following, before he reached for the pianist's clothing and the other man reached for him. He didn't know who stripped whom or what went where, only that suddenly there was only hot skin and cool sheets and the deliciously erotic friction of their bodies sliding together until they found that perfect lock where dips and angles of sinew intersected, every last one of Malcolm's hard edges finding a place in the sleek flow and stretch of the pianist's long, supple body, until their hips matched and mated so that every slow motion that brought them against each other kissed their cocks together in stroking fireburst caresses.

Like this the other man felt so *small* beneath him, and

there was something about that that inflamed Malcolm, that roused conflicting urges to dominate, to protect, to capture, to cherish. He would never see this man again after tonight…but for tonight, at least, he touched him as if he would remember the slope of his stomach and the angle of his hip and the soft dip of flesh behind the bend of his knee for the rest of his life.

And when Malcolm hooked his fingers beneath one long leg and drew it up to flank his hips, the man opened for him willingly, spreading himself in clear anticipation. Sightlessly, Malcolm dug the bottle of lube from the nightstand drawer and coated his fingers in a slick layer, while those wide blue eyes watched him with lashes trembling in a touch of trepidation, nervousness—nervousness Malcolm kissed from the pianist's lips, plying him slowly, gently, coaxingly.

So that when he slipped the first finger inside that waiting, wanting body, the cry that melted against his lips would be one of pure pleasure, rather than fear or denial.

"Relax for me," Malcolm whispered, as the man arched his back, tensed his entire body, shaking and spreading his thighs wider until he was a pale, divine offering. "Relax."

The only answer was a keening, breathless whisper and the bite of nails into Malcolm's shoulder blades. He hissed, pain spiking right to his gut with little needles of desire, but still made himself move slowly—easing his finger into that tight heat, testing just how much the writhing man beneath him could take, listening to those broken, strained whimpers and harsh breaths through clenched teeth.

They were the music notations guiding him in playing the pianist's body, telling him when to slow down, draw it out, savor every quiver of taut flesh and every clench of tight muscle gripping at him—and when to push for more, adding a second finger, a third, stretching and working them inside the man's body until he was yielding and soft and ready. Until the pianist was thrashing against the sheets, his fingers knotting up ridged handfuls, his cock hard and swollen against his belly and the tip leaking in clear threads against his skin like melted sugar.

Malcolm caught that succulent lower lip between his teeth, drew it into his mouth, rolled the taste of a whimper over his tongue, and gently eased his fingers free.

"Enough?" he asked, trembling with the effort to contain himself.

The pianist nodded slowly, his eyes wide, his body slicked with sweat until he gleamed in the faint street lights coming through the long, low windows, his hair a sheaf of pure darkness tossed across Malcolm's pillows as if it had been scattered there by the handful.

"Enough," he breathed raggedly. "Please...don't make me wait."

"You wanted me cruel," Malcolm said, but couldn't help but smile—only to hiss, as he poured a fresh pool of lube into his palm and slicked it over his cock, his own fingers almost more than he could stand when the heat of his own body turned the oil into a burning, licking caress against his painfully hardened flesh.

"Maybe," the pianist murmured, reaching up for him, his longing so clear, and for one bitter moment Malcolm remembered a heated, hungry kiss like two storm fronts meeting, cold black eyes, a coolly dispassionate voice saying *I felt nothing* while this lovely thing beneath him gave everything. The pianist drew him down, kissed him softly, twined his fingers into his hair. "But now I just want you."

Malcolm settled between his thighs, sliding his hands down slender hips and lifting them, angling them just right. He didn't answer. He couldn't answer, not when his head and heart were full of bitter things and all he wanted was to drown them in sweetness.

And so he claimed the pianist's lips once more, and lost himself in that ready, pleading body.

He was ready for the cry, for the tension, for the desperate, grasping clutch of slim hands as he sank slowly into tight heat—taking his time, torturing them both, easing past stretched, softened muscle turned slick by the passage of body heat-warmed oil. The pianist's body was so tight it nearly choked the breath from Malcolm, and their rough, needy, frantic gasps mingled and mated with biting, desperate kisses as Malcolm buried deeper and deeper into heat that threatened to melt him down to his bones.

Somehow one inch at a time became one breath at a time. One breath at a time became one thrust at a time, slow and easing between them, the need rolling through Malcolm's body in powerful waves enough to move them both as he sank into that quivering flesh again and again, coaxed that tight-gripping sheath of muscle to open for him, to take him again and again.

And sharp teeth of pleasure bit him again and again, savaging him, his body a thing of heat that burned from a deep inner core, washing over him in waves each time flesh and fire enveloped him—but it was those soft, hungry, gasping cries that stoked him higher. That urged him faster. That drew him deeper, as the lovely man's thighs clutched against his hips and his fingers raked over Malcolm's back and every lift of his hips and shiver of his body and wordless plea in his voice said *I want you.*

No questions. No doubts. No hesitations. No complications.

I want you. I want you. I want you.

And Malcolm gave—one hand braced against the headboard, his knees spread wide, arching over the pale flesh beneath him as he poured his entire body into each deep thrust, trembling to control himself, to control the pace, to keep his pretty captive for the night wholly on edge. He wouldn't let himself go even when his cock was throbbing, tight to the point of pain, need building up in that deep hard knot that said he was going to lose himself at any moment. Not yet. Not *yet,* and even as he angled his hips to surge deeper, to make his nameless lover arch and gasp and clutch at him harder still, he wrapped his fingers around the pianist's stiff, pulsing cock, stroking, demanding, finding every spot the man had taught him would make him writhe just minutes before and drawing every pleasure he could from those keening, panting lips with each touch.

But his control shattered as the pianist arched his entire body, every muscle locking tight as he gave in to Malcolm's demands with a hoarse, broken cry. His cock jerked against Malcolm's palm, and suddenly his fingers were wet and his body was on fire as the other man drew up tight and locked his cock in a searing vise. Malcolm curled forward, pressure crushing him, shattering him, breaking him like a sledgehammer smashed into the stone of his reserve. He held off for a moment longer, just long enough to drag the pianist up, stealing his mouth for another ravaging, deeply hungry kiss.

Then he was lost, white-hot sensation consuming him, until he knew nothing but the tight-clutching ache at his core and the low, deep, painfully intimate sensation of everything he *was* concentrating down to a single moment, a single point, a single breath—and spilling from him into a complete stranger's body.

[8: SAY LESS]

SLEEP CAME FAST, ONCE THEY'D disentangled and cleaned themselves, the bed, each other. The pianist tried a few teasing comments, but was half asleep before he could even finish a complete sentence, passing out on his stomach in a drowsy tangle with his arms looped around a pillow and his face buried into the crook of his elbow.

Malcolm watched him in silence for long moments, unable to help a touch of weary, amused affection, before he stretched out on his back with a sigh and tried to will himself to just...sleep.

Sleep, and not let his thoughts wander in brooding circles.

Normally he'd be a melted, sated heap by now, his brain blessedly empty—the only time his mind ever quieted itself, leaving him tired and drifting off to sleep. It was a good way to shake his demons out after a hard case, but right now...

Fuck. *Fuck.*

He touched his lips. His kiss-bruised, swollen mouth, tender and aching, but the taste he remembered wasn't of whiskey and vodka meeting and shared in needy, biting kisses between strangers.

It was the taste of overripe strawberry lips, the scents of diesel and maleness, the flash of light catching in enigmatic black eyes.

Fuck, he repeated to himself, glancing at his nameless moment of frustrated, reckless, *unprotected* impulse sleeping with the sort of bliss Malcolm envied.

Forcing his mind to blank, he rolled over, dragged the covers up, draped an arm over the pianist's pliant body, and willed himself to sleep.

HE WOKE EYE TO BLACK, cool eye with Seong-Jae Yoon.

Malcolm's eyes drifted open to the painful glare of morning sunlight—blocked by the outline of a tall, angular body leaning over him. He blinked dully up at Seong-Jae, muddled thoughts registering only that he was sleepy and for some reason Seong-Jae was *there,* bent over the bed and looking down at him dispassionately.

"Good morning, Malcolm," Seong-Jae said flatly. "Did you enjoy yourself last night?"

Malcolm blinked.

His head cleared in an instant. His stomach sank. He rolled his head to the side; his one-night stand was still out cold, sleeping soundly on the pillow next to him, while Seong-Jae stood over the bed, calm and unflappable in his usual all-black, the door of the apartment wide open.

And Malcolm buck-ass fucking naked under the covers.

He groaned, closing his eyes, and scrubbed a hand over his face. "What the fuck are you doing here?"

"You left your door unlatched," Seong-Jae retorted smoothly. "And you did not answer when I called."

"I muted my phone for a reason." Malcolm sighed and elbowed the pianist. "You. Wake up."

The pianist snuffled sleepily. "Nngh?" He blinked, slow and drowsy, yawning, before slumping against the pillows with a sleepy smile. He opened his mouth—only to freeze as his gaze moved past Malcolm and locked on Seong-Jae. He scrambled to sit up, clutching the covers to his chest, eyes wide. "Oh fuck. Oh fuck, is that your boyfriend?"

"*No*," Seong-Jae answered vehemently, just as Malcolm said,

"No. He's my partner." When the pianist went pale, horror washing his expression blank, Malcolm swore. "For fuck's sake, not like that. For work."

"Oh." The pianist looked rather confused, and rather chagrined. "Uh. I...uh."

He stared between them, then offered a sheepish smile and wiggled sideways out of the bed, dragging the sheet with him—and nearly pulling the duvet off Malcolm, before Malcolm grabbed it and hauled it back over his lap. The pianist managed to squirm to his feet with the sheet for a shield, and cast about quickly before coming up with his pants and shirt, clutching them to his chest with that same frozen smile.

"I'll…get my things and go," he fumbled out.

"That would be wise." Sighing once more, Malcolm sank against the headboard and jerked his chin toward the Moroccan folding room divider across the room. "Bathroom's behind that screen."

"Thanks," the pianist said—then cast one more wide-eyed glance at Seong-Jae, before nearly scampering away and vanishing behind the screen.

Seong-Jae's expression never changed, his voice as toneless as ever, and yet it set Malcolm's teeth on edge when he asked mildly, "Friend of yours?"

"I don't think that's any of your business," Malcolm grit out. "You gonna stare at me, or get out so I can get dressed, too?"

Seong-Jae's gaze dipped down Malcolm's naked chest, and for a moment lingered at the line where the duvet covered his lap, and Malcolm couldn't help the heated surge of interest making his cock throb at the obvious once-over before Seong-Jae's gaze rose to meet his eyes again.

"You have my apologies," he said, and pivoted on his heel to stride toward the door.

"Hey," Malcolm barked after him.

Seong-Jae paused, poised mid-stride, and glanced back. "Yes?"

"Don't apologize if you don't fucking mean it."

"Very well, then. You do not have my apologies," Seong-Jae retorted. "And I will not be pleased if you are hung over and as foul today as you were yesterday."

"I already told him you're not my boyfriend. You don't get to nag like one." Malcolm snorted. If this wasn't fucking déjà vu all over again. "*Out*, Seong-Jae."

Seong-Jae only made that soft *tch* sound under his breath, walked out, and closed the apartment door in his wake.

Malcolm told himself he was imagining that the door slammed just a little harder than it had to.

His entire body felt heavy, as he rolled himself out of bed and picked up his slacks, hoisting them up around his hips; his head was fucking killing him and he needed a shower, but there was a puppy-eyed prettyboy in his bathroom. So he settled on starting coffee, scrubbing a hand through his sleep-mussed hair as he padded around the kitchen. A few moments later the pianist emerged from behind the screen, dressed with his shirt untucked and only half-buttoned, slacks dragging over stocking feet. He peered across the apartment with wide, somewhat nervous eyes, then seemed to relax, smiling shyly and rubbing at one arm as he padded toward the kitchen.

"So," he said lightly. "He was hot."

"I hadn't noticed." Malcolm dumped a scoop of Kona blend into the pot and flicked it on. "Professional boundaries."

"So, uh..."

Malcolm glanced up. The pianist was watching him with that same curious, shyly eager look as last night, that sense of an unspoken question on his lips. Malcolm exhaled, shaking his head with a rueful smile.

"No. You can't have my number."

The pianist laughed. "Damn." Then he cocked his head toward the door. "What about your partner's?"

"Get *out*," Malcolm snarled, struggling not to laugh. "I'm surrounded by insolent wretches."

With another laugh, the pianist circled the kitchen counter and stretched up on his toes to kiss Malcolm's cheek. In that kiss was a silent message: *I understand, it is what it is, I had a good time, thanks for the night*. But still the pianist teased, "No morning-after breakfast?"

Malcolm hooked an arm around his waist, pulled him in close, and slid his hand up his back to cup his nape, fist a handful of his hair, gently drag him back—capturing him just enough to kiss him, just enough for one last taste to take the edge off, just enough for the satisfaction of feeling him go weak, fingers clutching and sliding over Malcolm's bare shoulders, mouth lax and gasping and sweet.

Then he pulled away, letting the pianist go with one last light stroke down the side of his throat. "No time or I'd eat you," Malcolm said. "I'll call you a cab. On me."

The pianist stood there for a moment, a bit wide-eyed, lips parted, before he let out a touch of an incredulous laugh and ran a hand through his hair. "Thanks." He was already backing up, casting around for his shoes before finding them, flung halfway across the room and fetched up near the coat closet. "See you at Blue again some time?"

"Maybe," Malcolm hedged.

Maybe seemed to be enough—for with another laugh, low and soft, the pianist slipped his shoes on and let himself out.

Malcolm sank forward until his forehead hit the raw wood countertop, and let out a low and tired groan.

"God *damn* it," he muttered.

Just...just...

Damn it.

SEONG-JAE LEANED AGAINST THE WALL outside Malcolm's apartment and waited.

He never should have come here.

Even if there had been a certain sadistic pleasure in waking Malcolm the way he had, he'd also been rather…annoyed. Annoyed that he had had to come fetch Malcolm at all only to find him lounging in bed with some dalliance, when it was highly unprofessional of him to shut his phone off. That was the only reason.

The *only* reason.

Nonetheless he tensed as the door to Malcolm's apartment opened and the pale, rather elfin young man who had been occupying Malcolm's bed came slipping out, his movements sheepish as he buttoned the cuff of his shirt. He turned—then froze when he saw Seong-Jae, his eyes widening, cheeks flushing.

"Oh. Uh. Hi?" He offered a sheepish smile. "Sorry if I made him late to work."

Rather than *sorry*, however, he seemed almost proud of himself, and something about the possessiveness in *Sorry if I made him late…*

Seong-Jae shoved the thought away irritably. He was being entirely irrational, simply because he was not overly fond of wide-eyed, wet-nosed little prats, soft about the edges.

Malcolm Khalaji seems rather fond of him, though. Do you think that is his type?

As if he gave half a damn.

He just needed Malcolm to show up and actually do his job. They had a case to close, half a dozen leads left unexplored, and the last thing he needed was his increasingly erratic partner to go even farther off the rails.

Seong-Jae realized he was just *looking* at the prat—and

the longer he looked at the prat, the more stiff and pale the little thing grew. Blue eyes widened, before the young man swallowed thickly and let out a nervous little laugh.

"I'll…uh…I'll just go."

Seong-Jae narrowed his eyes, then looked away with a soft "tch."

And didn't look back, while the mousy, annoying little thing escaped down the stairs.

Approximately ten more minutes passed—minutes in which he caught the sound of a running shower from inside Malcolm's apartment, and the scent of brewing coffee. Finally Malcolm emerged carrying a travel mug in either hand, the disheveled naked behemoth of lazy sexual energy replaced once more by the old wolf in sheep's fine-pressed wool suit. Stark black today, threaded subtly with the thinnest of silver pinstripes and buttoned over a pale gray shirt with a darker gray tie.

Once again that tie irritated Seong-Jae no end and for no reason, and he could very easily see himself curling it around his fist and *choking* Malcolm with it.

He swallowed back the growl building in the back of his throat, flicked Malcolm over with a sharp look. "So."

"Not a fucking word, Seong-Jae," Malcolm growled, tucking one of the mugs into the crook of his arm and freeing a hand to fit keys to lock and close up the apartment. His hair, still unbound, fell across his face in a half-dried tangle, shadowing flinty eyes that swept Seong-Jae irritably. "There a reason you couldn't wait to meet me at the office?"

"I did," Seong-Jae said. "You were late."

Malcolm dragged the cuffs of his coat and shirt back to check the thick leather-banded watch on his wrist. "No, I'm on time. I usually get there early. It's not a crime if I clock in on time for once."

"You were late for *you*."

Malcolm just stared at him, then burst into soft, almost whispered curses in that musical language he occasionally switched into when Seong-Jae had particularly annoyed him—Persian, he had said it was. Finally he trailed off, fixing Seong-Jae with a baleful look. "Don't come in my apartment unless I explicitly invite you. Understood?"

"Mn." Seong-Jae only shrugged, but deep down there was a part of him that rather took pleasure in Malcolm's irritation. "Are you planning on seeing the departmental therapist today?"

"I told you you don't get nagging rights." Malcolm grumbled and leaned against his apartment door. "Why are you here and where are we going?"

"We should attempt to once more gain access to the Wellington residence to speak to the husband."

"Guess he's our most likely suspect after Lillienne herself. They say it's always the husband." He thudded his head back against the door hard enough to rattle it in its frame, then grimaced; Seong-Jae almost winced in sympathy. "It's almost never the husband."

"Statistically, perpetrators of violence in situations involving domestic couples are overwhelmingly a male partner, even if the victim may not be the other partner."

"Do you really think we're lucky enough that statistics will line up that easily?"

"One can hope," Seong-Jae said. "The scenario is almost textbook, and the motive is undeniable."

"Honestly, I wouldn't mind closing this quickly and getting it off my back." Malcolm straightened and brushed past Seong-Jae, heading for the stairs, but not without pressing one of the travel mugs against his chest. "Here."

Seong-Jae had to snap both hands up to catch the mug before it could drop; he frowned, sniffing at the faint steam rising from the opening in the lid. Faintly bitter, mostly creamy. "What is this?"

"Ten percent coffee, twenty percent sugar, seventy percent whole milk," Malcolm threw over his shoulder, already disappearing down the stairs.

"…oh." Seong-Jae stared at the mug. Why had Malcolm gone to the trouble? But he took a tentative sip; the taste of the coffee was different from the typical diner fare, a subtler blend that was actually not unpleasant when it was only an accent to the sugar and milk, creamy on his tongue. He made a thoughtful sound, trailing Malcolm down the stairs. "It is not overwhelmingly terrible."

"I'll take that as a compliment." Malcolm paused at the foot of the stairs, reaching back to hold the door for Seong-

Jae. "Did you drive here?"

He slid past Malcolm and out onto the sidewalk. For a moment their bodies brushed; Seong-Jae flinched, and told himself he imagined Malcolm flinched as well. "Cab."

"Do you even own a car?"

"No."

"Here."

Malcolm tossed his keys toward Seong-Jae; Seong-Jae caught them out of the air, folding them against his palm and arching a brow.

"I'm too hungover to deal with traffic yet," Malcolm said, rubbing his fingers against his temples.

"And whose fault is that?"

"Shove it, Seong-Jae."

"I think," Seong-Jae said, flicking the Camaro's alarm and rounding to the driver's side, "you have done quite enough of that for both of us."

"Fuck off."

"You seem to have done quite a bit of that, as well."

Malcolm only gave him a surly, almost sullen look, and yanked the car door open to stuff himself into the passenger's seat.

Seong-Jae hid his smile behind his mug, and slid smoothly behind the wheel.

MAYBE IT WAS THE HANGOVER talking, but Malcolm was beginning to deeply regret letting Seong-Jae drive his car.

The man drove like he couldn't tell the difference between city streets and a Formula 1 track: staying barely half a notch below the speed limit and zipping smoothly in and out of traffic, treating the cars like an obstacle course and narrowly missing scraping bumpers, fenders, the fucking *sidewalk*. Malcolm wasn't accustomed to the perspective from the passenger's side, and to his knotting stomach they always seemed at least three inches too close to the curb and on the verge of smashing into a street lamp. He kept one hand on the oh-shit handle, one hand on his throbbing skull.

And both eyes firmly closed, rather than looking at the rush of traffic—or at that stone-set, calm face.

Fuck a stranger to stop thinking about Seong-Jae, and wake up with Seong-Jae standing over his bed, watching him with the same analytical impassivity with which he might watch a crime scene.

For fuck's sake.

Not exactly how he wanted to start his morning.

Although he wasn't sure why he gave a flying fuck. His

private life wasn't Seong-Jae's business.

And the damned man needed to learn how to *knock.*

He didn't open his eyes until Seong-Jae slowed to a more sedate speed. Malcolm cracked one eye open. Chinquapin Park, the block-spanning brick wall surrounding the Wellington estate just up ahead. He touched Seong-Jae's arm lightly, then jerked back.

"Stop here."

Seong-Jae eased on the gas. "But there is parking closer to the gate."

"We're not going in the gate, and I don't want them to see us. Turn at the next block and park down the cross street."

Seong-Jae gave him a skeptical look, but complied—taking the next right and easing the Camaro into a smooth parallel park before killing the engine. "Malcolm, what are you planning?"

"Do you really think the security guard's going to let us back in without a signed and stamped warrant?"

Seong-Jae's eyes narrowed. "What you are suggesting qualifies as breaking and entering."

"Not if we call it a city inspection of their security system." Malcolm levered himself out of the car. "Come on."

He caught Seong-Jae's borderline disgusted sigh before the car door closed. A moment later Seong-Jae emerged, giving him a long, measuring look before shaking his head.

"As you say," he muttered.

"As I goddamn well say."

Malcolm led the way down the sidewalk, once more lifting his gaze to scan the trees that flourished over the top of the fence, their branches reaching beyond the upper ledge of the brick, green leaves making dapples on the sidewalk and now and then whispering in the breeze. But he paused when he caught sight of what he was looking for:

A security camera, turned inward.

And its cabling completely destroyed by branches that had grown through it and around it, puncturing the wires connecting it to other cameras along the perimeter. Several other wires hung frayed and loose as well, likely part of a motion sensor system.

"Sloppy maintenance," he said, nodding toward the mess.

Seong-Jae tilted his head back, looking up, before his brows knit and he shot Malcolm an almost accusatory look. "This is why you were watching the trees as we entered on foot yesterday. This entire segment is not covered by the security system."

Malcolm grinned. "Now you're catching on." He stretched up to test the height of the fence; the upper ledge was just beyond his reach. "Want to boost me up?"

Seong-Jae let out a long, slow sigh, then sank down to one knee and cupped his hands together. Malcolm slipped his heel in carefully, then yelped as Seong-Jae hoisted him up with surprising strength; he nearly lost his balance, only to catch at the upper edge of the wall and stabilize himself. He shot a glare down over his shoulder.

Oversized asshole had done that on purpose.

He grasped one of the branches overhead, braced his other hand on the top of the brick wall, and hauled himself up to crouch on the edge. Keeping his grip on the branch to for leverage, he leaned down, offering his hand to Seong-Jae.

"Here."

"No need," Seong-Jae said, and reached up to grip the edge of the fence. He fit the toes of his boots into the cracks of the brick, then hefted himself up neatly, effortlessly, pulling himself onto the wall to rest on one knee at Malcolm's side, the crow perched there lightly and on the verge of taking flight.

"Showoff," Malcolm muttered.

"My height does have its advantages," Seong-Jae replied, then vaulted lithely over the side and dropped down into the grass. Straightening smoothly, he held his arms up. "Would you like me to catch you?"

"I hate you."

"Do you?"

Malcolm only eyed him, then dropped himself over the side, carefully hitting on the balls of his feet so his dress shoes wouldn't slip in the grass. He landed in a scattering of leaves, sinking down to catch the bulk of the impact in the tension of his thighs, then straightened and dusted himself off, straightening his coat.

"Let's go," he said. "Stay close to the wall. Under the

trees."

He slipped along the wall, lifting his gaze to search the boughs for additional cameras. With the circuit interrupted this entire wall was probably out; it was rather odd that a family with as much money as the Wellingtons didn't bother to have someone out to repair this instantly. The last time he'd been here he'd taken note of the bank of security monitors in the gate guard's station, and surely any one of the guards on duty had reported that an entire wall of cameras was out.

Would the Wellingtons have left the cameras down on purpose?

Why?

Seong-Jae trailed after him, soundless save for a faint rustle of leaves. "This is highly illegal, Malcolm. We are trespassing on private property without a warrant."

"Probable cause, husband is a suspect," Malcolm said.

"That is abuse of probable cause."

"It's the easiest way to avoid conflict with Wellington Senior and still do our jobs." He sighed, stopping and looking back. "I know. I know it's shady. It's somehow even more shady than Vasquez and Huang, because we're trespassing on a private citizen's property. I *know*. And I'm not comfortable with it." He shook his head. "But we're here. So let's find the husband and get out."

"Malcolm?"

"Yeah?"

"Perhaps on matters that prick your conscience, you

should make a point of discussing with me as your partner before simply taking action."

Malcolm drew up short, just looking at Seong-Jae. The man was as withdrawn and impassive as ever, but there was a faint, odd knit to his brows, a strangeness to how he looked at Malcolm, standing underneath the shadows of pale green leaves with dapples of sunlight reflecting from his eyes like light striking the shimmer-black surface of a pool of oil. Something hovered about him, a waiting stillness, a question he wasn't quite asking and that Malcolm couldn't quite read. But whatever that strangeness was, it halted Malcolm's growling retort, drying it to nothing on his tongue.

"I...yeah." He looked away. "Maybe I should."

"I would appreciate it."

"Okay."

Seong-Jae inclined his head. "Shall we, th—"

The sound of shouting cut him off. Lillienne Wellington's voice, drifting from the house.

Malcolm and Seong-Jae exchanged glances, then took off running across the grass.

As they drew closer, the sound pulled them around to the side of the house. Her voice was raised not in distress, but in anger, from the tone—and they skirted the carefully cultivated bushes flanking the house until they came to an open first-floor window that looked in on a large dining room with a massive, gleaming table set with various crystal fineries that looked as though they'd been put out for show. The

Wellingtons didn't seem like the type of family who regularly ate grand meals together.

Especially when, at the head of the dining room, Lillienne Wellington stood gesturing wildly, furiously, tears streaming down her face as she shouted at a man who stared at her with dull, almost empty eyes, weary and patient to the point of being broken. He was her height, maybe an inch or two shorter, with a solid, muscular build, top-heavy with brawny, hairy arms and a short shock of brown hair almost the same color as his sun-tanned skin. His face was handsome in a crude way, square and blunt, and he made Malcolm think of nothing more than a tired dog with a volatile, unpredictable master.

Malcolm sank down on his haunches, just barely peering over the windowsill; Seong-Jae joined him, the close-trimmed hedges pushing them into each other until they were almost leaning on each other to stay upright, crouched and sharing body heat as they listened.

"Why do you even care?" Lillienne demanded. "Why do you even care how I feel?"

"You're my wife," the man answered with the quiet emptiness of someone who had said this a thousand times before. "Shouldn't I care?"

"You just want me to say it. Isn't that it? You want me to say it out loud so you can hate me."

"What do you think I want you to say, Lili?"

"Nothing. Nevermind. *Nevermind!*" She clenched her

fists, shaking. "Why are you like this? Why are you so passive? Why don't you *care?*"

The man said nothing, didn't even move, for almost thirty seconds while she glared at him, her entire body trembling. Then he sighed, looking away slowly, pointedly. "I don't want to argue with you."

"Of course you don't. You never want to argue. You never *want* anything." She gulped back a near-sob. "I don't even know if you want *me.*"

"I married you."

"Yeah? Well people change, don't they? Maybe I'm not who you married."

Once more he remained silent—but the sharp *crack* of flesh to flesh broke the stillness. Her hand snapped across his cheek hard enough to force his head to the side, hard enough to leave a mark against swarthy, stubbled skin, nearly glowing red. Still his expression didn't change, his gaze fixed blankly across the floor.

"Hate me," she hissed, then continued, her voice escalating to nearly a scream by the time she was done. "Hate me for being an awful person. Hate me for being a selfish, spoiled brat. Hate me for all the terrible things I've done. Just *hate me!*"

"No," he murmured.

Lillienne Wellington stared at her husband. For a moment Malcolm thought she would break—completely fall apart and either confess to the murder or accuse her husband, or at least give them more insight into *all the terrible things I've done*. The terrible things she'd done, and what she thought her husband was trying to pull out of her with his apathy.

Like murder.

But she only cursed, then turned on her heel, stalking away and leaving the man alone, the sound of her heels receding away sharply with staccato clicks. Malcolm glanced at Seong-Jae, arching a brow.

"So that was interesting."

"Quite," Seong-Jae agreed.

Lillienne's husband finally moved, sighing as he pushed himself away from the wall and disappeared in the opposite direction, heading toward the back. Malcolm tossed his head toward Seong-Jae, beckoning with two fingers, then moved quickly through the bushes, bent over low to the ground and edging toward the back of the house. They reached the end of the wall just as one of several back doors set into the house creaked open. The man stepped out onto a wide marble verandah scattered with various seating arrangements, looking out over a lush back lawn dotted with sculpted bushes, garden settings, a fountain, a small landscaped brook that circled around the edge.

Seong-Jae glanced at Malcolm and raised both brows. Malcolm nodded, and together they straightened and slipped around the side of the house, stepping into view.

The man immediately tensed. His eyes—dark, haggard—

hardened, watching them warily, but he made no attempt to run. He didn't even move, just leaning against a tall column and watching them as they strode across the marble.

"You the other half of Lillienne Wellington and partner?" Malcolm asked.

"I am." The man studied them measuringly, then said, "Paul Barker. I'm her husband. No, I don't know where she was night before last, except in Marion Garvey's bed."

They drifted to a halt with a safe few feet of distance between them and Barker. Seong-Jae cocked his head. "The fact that you are volunteering that information says you understand who we are, and why we are here."

Barker let out a bitter snort. "You're cops. My wife ran from a murder scene. You think I killed the guy she was fucking."

"If you wish to put it that crudely," Seong-Jae said, "yes."

"I didn't," Barker said. "You're not supposed to be here. How did you get in?"

Malcolm tossed his head toward the wall. "Your security's a little lax."

Barker's lips creased bitterly. "You found the hole in the wall."

"You knew about it?" Malcolm asked.

"How do you think Garvey snuck in and out all the time?"

"Your wife did not want the breach repaired," Seong-Jae

observed. "And so it was pointedly overlooked. Who else knows about it?"

"Everyone in the family. Most of the household staff."

"That had to be embarrassing." Malcolm folded his arms over his chest. "This open secret with your wife's lover sneaking in and out of the house."

Barker just looked at him with those weary, flat eyes for long moments, then looked away, staring glassily across the lawn. The twist of his lips was bitter, cold. "About the only courtesy they gave me was not using the front door."

"When they weren't at the hotel together," "Malcolm added.

"Yeah."

"So you knew about that, too."

Barker's eyes closed. "...yeah."

"What do you do for a living, Mr. Barker?" Seong-Jae asked.

"Auto repair technician."

Seong-Jae tilted his head in that puzzled, curious way of his. "You have the luxury to never work a single day in your life, and yet you choose a low-paying occupation in skilled labor."

Barker's eyes slipped open with a humorless, near-silent laugh that shook his shoulders. "I'd be even more useless then, wouldn't I? Just keep me in my box and take me out when someone needs me for something. Not that anyone ever needs me for anything." He considered for long moments, then pushed away from the column, straightening. "You gonna want me to come down to the station or not?"

"You volunteering?" Malcolm asked.

"Might as well get this over with." His shrug was pure, defeated acceptance, listless and lifeless, though he offered another smile—more self-deprecating this time, almost pained, grieving. "Out the gate, if you don't mind. I'm not going over the wall. Bad back."

It was that smile that caught Malcolm. That was the smile of a guilty man with remorse riding his shoulders; a man who'd never thought he could be capable of terrible things until he'd done them in a moment of rage and passion.

That was the smile of a man who'd turn himself in rather than run from the cops. The smile of a man who'd confess to murder.

Even a murder he didn't commit.

God damn it, *nothing* about this case felt right.

He stepped closer, taking Barker's arm gently—just a precaution, when he didn't think he would run. "Come on," he said, tossing his head.

Barker went without a word, head down, falling into step with Malcolm without a single protest or hesitation.

Seong-Jae took up a flanking position on Barker's other side, and together they rounded the house to the front pathway. Just as they stepped onto the lane, however, the front door of the house opened. Rather than the scarecrow of a butler, Maximilian Wellington strode out, chest first. He stood at the top of the steps, looking down at them as if in absolute judgment, Zeus looking down from Mount Olympus to condemn the petty and useless affairs of mortals who dared to lay themselves at his feet.

"Detective Khalaji," Wellington said coldly. He looked right past Barker as if he wasn't even there, fixing his icy steel gaze wholly on Malcolm. "I thought I told you I would have your badge if you bothered my family again."

"Technically," Malcolm said, keeping his voice pleasant, "Mr. Barker here isn't related by blood. We're just having a voluntary conversation."

Wellington watched him with hooded eyes. In that heavy gaze was the promise he'd made at the station: that he would ruin Malcolm, have his badge and his career and leave him in disgrace. Malcolm met his gaze unwaveringly. It wasn't his goddamned job to keep rich people's names out of the news, or suppress scandals.

It was his goddamned job to track down murderers, and he was going to do that no matter who pressured him.

After a moment, however, Seong-Jae stepped forward. If Wellington was ice, Seong-Jae was subzero glacial, his gaze as hard as black diamonds as he flicked Wellington over with an assessing look that said he saw nothing worth noting, before fixing on his face again as he spoke softly, a subtle undercurrent of menace in his dispassionate, husky voice.

"If you would like, Mr. Wellington, you may have my badge number before I arrest you for attempted obstruction of justice."

Malcolm was hard-pressed not to stare at Seong-Jae. It wasn't hard to see what this was: not a genuine threat, but a quiet affirmation of solidarity. He was making a pointed choice to stand with Malcolm, to have his back.

And Malcolm couldn't help the faint warm flush that went through him, even as he kept his gaze steady on Wellington.

Wellington looked at Seong-Jae through narrowed eyes, then peeled his lips back with a disdainful sound and transferred his gaze to Barker. "Paul," he clipped out, not an ounce of love wasted on the single syllable.

"Max," Barker answered just as coolly. "It's fine." They stared at each other, something passing between them, before Barker said, "Since I didn't do anything, it's fine." He fixed haunted eyes on Malcolm. "Let's go."

Wellington said nothing else.

But his gaze followed them, heavy and penetrating and thoughtful, as they led Barker down the winding lane, through the gate, and away from the Wellington estate.

[9: OFF IN MY HEAD]

SEONG-JAE RETURNED MALCOLM'S KEYS FOR the drive back to the station, and settled in the passenger's seat to watch traffic pass.

In all actuality, however, he was watching Paul Barker in the back seat of Malcolm's car, studying his motionless reflection in the rear view mirror. The man's curious *blankness* was eating at him. This entire case was eating at him. It should be simple open and shut, but everything felt like surface over something deeper. As if the entire case were some kind of pantomime, everyone playing their exaggerated parts to some strange end.

He didn't like it.

And he didn't like how passive Barker was, as if he already had some conclusion in mind and would see this through to that outcome regardless of the truth.

He let his gaze tick over Barker—his build, his height. He would place Barker at approximately five foot seven. With the brawn hewn into his arms, he could easily have thrust a knife into Marion Garvey's chest hard enough to leave those deep scrapes on the sternum before severing the sternocostal joints to strike the heart and lungs. He was approximately the right height for enough leverage and a straight stab with a slight downward angle.

And he had motive.

Open and shut.

But no prints, no video, no evidence.

Only probable cause, and people behaving in ways inappropriate for the positions they were in.

So what was Lillienne Wellington hiding? She had not behaved as if she suspected her husband of the murder. The dynamic between them was strange, confusing. Not that Seong-Jae was an expert on relationship dynamics; his last had been far too long ago, and nothing he wanted to relive. Nothing he could compare Lillienne Wellington and Paul Barker to.

Nothing he could compare anything to at all.

One green, one blue.

The words Sarah Sutterly had spat at him. Memories he'd excised. Memories he didn't want back.

For a moment, Paul Barker met his gaze in the rear view mirror. They watched each other in silence, something in Barker's eyes seeming to say he knew Seong-Jae's every tired, aching thought.

Knew, and understood.

Seong-Jae turned away from the mirror, and fixed his gaze straight ahead.

At the station, Barker remained passive as they led him

to the very same interrogation room his wife had occupied the day before. Without being told, he settled in the chair, clasped his hands together on the table, and watched them expectantly. Malcolm started the recorder, but when he hesitated, looking at Barker oddly, Seong-Jae chose to take the initiative.

"Why did you volunteer to come to the station, Mr. Barker?" he asked.

"You were gonna haul me off in cuffs if I didn't." Barker shrugged listlessly. "I'm the easy suspect, right? Jealous husband. It's always the husband."

Seong-Jae arched a brow. "Is that a confession?"

Barker remained silent, parting his lips as if he had started to say one thing, then chose another—and after a moment he slumped. "No." His gaze lowered to his clasped hands. "I didn't even know the name of the guy she was fucking, until she came home crying about him being dead."

Malcolm leaned casually against the wall next to the one-way glass of the observation window, hands slipping into the pockets of his slacks. "Your wife came home crying to you over her dead lover," he mused. "How did you feel about that? That had to sting. You've got a wife who wouldn't even take your last name. Like it wasn't worth anything next to the Wellington name. And now she's sobbing to you because someone killed the rich guy she picked over you."

Seong-Jae watched Barker for any hint of reaction. He was starting to understand Malcolm's techniques; where

Seong-Jae preferred to herd witnesses with flat logic and reasonable conclusions, letting them expose themselves trying to escape from their own tangles, Malcolm repeated the truth back to them in that casual, almost taunting drawl to goad them into exposing themselves in a fit of emotion. Prodding at open wounds, as it were.

Yet Barker exposed nothing; no change in expression, no shift in that resigned demeanor. All he said was, "It is what it is."

"Perhaps because you took satisfaction in her grief," Seong-Jae said, "considering that you had already disposed of him."

"I told you I didn't even know the guy's name."

"You do not need to know someone's name to kill them."

"That's true," Barker acknowledged, far too easily. "Doesn't change that I didn't do it."

"Do you have an alibi for the time of death?" Malcolm asked.

"That would depend on when the asshole died, wouldn't it?"

There. A quick flare of emotion on *the asshole,* a touch of a snarl, of loathing, of bitter and broken pain.

"According to surveillance video," Seong-Jae supplied, "he died between nine thirty and ten PM, the night before last."

Barker's gaze swung to him. "If you've got surveillance

video, why can't you find who killed him?"

"Because," Malcolm answered. "Your wife had the video shut off for a fifteen-minute window so she wouldn't be caught on camera meeting up with her boy-toy."

Barker's jaw clenched. The muscles in his forearms bunched, his laced fingers tightening until the knuckles went white. Perhaps if Malcolm continued to prod him, he would snap. Seong-Jae held his tongue. Barker's gaze darted between them, his shoulders growing tighter and tighter, before he let out a soft, frustrated growl.

"You really want to know where I was then?"

Malcolm shrugged. "Might help, Barker."

Barker's lips twisted in a self-loathing smirk. "At home jacking it to internet porn in a fucking empty California king, on sheets that cost more than I make in a year."

Malcolm's gaze sharpened. "Can you prove that?"

"Not unless you can carbon-date the stains on the sheets."

"Lovely," Malcolm retorted dryly.

That ugly smirk was still on Barker's lips, tainting a rather earthy, handsome face with the shadow of disgust. Years, Seong-Jae thought. Years eroding at his self-esteem until he despised himself for loving the woman he had married, for allowing her to treat his feelings so callously. That sort of emotion could build up into a cathartic expulsion of violence, only to drain away into a tired calm once the last of the rage had expelled itself on a suitable target. Seong-Jae could see Barker tailing Lillienne Wellington to the hotel just to confirm what he knew had been happening under his nose the entire time, only to fly into a rage and murder Garvey in a crime of passion.

Only the timeline didn't match up with the video. Barker would have had to arrive before Lillienne Wellington, meaning he knew of their plans for the night and intended to disrupt them with a confrontation before his wife met with her lover. That would have given him a very narrow window. Almost too narrow a window, even though it was possible.

Possible, but it didn't feel probable.

Frustration was an unfamiliar feeling, twisting in the back of Seong-Jae's thoughts and making tangle after tangle.

None of this felt right.

"Do you resent your wife's wealth, Mr. Barker?" he asked.

"Resent it?" Barker blinked, clearly taken aback by the diversion, then shook his head. "Nah. I just didn't realize what I was getting into when I married into money." He grimaced. "It's...a lot. It's like marrying into monarchy when you're a goddamn peasant. That's how I feel, most of the time. Like a peasant."

Seong-Jae lingered on that note of resentment undercutting every word. "Did you know that your wife's lover was a very wealthy man?"

"Was he? That's..." Barker shrugged. "...yeah. I'm not surprised, I guess. I knew the novelty was wearing off.

Slumming it is only fun for so long when your little slum dog doesn't let you dress him up and do tricks on command. So it doesn't surprise me she was shopping for an upgrade." His tongue darted over his lips; his Adam's apple bobbed. He stared down at his clasped hands. "She left me divorce papers the other night, before she went to meet him," he whispered. "I knew it was coming."

"So you found the papers," Seong-Jae said, "then flew into a rage, followed her to the hotel, and murdered Marion Garvey."

"Nope," Barker answered, almost cheerfully.

"You are remarkably calm for a man being interrogated as the prime suspect in a murder."

"Because I know I didn't do it," Barker said simply. "I dunno how to prove it, so either you're gonna do what you're gonna do and I'll go down for it, or I'm gonna walk free."

Malcolm stroked his beard. "It must be hard to care about prison when you've felt like you've lived in a prison for years, isn't it?" His eyes narrowed. "That's why you still work. It's your independence. The one thing you can do not to feel trapped any longer."

Barker eyed Malcolm warily. "Something like that."

"How did you and Lillienne Wellington meet, Mr. Barker?" Seong-Jae interjected.

Barker paused. He was visibly off-center, rather clearly uncomfortable being pulled between Seong-Jae's and Malcolm's different lines of questioning, and Seong-Jae rather wanted to keep him that way.

Keep him spinning, until he gave away something that made this entire fiasco make *sense*.

After several frozen seconds, Barker exhaled. A rueful smile crossed his lips, one that was part nostalgia, part regret. "She came into the shop looking for someone to buff out a ding," he said. "Freaking out the whole time over her big bad Daddy finding out she banged up a million-dollar car. Max is a fucking skinflint. Treats everything he owns like it belongs in a trophy case, untouched. Even his goddamned daughter. So I helped her. Suctioned out the ding, buffed the scrape, and…"

He shrugged. His laced fingers clenched. He glanced at the recorder as if he was uncomfortable saying what came next, then continued.

"I dunno. It was a thing, I guess. She got hot for the dirty, sweaty, greasy guy. She said she lived in a glass cage and couldn't ever get dirty. I made her feel dirty in a way she liked. And we just…" A faint, almost soundless laugh, a pained quirk of his lips, his eyes darkening. "We'd get to talking. I thought she was just a spoiled piece of ass at first, and then I got to know her." He lifted his eyes to Seong-Jae; they were wet about the edges, and his gaze pleaded, as if begging him to understand. "She's not who she pretends to be. She's not all the shallow bullshit and the expensive clothing and nice dinners and fake laughter. She's just…*more*, and she's stagnating under Max's thumb." He looked away then, suddenly stiff, as if his pride had caught up to that moment of weakness. "I think if I'd tried to take her out of there instead of going under that damned glass dome with her, we'd have been okay."

"You really love your wife, don't you?" Malcolm asked gently.

"Yeah." Barker's smile was pure torture. "It's pathetic, isn't it? I'm a pet to her. She was going to leave me for a man with money. Her father hates me and makes us miserable, until we're always at each other's throats." His voice hitched, and he closed his eyes, dragging his hand over his mouth. "But god damn, I love her."

Malcolm pushed away from the wall, hands slipping out of his pockets. "You know that love gives us grounds to hold you, doesn't it?"

"It's motive, isn't it?" Barker asked. "Would you believe I love her so much I'd never hurt her like that?" He sank down deeper in the chair, tilting his head against the back with a desperate, bitter laugh. "If he made her happy, I wouldn't take that away from her."

Something in his demeanor changed, then. Something resolute, something quiet, something heavy and tired. As if he'd come to some sort of decision, and his shoulders were stiff, his expression curiously blank as he straightened and looked from Malcolm to Seong-Jae once more.

"Besides," he said. "She's the only other suspect, right? I'm the easier one to lock up, aren't I?"

Seong-Jae sighed. Instead of more clarity, this had only muddied the waters further. "Are you trying to protect your wife, Mr. Barker?"

Barker fixed him with a frank, penetrating look. "If you loved someone...wouldn't you?"

Seong-Jae had no answer for that.

No answer at all.

MALCOLM DIDN'T WANT TO LOCK Paul Barker away.

But the man was giving him no choice.

He'd practically willingly put himself in cuffs. He'd given them more than enough motive with little to no alibi, and no matter that he'd said he hadn't done it...

He'd set himself up as the most likely suspect, and if they were going to jail someone on suspicion then Barker was the most obvious option.

Obvious almost never meant *right*.

After handing Barker over to a uniformed officer to be booked into holding, Malcolm drifted back to the homicide bullpen and his desk, hardly aware of Seong-Jae in his wake. He took a moment to hook his phone up to the desktop via

USB and offload the files on his phone to Sade's document dump repository, then sent the little monster a quick text.

Hey. Just sent you some surveillance footage from the Garvey case. Looking for footage of Barker, Paul. Just booked into holding. Entering or leaving hotel before and after time of death.

His phone rattled back moments later. Just a GIF—that little blond kid from that show from the nineties, thumbs up, flashing caption.

You got it, dude.

Malcolm smiled faintly, then settled his phone on the desk and just...stared at his screen until it timed out and went black. He chewed on his thumbnail, gaze fixed on his dark, sleeping desktop screen. Seong-Jae settled to sit on the edge of his desk, watching him curiously.

"Get your own desk," Malcolm muttered absently.

"I told you I like yours," Seong-Jae replied. "Do you believe Barker is the perpetrator?"

"I don't know." Malcolm let out a frustrated growl, and his dimmed reflection in the monitor scowled at him. "He's the easy suspect. There's also that arc of descent to think about. He's shorter than Garvey. He could've hit that entry angle without dislocating his shoulder, easily. But so could Lillienne Wellington. With a sharp enough blade, and enough anger behind the thrust..." He lost words, for a moment, his mind swirling, before he settled on one thought. "But he's harboring guilt over something. I just don't know if it's murder." He raked his hair free from its tail; it was giving him a fucking migraine, pulling at his scalp every time he scowled. "None of this feels right. Not a damned thing. Something's going on between Barker and Lillienne Wellington, but I'm not sure I buy either of them for murder. Did you notice he didn't seem worried about the surveillance video? Surprised, but not worried."

Seong-Jae dipped his head in a brief nod. "Either he knew about the arranged windows, or he did not know the hotel had security cameras. He only knew he was not on them, because he was nowhere near the crime scene."

"So we don't want him for this? Not even the jealousy angle?"

"I..." Seong-Jae's gaze darted away from Malcolm. Subtle—he almost missed it, almost lost it in the natural motions of Seong-Jae adjusting his position, settling more fully against the desk and stretching his legs out, gripping the edge with both hands and gazing across the busy bullpen. But there was something odd in Seong-Jae's voice, something soft and withdrawn and pensive, when he murmured, "I would believe that she committed the murder and he is covering for her, out of some misbegotten loyalty. But I do not believe he committed the crime."

Malcolm eyed him. "Seong-Jae..."

"It is nothing," Seong-Jae said, which meant it was very much something and he just didn't want to talk to Malcolm about it. He continued smoothly, "We should subpoena for the security tapes from the Wellington estate; it is extremely unlikely their patriarch will deliver them willingly. Perhaps we can verify his alibi if there is no record of him entering or leaving the estate during the appropriate time range."

"But he knows about the hole in the security coverage. Everyone knows about the hole in the security coverage."

"That does not mean we should not look. There may be areas of the grounds where we might see him or Lillienne Wellington en route to the dead zone in their security, and the exit over the wall." Seong-Jae glanced at Malcolm, then away, with a rather telling stiffness. "But I believe there is another connection we may have overlooked."

"Yeah? What is that?"

"I am not certain yet." Every word slow, carefully chosen, until Malcolm felt like he was being *handled* somehow, with every syllable Seong-Jae spoke. "I would like to return to the crime scene. We departed far too hastily for a proper assessment."

It took a moment to sink in—but when the meaning processed, Malcolm flushed, heat simmering under his skin and building in his temples, until the throb of his pulse was almost loud enough to drown out the grind of his teeth resonating into his skull.

He made himself take a slow breath, reining himself in, focusing his energy on pushing his chair back and standing, bringing him to eye level with Seong-Jae.

"You saying I did a sloppy job, Yoon?"

Seong-Jae stood—and if Malcolm didn't know better, he'd think the fucking asshole was deliberately using those couple of inches in height on him to overshadow him. Seong-Jae looked down at him coolly. "I am saying that you were not as thorough as you could have been."

A retort rose on Malcolm's lips. He bit it back, swearing mentally, and closed his eyes. Deep breaths. *Deep* breaths. If he was honest with himself, Seong-Jae was right. Malcolm was all over the place with this case, and he'd been in such a fucking mood at the Wellington hotel that he'd just gotten out of there as quickly as possible.

God *damn* it.

"Fine," he grit out, and pushed away from the desk, circling around Seong-Jae at a wide berth and heading for the door. "Let's go back to the hotel."

"Stop," snapped sharply at his back.

Malcolm whirled back, glowering at Seong-Jae. "What?"

"Stop your masculine posturing. Your offended ego." Seong-Jae closed the distance between them on gliding, purposeful strides as if stalking him, until he drew so close they stood almost chest to chest, eye to flat, penetrating black eye. "I am aware that, at thirty-three, I am ten years your junior, and likely not the portrait of American masculinity that most are inclined to submit to." Those swollen strawberry lips shaped each word so clinically, so dispassionately, that their very emptiness almost dripped with scorn. "But I earned my rank as your superior, and I am tired of dancing around your sulking masculine ego."

"Sulking masculine ego." Malcolm repeated each word—if only to be sure he'd heard them right. They tasted foul, and he was hard-pressed to keep from descending into a snarl. He didn't lose his temper. He made a *point* of never losing his temper, but Seong-Jae was pushing him toward the trembling edge. He swept a glance over the bullpen. The few detectives at their desks were watching surreptitiously, but it was Anjulie in her office, eyeing them over the stack of papers in her hand, that made him curse under his breath and turn away from Seong-Jae, striding for the door. "This is not the place for this conversation."

Seong-Jae said nothing.

But he followed Malcolm from the room, out into the hallway and then the stairwell.

Malcolm made it down one flight of stairs before he turned back, stopping on the landing with one foot braced on the step above, the stair rail cold against his palm—so cold that he felt like his entire body must be overheated with the irritation threatening to boil into fury inside him and incinerate the last of his restraint. He glared up at Seong-Jae, who paused a few steps above with the faint lights mounted on the walls framing him like a halo, casting white glints off the onyx oil slick of his hair.

"You think I'm upset with you over my ego," Malcolm growled. "You think I'm so up in my goddamned testosterone that I can't handle partnering with a kid who outranks me?"

Seong-Jae descended a few more steps. "If that is not your problem, then why have you been so irritable with me?"

"Do I need to remind you that I didn't *want* you?"

Malcolm mounted two more steps until there were none between them, Seong-Jae just one step above him, and he was so tempted to—to—he didn't know. Shake him. Kiss him. Anything to silence that hateful, cold voice that said he saw Malcolm as so little, so base, so disreputable, so *foul* that he was some out of control asshole counting his thoughts to the swing of his balls. But Malcolm held himself in place by a single trembling thread of control, even if his jaw was locked so tight it felt like prying apart rusted iron hinges to make himself speak.

"You were thrown at me," he bit off. "You practically forced your way onto my turf, and then we got stuck together. I accepted it because we work well together. When we aren't at each other's throats."

Seong-Jae's gaze flicked over him, settled on his mouth for a single unreadable moment, then rose to his eyes. "Then that is truly the cause of your surliness. Simple inability to adjust to having a partner."

"Some of it." Fuck. Fuck, with how *close* they were Malcolm could smell that hot diesel scent again, and that something *else* that was still caught on him no matter how many pretty pianists he fucked to erase it. He pulled back sharply, retreating to the stairwell and turning his back on Seong-Jae, gripping the stair rail and leaning hard on his stone-stiff arms. "I have a life outside you, Yoon. Sometimes it affects my mood."

"Interesting," Seong-Jae murmured.

Malcolm groaned, tilting his head back and staring up at the underside of the stairs above. "You only say that when you're about to psychoanalyze me again."

Seong-Jae said nothing. Malcolm shot a look over his shoulder, but Seong-Jae was only watching him like a peculiar and particularly inquisitive bird of prey.

"What," Malcolm bit off. "*What*. Just out with it."

"You called me Yoon, rather than Seong-Jae. Attempting to distance and depersonalize me." Seong-Jae descended the steps and drifted to Malcolm's side, looking out over the stair railing. "As if I am, somehow, at the core of your problems regardless of your assertions."

Malcolm sighed. "...you're not going to figure me out from a slip of the tongue, *Seong-Jae*."

"No. I suppose not." Seong-Jae slipped his hands from the pockets of his long black coat and leaned forward, bending his lanky frame almost in half to rest his folded arms on the rail of the landing. His gaze remained fixed outward as he murmured, "You do know that in my culture, being allowed to use one's given name is something of a privilege?"

Malcolm eyed him, then sighed again. God damn it. Fine. If they weren't going to fight, they weren't going to fight, and if Seong-Jae wanted to be circuitous then Malcolm was going to let him be fucking circuitous.

That didn't change that that accusation *stung.*

He struggled with himself for long moments, just trying to tamp down his annoyance, his knotted, messy feelings, so he could keep his voice even when he said, "I've heard." He watched Seong-Jae sidelong. "So why do you let me?"

"Partially because I have grown accustomed to American ways, and very few Americans will even stop to question if they should use my given name upon learning of it. One adapts, or one spends a great deal of time perpetually angry. I only have so much energy to spare for that." Seong-Jae shrugged. "Yet partially because I was attempting a…peace offering, I suppose. Even if I was not certain if you would recognize the significance of it."

Malcolm looked away from that maddeningly distant, remote expression and looked out over the stairwell as well. "It seemed like something. And it seemed like something when you started calling me Malcolm."

"Yes. 'Something.'"

"You don't have to do that." Malcolm shifted so he was leaning on his arms as well, almost arm to arm and shoulder to shoulder with Seong-Jae. "Not if it makes you uncomfortable."

"No, Malcolm. It does not make me uncomfortable to permit you to use my name. Nor does it make me uncomfortable to use your name. We are partners."

Malcolm guessed that, too, was another peace offering. Dealing with Seong-Jae was strange; his expression almost never changed, whether he was accusing Malcolm of being a testosterone-raging asshole or calmly offering to subsume his own cultural traditions and comfort for the sake of keeping things at ease between them. Malcolm had heard it was outright *rude* to use someone's first name in Korean culture unless they were family, close friends, or lovers.

So it felt strange to know the taste of the soft, sighing sounds of *Seong-Jae* on his tongue, and know that every time he called the man's name he was speaking to him with an intimacy that only Seong-Jae himself fully understood.

And he didn't know what to do with that, and so all he said was, "All right, then."

"As you say," Seong-Jae replied, implacably as ever. "So then you have been irritable because—"

"Stop right there," Malcolm said. "You need to learn to quit while you're ahead."

"I stop when I find the answers I seek."

"That works with suspects, most of the time." Malcolm turned his head, watching Seong-Jae, lingering over the sloping, graceful lines of his profile. "I'm not a suspect. Sometimes, when you're trying to form a relationship with someone, you need to learn when to stop and when to let things go."

Dark eyes slid toward him, catching him for a moment of pensive eye contact. "Is this a relationship, then?"

"Every partnership is."

Seong-Jae lofted one black dash of a brow. "You hardly

seem the expert on partnerships."

"Ha fucking *ha*." Malcolm snorted. "I've had partners in the past."

"Did something happen, to make you so vehemently against them?"

"Seong-Jae?"

"Yes?"

Malcolm leaned over enough to nudge him with his elbow. "Remember what I said about knowing when to stop?"

"Yes."

"This is one of those moments when you should stop."

"As you say, then." Seong-Jae inclined his head. "But Malcolm?"

"Yeah?"

"Either I am your partner or I am not." That cool voice took on a touch of firmness. "I am not conveniently invisible when you do not want me there, or do not want to listen to me. I am aware that I have a tendency to self-efface, but if anything you seem determined to push me to the fringes."

"That's fair," Malcolm admitted. Fuck, he was an asshole, but he hadn't meant to be *that* kind of asshole. "I'm sorry. I am. I'll try harder."

"Thank you," Seong-Jae replied.

Malcolm said nothing. He couldn't acknowledge thanks for just agreeing to do the bare minimum he should have been doing in the first place.

Yeah. He really wasn't in the best place to be making decisions, right now. He'd been fucking things up more and more since the McAllister case had closed, all because he wouldn't unbend his pride long enough to go see Ryusaki. He didn't know why he was so against it. He'd been seeing Ryusaki for over a decade. She *knew* him.

Maybe that was the problem.

She knew him, and had been there for him during things he'd rather forget.

Malcolm parted his lips to speak—but the door one flight above slammed open hard enough to ricochet off the wall, the rattle echoing. He winced. He didn't have to look back to know who that was.

"Mal," Captain Zarate snapped, her voice hard-edge and seething. "I just had *my* job threatened because you were on the Wellington grounds. *Don't fuck this up.*"

Malcolm turned to face her, leaning his elbows back against the rail. He didn't blame Seong-Jae for keeping his back to Anjulie; maybe now would be a good time to be actually invisible, or at least unobtrusive enough to escape notice. Anjulie stood at the head of the stairs, her tall, razor-sharp frame imposing, her angles sharp enough to cut, her eyes snapping with authoritative fire. Her bold, assertive personality was one reason Malcolm respected her so much; he'd watched more than one male officer and politician try to cut her down a peg and make her feel small, smaller than them, and they'd never managed to dull even the slightest edge of her wit and ferocity.

But god damn, was it hell having that ferocity turned on him.

He studied her, trying to work out how angry she actually was versus when she just wanted him on his toes. Pretty fucking angry, he thought from the twist of her lips and the plant of her fists on her hips.

"Do you trust me?" he asked.

"No," she retorted immediately.

"Anjulie. C'mon."

"Don't. Fuck. This. Up," she repeated. "You do your job, and you do your job right."

"I've got Paul Barker in holding. I'm doing my job right."

She drew up short, blinking. "Who?"

Malcolm blinked right back. "That's not who you're threatening me over?"

"No. The DA didn't say a damned word about Barker." She shook her head. "Just that Wellington was pissed you were sniffing around again. He wants to have you fired."

"Am I?"

"Are you what?"

"Fired."

"Do you see me kicking your ass from here to next Tuesday yet?" She transferred her glare to Seong-Jae's back. "I'm sorry. I'm sorry for putting you with him. I can reassign you by morning."

Seong-Jae looked over his shoulder, his expression almost too bland. "I am not particularly disinclined to my current assignment."

"If you shoot him," she said, "I'll look the other way."

"Anjulie!" Malcolm protested.

Seong-Jae's expression didn't change. "I do not find that particularly humorous."

"You wouldn't," Anjulie muttered. "Get out. *Fix this*," she snarled. "Or I'll shoot you myself."

Then the stairwell door banged closed, its booming rattle echoing and then fading, leaving them alone.

Seong-Jae eyed the door for long moments, before looking at Malcolm. "...she does not mean that, does she?"

"I've never really wanted to find out," Malcolm said, but he couldn't help chuckling. Fuck, the Captain was something. Exhaling heavily, he caught the stair rail and headed down the next flight, tossing his head to Seong-Jae. "Come on. Let's follow up your hunch and see what we missed at the hotel."

[10: A SILVER RAIN WILL WASH AWAY]

FOR A MOMENT, SEONG-JAE ALMOST wished he hadn't said a thing to Malcolm.

Perhaps if he hadn't, Malcolm would be more willing to intimidate his way past the obstinate, snooty, entirely self-righteous little troll of a man currently barring their entrance to the Wellington hotel.

"Absolutely not," Caldwell Brixton repeated for what had to be the fifth time. He had positioned his entire body in the doorway, and only allowed it to open far enough to sandwich him in shoulder to shoulder between the door and the frame, as if he were a strange vertical doorjamb of flesh. "I've already put your people out once, and Mr. Wellington was quite clear. The Baltimore Police Department is not allowed on these premises without a warrant, and you do not have a warrant." He looked uncertain for a moment. "Do you?"

"We don't," Malcolm said patiently. "And I understand your devotion to the Wellington family. I sincerely do. But the longer this case drags out, the more likely it is that certain things will leak to the media, and they'll sensationalize it as much as possible. The Wellington name means headline clicks. There are probably a dozen paparazzi in the bushes stalking half your clientele right now, and the longer we're standing out here in plain sight, the more shots they have to draw all the wild conjecture they want. In the interests of avoiding that, we're trying to find as much information as we can to rule Lillienne Wellington out as a suspect. You let us do that, and we can avoid a scandal."

Brixton sniffed. "If I let you in I will more than likely *cause* a scandal. I don't trust you not to have photos of the room plastered all over the gossip rags by morning."

"I'm a cop, not a reporter." Malcolm spread his hands. "Work with me, Brixton. What do I have to do to get in? Book a room?"

"As if I would even *allow* someone like you—"

Seong-Jae bit back an impatient sound under his breath and stepped forward, insinuating himself between Malcolm and Brixton—which meant pressing almost chest to chest with Brixton, even if it was more nose to chest when Brixton barely came up to his shoulder. He stared down at the man, clenching his hands into fists in his pockets and biting back every cruel, scathing, irritated thing he wanted to say. He did not like when someone put their personal politics in the way of solving a case.

He wanted in that room, and he was getting in that room.

"*Move,*" he ground through his teeth.

Brixton stared up at him, his face purpling briefly with a flash of temper—but the longer he stared at Seong-Jae, the paler he turned, his eyes widening. He faltered, the bravado draining out of him like a deflating balloon. He looked past Seong-Jae at Malcolm as if he would find help there, but Malcolm said nothing, and Seong-Jae silently thanked him. When Brixton stared at Seong-Jae again, though, Seong-Jae said nothing else, only narrowing his eyes and waiting.

He was not moving.

Not unless Brixton had him physically removed, and that would have interesting consequences indeed.

Brixton mad a faltering sound. "I..." He physically shrank back from Seong-Jae, then sniffed haughtily, turning his face to one side as if he had condescended to this decision himself. "Very well. This is the last time, you understand? If only for the sake of clearing the Madame's name."

He pushed the door open wider, stepping back to make room for them. Malcolm stepped forward, but as he passed Seong-Jae he muttered from the corner of his mouth. "And you call me a bully?"

"Not one word," Seong-Jae hissed to his back, as Malcolm ducked through the door.

Seong-Jae followed him with one last look for Brixton, but Brixton's gaze skittered sullenly away—and rather than lead them to the service elevator this time, Brixton just handed over the master room key without a word, then flicked his wrist in a dismissive yet oddly defeated gesture, shooing them toward the main elevators. Neither said a word until they were in the lushly appointed, oak-paneled elevator, the carpeted floor jolting underneath them as the doors closed and the lights overhead came up bright. Malcolm tilted his head back, shifting restlessly—what *was* his aversion to elevators?—and watching the numbers.

"In a mood, Seong-Jae?" he asked mildly.

Seong-Jae shrugged stiffly. "I have a feeling, as you would say."

"Yeah?"

"Something is bothering me. Something about this hotel."

Malcolm seemed to be expecting more, from the way he watched Seong-Jae sidelong, amusement glittering in his eyes. Seong-Jae glanced away, muttering under his breath.

"…and he was in my way."

Malcolm's only answer was a sharp, almost delighted huff of laughter, as the elevator dinged on the fourteenth floor and let them out into the hallway.

At the honeymoon suite, Malcolm fit the key card to the lock—but Seong-Jae stopped, frowning at the wall outside the suite. The pale blue-gray, lightly textured wallpaper had already been scrubbed free of blood, but an echo remained, soaked into the paper. He lingered on the smear patterns. For the most part they seemed congruent with Lillienne Wellington's movements; she had exited the room, backing out, her fingers covered in blood as she reached out clumsily for something to grasp on to, only for her hand to fall away in a trailing streak. But there was part of the blood pattern that didn't match. Part that just...didn't look right. He would have to get the forensics photographs from Stenson, but...

Just in case, he retrieved his phone from his pocket, opened the camera app, and lined up a shot, capturing the downward-streaking lines that had caught his attention. Maybe it was something. Maybe it was nothing.

But that sense of prickling unease sank deeper, itching under his skin.

Unease, and familiarity.

Malcolm glanced back as the door came unlatched. "Seong-Jae?" he asked. "What is it? Did you find something?"

"No. I was simply interested in the blood smear pattern." Seong-Jae closed the camera app on his phone and dropped the device back into his pocket. "I am currently reading a book on blood spatter analysis."

"Mm."

That single sound and Malcolm's long, dubious look said he didn't believe him.

But he did not press the issue, and that was all that mattered to Seong-Jae.

He strode to the door to the room. "Shall we?" he said, and stepped inside. Malcolm followed.

And immediately began to swear.

The room had been completely turned out—all traces of

the crime erased. The carpet was spotless, the sheets changed, the debris cleaned away. Seong-Jae would hazard a fair guess that the room had been steam-cleaned, pressure-washed, anything that would wipe out all traces of evidence. He frowned, scanning wall to wall, but it might as well have been any other featureless room in any other featureless hotel.

"Did forensics give the clear to tear down the crime scene?" he asked.

"I doubt it, but since when do these fucks listen to lowly cops?" Malcolm closed his eyes, pinching the bridge of his nose. "I'm gonna kill the uniform who was supposed to be on watch here. Probably some rookie who let Brixton bully them off the property. We're not going to get anything out of this room. They've scrubbed it right down to shampooing the carpets. We're too late." His hand fell away, stark slate blue eyes opening to fix on Seong-Jae, dark with regret. "Fuck. If I hadn't been such a stubborn ass..."

"We would not have been able to rule out Paul Barker so easily."

Malcolm blinked. "What?"

"Think," Seong-Jae said. "Barker made it clear that he is powerless in the Wellington family hierarchy. He would not have had the authority to command the hotel staff to override police protocol and scrub the room down to—"

"—destroy any additional evidence," Malcolm finished, expression clearing, eyes widening. "But Lillienne Wellington could."

"Which gives credence to the theory that she is the murderer, and Barker is only attempting to cover for her. To take the fall, as it were."

Malcolm and Seong-Jae looked at each other for long moments; it wasn't hard to read the question in Malcolm's gaze. A question he echoed out loud as he said,

"...that's all a load of bullshit, isn't it?"

"Yes," Seong-Jae replied, and Malcolm growled, pacing a few short steps toward the bed, then away. His hair lashed around his shoulders, still left loose in tumbling waves of ash and chestnut.

"What are we overlooking? *Who* are we overlooking?"

Seong-Jae weighed the option of continuing to hold his silence for only a moment before he said, "Brixton."

Malcolm turned back. "You're kidding me. He almost puked all over the crime scene."

"People are capable of acts in a moment of passion that would revolt them at any other time. Disorganized offenders often feel sickened by their own actions. And not only has he repeatedly attempted to bar us from the crime scene, but..." Seong-Jae swept a glance around the spotless room. "He had perfect access to remove the evidence once he regained composure."

"But Brixton? What's the motive?"

"I had been turning over the possibility of a member of the hotel staff fixated on Lillienne Wellington, and jealous of her tryst with Garvey. The most likely options were a member of the security staff, or Brixton himself. With the takedown of the crime scene on someone's authority, that leans the theory more toward Brixton."

Malcolm eyed him oddly. "How long have you been sitting on this?"

Seong-Jae considered dissembling for only a moment before he admitted, "Since yesterday."

"And you didn't *say* anything?"

"You did not seem particularly receptive."

"That's fair. But the next time you keep information from me in a developing case, I swear to all hell I'm going to kick your ass," Malcolm growled.

"That, too, is fair," Seong-Jae agreed. "I was not certain of my footing or my unease at the time, so I chose silence until I could assess why I was off-center."

"Because I was being a jackass, I know. We don't have time for that right now." Malcolm sighed, one hand on his hip, the other pressed with knuckles curled to his mouth. "Brixton, though. He's so short…"

"If the blade were lifted over his head, the estimated arc of descent and impact angle would still be possible." Seong-Jae stepped closer to Malcolm. "Here. You are shorter than I am. Let me show you."

Malcolm shot him a glower. "I'm six feet fucking tall. Plus an inch."

"And I am six foot three. The discrepancy is not enough for the discrepancy between Garvey and Brixton, but it will serve to illustrate. Here." He settled facing Malcolm, then turned away—as he imagined Garvey must have been when he heard his perpetrator entering the room. "You are Brixton. Coming behind me with a knife. As Garvey, I hear you, thinking you are Lillienne Wellington, and turn with my arms spread in welcome." He did so, turning to face Malcolm, spreading his hands and arms as if he would embrace a lover. "You see your moment, but you are inexperienced with a knife and your first instinct is to slash, not stab."

He waited. Malcolm looked at him blankly, then seemed to get the message after a moment. His expression darkened, and he looked away, grumbling as if he would refuse—before his shoulders slumped, he sighed, and he curled his hand, pantomiming holding a knife, and made several slashing gestures toward Seong-Jae, powerful shoulders bunching against his suit coat. Seong-Jae brought his hands in quickly as if attempting to push the knife away and ward off a mortal blow.

"And so," he said, "we see the defensive wounds on the hands. You, realizing that I am larger and you will not be able to force past the guard of my arms, instead make a desperate lunge. A stab, raising the knife overhead in a moment of fury and making a direct downward jab. One that breaks past my uncoordinated, inebriated arm movements, sinks into my chest over the sternum, bounces off bone, and carries the momentum to one side to sever the sternocostal joints, graze my heart, and plunge into my lungs."

He arched his brows, waiting. Malcolm rolled his eyes,

but then let out a sigh and made a good effort at mimicking the thrust, raising his arm overhead and coming down, catching an open spot in Seong-Jae's criss-crossed arms. Malcolm's heavy fist came to rest against his chest, as if he'd plunged a knife in to the hilt.

"Like this?" he asked.

"Just so," Seong-Jae said, then clutched at his chest—ending up clutching at Malcolm's hand, the fine bristles of hair on his knuckles teasing at Seong-Jae's palm. "Now you pull your hand away, and there is only me, the knife…and the fall." Seong-Jae let himself fall backward—only Malcolm was there, suddenly behind him, catching his body against his chest and embracing him in hard-corded arms, the pressure of Malcolm's breaths and his heat against Seong-Jae's back.

"And then I catch you and drag you over to the bed?" Malcolm asked, his voice a rumbling seismic quake working through Seong-Jae, the sound husky against his ear. Malcolm's beard scraped and tickled his throat, and Seong-Jae's pulse jumped.

His chest felt tight, strange. What was *wrong* with him?

He pulled himself back on track, turning his head to look over his shoulder at Malcolm, the other man's breaths warm against his cheeks, his lips. "I actually am not quite certain," he said. "From what I recall of the debris pattern, it is equally possible that Garvey fell to the floor atop the rose petals, which caught much of the initial blood spatter…or that the perpetrator caught him and dragged him. It would have been difficult for someone of Brixton's size to dead-lift Garvey from a prone position…but equally as difficult if he had caught the full force of Garvey's weight."

"Ah," Malcolm said. Were his arms tightening, or was Seong-Jae imagining that? "So that lessens suspicion on Brixton."

"Lessens, but does not remove." Seong-Jae met Malcolm's gaze over his shoulder, lingering on slate blue eyes that crackled electric with storms. Malcolm had tasted like storms, he thought distantly. Like the cold breath of ozone-laden wind blowing in as the sky turned dark and the air shivered with portent to prickle the skin. "Malcolm?"

"Ah?"

"…I believe the last time we were in this position, you reminded me that I could let you go now."

"…ah."

But Malcolm didn't let him go. Instead his gaze dipped downward, a near-palpable touch to Seong-Jae's lips, paired with an audible hitch to his breaths, their edges turning ragged. Malcolm's hands clenched against Seong-Jae's clothing, just a subtle flex of strength as his fingers dug in, and the pit of Seong-Jae's stomach turned far too warm, heat stealing over him.

"Seong-Jae," Malcolm breathed, and the rough, hungry edge on his name made Seong-Jae's heart give an entirely distressing flip.

"…Malcolm…?"

The sound of his name seemed to snap Malcolm from a trance. He stiffened, his entire body going hard against Seong-Jae's back, before with a soft, vicious-sounding word under his breath in quietly inflected Persian he turned his face away, easing his grip on Seong-Jae until Seong-Jae found his feet, straightened, and pulled away. He turned to face Malcolm, straightening and smoothing his clothing, a question on his lips, a twist in his gut, but the unspoken things written in the deep furrows of Malcolm's brows stopped him. He only waited, wondering what Malcolm would say, what growls and furious deflections would fall from those subtly parted lips.

But Malcolm said nothing.

He only dragged his hair back out of his face, shot Seong-Jae an almost accusatory look, then turned and walked away.

Malcolm brushed aside the filmy curtains with enough force to make the curtain rod rattle, revealing the glass patio door to the balcony. The door squealed in its tracks as Malcolm jerked it open, then stalked outside. His back was a hard, tense line as he leaned against the balcony rail, looking out over the street below. The sun made stark edges of him, falling down on him as if it would kiss his roughness, his fury away, yet it only made him sharper. Malcolm, Seong-Jae thought, was not a creature of sunlight and brightness.

He, like most old wolves, was made to run under the silver light of the moon, then vanish unseen into the dark.

Seong-Jae drifted after him, moving to lean in the open

patio doorway, propping his shoulder against the frame. For some time he just watched Malcolm; Malcolm was utterly motionless save for the tendrils of his hair caught in a lazy midmorning breeze, drifting and eddying in wisps around his face and shoulders. So tense, Seong-Jae thought. So angry. With himself, considering a notable tendency to self-flagellate when Malcolm failed at his own ideals?

Or with Seong-Jae?

"Malcolm…?" he prodded gently.

Malcolm's fingers curled hard against the balcony. "I just needed some air," he said. "This case is getting to me."

Seong-Jae chose to let the obvious lie go.

Instead he let his gaze drift away from Malcolm, lingering on the high-rise buildings around the hotel, the way the sun turned windows glassy blue and reflected back the city in faded shadow shot through with sparks of glaring sunlight. Even with the reflections dimming his vision, he could see people moving around through the windows opposite, going on about their quiet lives when, had one of them been working late night before last, they might have had their small, simple world shattered had they glanced up at the right moment to watch a man tear another man to pieces on the edge of a blade.

If…they had glanced up…

It came together with a sharp *click*. What he'd been missing. His eyes widened, and he pushed away from the door, stepping forward. "Malcolm," he said. "Look." He nodded across the street at the glassy building just opposite. "What is that building?"

Malcolm took a moment to respond, his gaze cloudy. "Office suites, looks like." His eyes sharpened as they shifted to Seong-Jae. "What are you thinking?"

"Security cameras. Brixton and Wellington can control the cameras at the hotel, but not on someone else's property. Perhaps one would have caught the incidents last night."

Malcolm's sucked in a breath, but there was an edge of caution as he asked, "Would the image even show enough detail to be worth it?"

"It is a lead. Considering the murder took place at night, interior lighting would render the hotel's windows more transparent. We can try, can we not?"

"It's better than nothing. It's better than what we've had, bouncing between Barker and Wellington and just crashing into dead ends and improbable conclusions." Malcolm idly dug his fingers into his hair, gathering it up as he stared fixedly across the street at the building. "Why can't the bad guys just be...obviously bad guys?"

"Because humans do not work in such a fashion," Seong-Jae replied. "Very few people are unequivocally, unilaterally 'good' or 'bad.'"

Malcolm pulled an elastic from his pocket and stretched it wide between his fingers before snapping it over his hair in a trailing, disarrayed bun. "Then what are they?"

"Messy." Seong-Jae sighed. "I believe the best word I

could use would be 'messy.'"

But even he wasn't sure if he meant people in general…

Or just Malcolm Khalaji.

[11: CAN'T QUIT, TAKE SIX]

THE BUILDING ACROSS THE STREET didn't have a name—just a tall sign tower with the building number, names, and logos of its occupants lit up behind plastic, everything from bank offices to what looked like venture capital startups and a few phone-bank call centers for a couple of major brands. Malcolm stood on the milling sidewalk below, squinting up at the suite numbers through the bright sunlight, then shook his head and headed into the cooler shadows of the main lobby.

They were probably chasing a dead end, but it was a better lead than they'd get playing chicken with one of Baltimore's most powerful families.

And he wasn't going to ignore Seong-Jae's suggestions after the way he'd been treating the damned man lately.

As they stepped inside, the dark, cool gray floors threw up reflections and cast off steps that echoed around the tall, glass-walled room. An escalator led up to a terraced second floor that looked to have a number of open-front retail stores, while the first floor was nothing but a security guard station, a directory plaque, and a bank branch set back unobtrusively to one side, an ATM just outside its glass front doors.

Seong-Jae lightly nudged him with his elbow. "Malcolm. Look."

Malcolm tilted his head back, following Seong-Jae's line of sight. His reflection looked back at him, miniaturized and fish-eye warped in the curving black bubble of a security camera embedded in a high corner, the faint glimmer of its red eye barely visible through the smoky glass.

"Think they have those on every floor?"

"We can hope."

The security guard behind the station—older, with a grizzled Wilford Brimley mustache—eyed them, as if trying to decide if they were normal patrons trying to figure out where they were going or if they might end up being an actual problem. His expression when from dubious to outright wary when Malcolm touched Seong-Jae's arm, then turned and headed straight for the security desk.

Before the man could open his mouth, Malcolm flipped his badge out. "BPD homicide unit," he said, and pulled out one of his cards, sliding it across the desk. While the guard picked it up and stared at it, Malcolm continued, "Can we review your security tapes? We need…" He paused to think. "Twelfth, fourteenth, and fifteenth floor would do it, I think. From night before last, from nine to ten P.M."

The guard—his nametag said Elroy—blinked at him slowly, his mouth hanging open in a small slack pucker underneath that full Brimley, before he made a soft, glottal sound. He shook himself, then apparently decided to believe them, because he said, "No cameras on twelfth or fourteenth." His eyes were wide and confused and curious, gleaming with interest. "It's up to the clients who lease each floor if they're willing to pay for active security or if they'll pay for their own. Sometimes they skip it because it's cheaper." He turned toward the bank of monitors and the control terminal next to them, his short, stubby fingers quick on the keys. "Fifteenth floor does, though. Six standard cameras."

"Do any of them point west?" Seong-Jae asked. "Particularly, do any of them offer a view across the street?"

"I...uh..." Elroy blinked. "I don't know."

Malcolm rounded the desk. "Let us see."

The guard hesitated, then slid his chair to one side. Malcolm leaned over the keyboard, tabbing through the folder of security records the guard had brought up. Seong-Jae leaned over the side wall of the security kiosk, arms folded against the half-wall, his head almost bumping Malcolm's as he craned in to peer at the monitor. Malcolm froze, watching him from the corner of his eye.

"Do you mind?" he grit out.

Seong-Jae arched a brow. "I need to see."

Malcolm just bit back a growl and focused on sorting through folders that looked to be organized by date and floor. Seong-Jae was too *close*. Seong-Jae was always too close. And Malcolm was thinking not about the case, but about Seong-Jae falling into his arms and crushed close against his chest.

[229]

This distracting shit was why partners didn't get involved.

He forced himself to focus on the folders. The right date, and then…fifteenth floor. Seventy-two files, twelve for each camera; it looked like the security recording software truncated the file every two hours, saved it automatically by timestamp, and started a new one. He squinted at the thumbnails for the six for the window of the murder, then snarled under his breath and fished his reading glasses from his pocket, perching them on his nose.

Seong-Jae eyed him. "…poor vision is against regulatory codes for adequate physical condition for police service."

"I'm a little near-sighted with tiny words and pictures," Malcolm threw back. "I can still pass my firearm certification."

"Can you?"

"You want to test if I can hit a moving target at twenty paces, Seong-Jae? Because I could use a little practice."

The security guard made a strangled sound.

But for a second, Malcolm could almost swear Seong-Jae smiled.

Two of the thumbnails looked as if they captured a good view through windows opposite. Malcolm opened one, but it didn't take more than ten seconds of video to realize it was the wrong direction, looking out on the gray concrete walls of a nondescript older office building. He tried the other one—and was rewarded by the gold gleam of the Wellington's tall vertical emblazoned logo, the black sheen of its glass. It was distant, filtered through multiple layers of glass…but he could just make out the interiors of a few rooms with their curtains pulled, hints of beds and carpet and furniture and the soft golden glow of wall lamps, the windows' black tinting nearly invisible against night-lit rooms.

Seong-Jae leaned in further and pointed at one room, long index finger pressing against the screen. "That one. That is the honeymoon suite."

"Are you sure?" Malcolm asked.

"As reasonably certain as I can be with spatial projections, average calculations of room volume and dimensions, and the estimated location of the room on the specified floor."

"…will you talk like a human for once?" Malcolm muttered as he dragged the video player's timeline slider closer to the actual time of the murder.

"I am speaking like a human. I have reasons for speaking the way I do, and I would prefer not to discuss them here."

"Um," the security guard interrupted, goggling at them blankly. "Did someone die?"

"That would be why we're here," Malcolm said, then stopped the video just a few minutes before the time of death. "Here. This is it."

Seong-Jae leaned in again, his temple lightly brushing Malcolm's. Malcolm almost snapped something, only for the security guard to crowd in on his other side, shoulder almost jabbing into Malcolm's waist. Malcolm stared at him incredulously, but the man's gaze was locked on the screen, little images reflecting in his glasses.

Malcolm restrained a groan, rolled his eyes, and returned his attention to the screen.

In almost ghostly movements, people milled in and out of the room. He couldn't quite make sense of what they were doing at a distance, until he realized they were scattering something on the floor. Employees from the florists, he thought. Scattering those rose petals that had been on the carpet. He thought he caught a figure that had to be Garvey—darker suit, plus he recognized that body language from their interactions back during his narcotics days. That swagger, trying to look effortlessly casual but never quite hitting that note, arrogance and narcissism in how he carried himself. Garvey had always walked as if he'd like nothing more than to watch himself moving.

Yeah.

Yeah, that was him, pointing at the floor and making imperious gestures, commands the flower shop people scurried to obey.

Then they were gone, and Garvey was alone. He strutted around the room, preened in a mirror, brushed his hair back. Next a bellhop, room service cart there and gone. Malcolm held his breath. This was it. This was *it*, if they could get Paul Barker or Lillienne Wellington or even Caldwell Brixton on tape committing the murder, they had it. Open and shut case.

Well, not open and shut. The video was grainy, distant, and it would take a little work to convince a jury just who was on the video other than the shape of a man or woman who vaguely matched up with Barker's or Wellington's body type.

But it was more to work from than they'd had before, and if they were smart they could work around plausible deniability with an outright confession.

There—the door opening, just as Garvey bent over the room service cart, plucking and fussing at things. Whomever opened the door had keycard access, and Malcolm waited for Lillienne Wellington to come strutting inside.

Instead a man walked in. Short. Barrel-chested. Dark suit. Gray or blonde hair, hard to tell on black-and-white video. A tight, aggressive stride, one that took him swiftly across the room, past Garvey, knife snatched up from the cart while Garvey turned, arms spread. The man slashed at him— two, three, four, quick and sharp, left to right then right to left, then lifted his arm over his head.

The security guard made a strangled sound, clapping both hands over his mouth.

The knife plunged down.

Garvey's cry was soundless, yet rang in the back of Malcolm's mind nonetheless. He fell. Rose petals showered everywhere. The man stood over him and, with quick, businesslike movements, dragged the knife out of his chest, wiped the handle on a napkin from the cart, and dropped it to the floor before bending to hook his hands under Garvey's arms and heft him up, dragging him toward the bed.

"Oh my God," the security guard breathed, his mouth hanging open as he slumped back in his chair. "He killed him. He straight up mother fucking killed him."

Malcolm ignored him. "That's not Lillienne Wellington," he said grimly, straightening and looking at Seong-Jae. "It's not Paul Barker, either. Or Caldwell Brixton."

"Adult male," Seong-Jae said. "Older."

"I would peg that for Maximilian Wellington." And Malcolm's stomach sank, just saying the words.

Fuck. *Fuck.* He fixed his gaze on the screen once more, watching as the man—with Wellington's blocky bulldog build and tight movements—hauled Garvey face-down onto the bed. It was hard to get a clear look at his face, just a white smudge with impressions of features, but the head shape was right. Though proving that against high-powered million-dollar lawyers and Wellington's influence with the BPD higher-ups…

He groaned, scrubbing a hand over his face. "Fuck. What do you think?"

"I do not understand the motive," Seong-Jae said slowly, carefully. "But I believe it is grounds for arrest on probable cause."

"Probable cause and he'll slither out in five minutes or less. His lawyers won't even need to lift a pinky." Malcolm dug in his pocket for his USB cable. At this rate, he was going to need to get a larger microSD card for his phone. "Let's get this to Sade. We need a warrant." He glanced at the security guard, who was still white-faced and staring. "I'm going to copy these videos as evidence. If your employers or anyone else has questions, you can call the number listed on the card I gave you. Okay?"

Technically it was fudging the lines a little. Malcolm had the right to take evidence without a warrant if he felt the time it would take to obtain one would jeopardize the investigation, but he was playing fast and loose by reinforcing that with permission. Frankly this man's permission didn't count for shit when he wasn't the owner of the building, but when Malcolm had cause for warrantless seizure the consent was just covering his bases.

The guard blinked at him, then asked, "...if you catch the guy, will the news say I helped?"

Malcolm stared at him, swallowing back a laugh. "They might."

"Yeah," the security guard said, leaning down to flip the under-desk door open for the computer cabinet. "Yeah, sure! Take what you need."

Seong-Jae opened his mouth as if he might say something very typically Seong-Jae, but Malcolm shook his head, lips twitching.

Don't, he mouthed, then bent to plug in the cable. *Just don't.*

Some things were better left alone.

Too many things he thought, sobering.

Too many things between them; too many things he couldn't forget.

But *don't*, he reminded himself, too.

Just don't.

BACK AT THE STATION, MALCOLM nearly vaulted up the stairs, swearing under his breath the entire time. He'd tried to mail the files to Sade to get a head start and the fucking thing had refused, saying the files were too big. So here he was wasting precious minutes actually driving back to the station with a silent and maddeningly patient Seong-Jae in tow, just to hand the files over to Sade manually.

He didn't know why he was in such a hurry. Why it suddenly felt *urgent*, to get Maximilian Wellington under lock before he slipped away. He'd had enough time already, but if he was smart he'd have hung around to keep an eye on the investigation and not make it so obvious he was on the run or attempting to bury things.

That was why he was on the DA.

It wasn't the scandal at all.

It was guilt.

It *had* to be.

It was the only thing that made sense, and the only thing that settled right in the pit of Malcolm's stomach, that sense of a compass finding north that he'd been searching for the entire time he'd been spinning on this case.

And it had been Seong-Jae who had pointed them in the right direction.

Malcolm had just needed to listen to him, and trust him.

Wasn't that *why* he'd agreed not to fight Anjulie about this assignment? Because during that first case, he'd caught...*something*. This wild energy that happened when they put their heads together, pitted their brains and different perspectives against each other to track point and counter-point until they arrived at the right solution with laser focus. That kind of energy with a partner was rare, and he'd been willing to accept it for the sake of solving more cases and doing his damned job right.

And then he'd turned around and undermined it left and right because he couldn't get his shit together over his personal life.

He owed Seong-Jae another apology, but not right now. Right now, he stepped onto their floor, pausing only to hold the stairwell door for Seong-Jae, before ducking into the homicide bullpen and into Sade's den.

Where Sade was currently upside down in their chair, their feet hooked over the back, their back against the seat, head hanging upside down and deep brown hair trailing to the floor while they fiddled with something under their desk.

Without even looking up, Sade snaked one long, slim hand out from under the desk and waved. "Hi, Mal."

Mal cocked his head. "Little spider, what are you doing?"

"Encrypted dongle," Sade replied cheerfully, as if that made the slightest bit of sense to anyone but them. "I was trying to find a free USB port. Too many peripherals."

"Right. What you just said."

"You're so cute when you're clueless." Sade laughed, pushing the chair out, then righted themself in a feat of acrobatics and swinging legs that Mal didn't quite follow. Only that he was suddenly looking at Sade's impishly smiling face instead of kicking feet, while Sade gripped the chair between their spread thighs and leaned forward, eyes glittering wickedly against dusky skin. "Actually, you're pretty cute regardless. But you, Mal-oh-Mal-oh-Mal-means-bad, have been ignoring me." They grinned, then, wide and devilish. "Been paying more attention to your pretty new partner?"

"I don't—" Malcolm spluttered and darted a glance at Seong-Jae, but Seong-Jae remained impassive, looking at him mildly as if to ask, *what? Well, have you?* Scowling, Malcolm switched his attention back to Sade. "I've been out on cases. Don't be cruel."

"I *suppose* I'll still love you." Sade sighed. "Whaddya

got for me today?"

Malcolm passed over his phone. "Video. Grainy. The passcode is—"

"I got it." Sade was already unlocking the screen with tapping thumbs; Malcolm stared at them. That...was disconcerting. But not nearly as disconcerting as Sade immediately swiping to his nearly-empty photo album, grin widening. "So where do you keep the dick pics?"

"*Sade!*"

Sade laughed and shifted to sit cross-legged, tucking their feet up under them and tapping over Malcolm's screen. "So where is it? Card?"

"Yeah. I didn't have time to make a separate folder, but it's the dump in the most recent downloads."

Sade's lips twisted up as they spun their chair and felt about—without looking—for a cable on the desk, then fitted it to Malcolm's charge port. "You know I probably can't enhance the video, right?" they said. "If the data's not there, the data's not there. I can't make pixels that don't exist."

"I know." Malcolm frowned, keeping a close eye on Sade's desktop. He didn't quite trust the little monster not to copy something other than the files. How the *hell* had they known Malcolm's passcode? "I was thinking more facial matching. Can you at least map points enough to get a high enough degree of probability to be admissible in court?"

"You mean high enough for a warrant. You're going after someone."

"You know me too well."

"I'll try," Sade said. "Lemme see what I'm dealing with." They disconnected the phone, then offered it back to Malcolm. "Mal?"

"Yeah, little spider?"

"You're gonna owe me *so* much sex for this."

Malcolm smacked his palm against his face. "God *damn* it, Sade."

Seong-Jae blanched, looking entirely puzzled. "That is highly unprofessional and inappropriate."

"Which is why I say it," Sade chirped cheerfully. "You're not my type, Mal, but I expect chocolate, roses, and a foot massage. Who am I matching to?"

"Maximilian Wellington. Owner of Wellington Enterprises."

Sade whistled softly, eyeing Malcolm. "That's a serious can of worms to open. You know I could probably match this up to a blowfish and it'd confirm for an eighty percent positive value?"

"Try to do better than that." Malcolm pocketed his phone and turned away, gently nudging the crow of a man in the doorway out of his way. "I need incontrovertible proof, not confirmation bias."

"Where are you going?" Sade called after him.

"To find out where Wellington is." He glanced back. "Call me when you get the warrant."

"Me? But—" Sade went ashen, eyes widening. They

pouted. "The judges are mean!"

"Just use that Sade charm," Malcolm tossed back, heading for the exit.

"I hate you, Malcolm Khalaji!" came wailing out of Sade's den.

He chuckled. "No, you don't," he called, then swung himself out of the door and into the stairwell.

Seong-Jae followed him, almost crowding him on the steps, barely half a step behind. "Are they always so inappropriate?"

"It's a thing. It's why everyone loves them." Malcolm swung around the corner to the next floor, quickening his pace to take two steps at a time. That urgency was pulling on him, that gut feeling that said time was of the essence. "You can't tell me you don't like Sade."

"I find them...disconcerting." Seong-Jae made an odd, almost frustrated sound. "And yet oddly endearing."

"That's how it starts. They'll have you wrapped around their finger by the end of the month." Malcolm stopped at the next landing, then. It hit him like a strange blow to the gut, how little time Seong-Jae had spent in Baltimore. He wrestled with himself for a few breaths, then made himself ask, "Hey. Seong-Jae?"

Seong-Jae stopped one step above, hand on the railing. "Yes?"

"I never really asked..." Malcolm ducked his head, then looked away. "How're you settling in?"

"I have been here approximately a week and a half. I would not call it 'settling in,' but I am…acclimating."

"How's it compare to L.A.?"

"It is…" Seong-Jae exhaled softly. "I do not find it particularly objectionable."

Malcolm glanced back at him. Seong-Jae watched him, unreadable as always, his eyes dark with things that seemed to promise a thousand secrets, maybe a million lies. Malcolm didn't think he would ever know, when Seong-Jae kept himself so completely closed off.

"That's better than being miserable," Malcolm pointed out quietly.

"I would not call myself miserable."

"You never seem overly happy, either."

Seong-Jae's lips twitched faintly at the corners. "I have my moments."

"On your own private time that isn't any of my business, right?"

"Something like that."

"All right," Malcolm said—and it *was* all right. Boundaries were good. Boundaries were smart.

And it was just another reminder that he needed to get his head on straight.

He flashed Seong-Jae a smile, then turned to clatter down the stairs. The lobby was teeming as usual, people trying to find where they needed to go to post bail or contest a seizure or report a violation or whatever they came to the

BPD for, every last one of them looking vaguely lost, vaguely afraid, as if somehow just by stepping into the building they would be found guilty of something and subjected to arrest.

With the BPD's reputation, Malcolm couldn't blame them for that fear.

That didn't mean he liked seeing it.

He was so focused on the people around him that he almost missed the man planting himself directly in Malcolm's path—but he pulled up short as he registered the sharp-cut, quietly imposing figure standing in front of him.

The District Attorney wasn't a large man, but he had *presence* nonetheless—trim and quietly controlled with a certain calm power in how he carried himself, a certain razor-edged confidence in the way he wore his fine suits, a certain stubbornness in the square cut of his jaw. His dark eyes gleamed with intelligence and a particular sense of *knowing*, as if he saw things people hid in a single glance.

And those eyes were currently locked right on Malcolm, as if DA John Matheson knew exactly where Malcolm was going and just how much trouble he was about to make.

"Detective Khalaji," Matheson said coolly, eyeing him up and down.

"DA Matheson," Malcolm answered, just as coolly. "I'm surprised you remember my name."

"Hard to forget when you're always making things difficult." Matheson's smile was forced and false, a lie when paired with the stern, commanding tone in his voice. "You need to stop pressuring the Wellingtons. They're one of our largest donors." His peaked brows twitched pointedly. "They essentially contribute to your paychecks by freeing up budget funds we need for equipment."

Malcolm shrugged. "Then I'll take a pay cut, sir, because I'm putting in for a warrant for Maximilian Wellington's arrest."

Deep furrows cut into Matheson's brow. "On what grounds?"

"Recorded video evidence of him committing a murder."

Matheson stared at him, long and hard, as if trying to stare him down, break him. Malcolm stared right back, lifting his chin. Matheson broke first, swearing, closing his eyes, pacing a step back before exhaling heavily and glowering at Malcolm. "You'd better be right about this, Khalaji."

"You can fire me if I'm not."

"I may fire you if you are." Matheson's gaze darted from Malcolm to Seong-Jae in an assessing once-over. "Who is this?"

Malcolm bit his tongue against a sudden defensive urge to snap at Matheson for the way he spoke to Seong-Jae: speaking *about* him as if he wasn't right there, discussing him without addressing him. He kept his mouth shut, though. Nothing good would come of him barking at Matheson, or talking over Seong-Jae.

Seong-Jae regarded Matheson with glacial calm, then answered shortly, "Lieutenant Detective Seong-Jae Yoon."

"The transfer." Something darkened Matheson's voice as he spoke, something close to contempt, and he gave Seong-Jae a longer look from head to toe. "I heard about you."

Seong-Jae could have been royalty addressing a peasant, from his icy distance and unflappable composure, from the way his toneless words almost mocked. "And what, exactly, did you hear?"

"Nothing good," Matheson retorted, before tossing Malcolm a baleful look. "Khalaji. Fix this."

"The only solution you'd be happy with is Wellington innocent and lining our pockets."

"I'd also be satisfied with your badge, your gun, and your ass on the curb."

"Duly noted, sir," Malcolm shot back—but Matheson was already brushing past him, heading for the elevator on swinging, high-impact strides, bristling with irritated energy.

Strange…what had he heard about Seong-Jae? Somehow Malcolm doubted actually asking Seong-Jae would yield anything, and he sure as hell wasn't asking Matheson. Not when the man was such a prick.

"You know, he actually used to be a decent person," Malcolm murmured.

"What happened?" Seong-Jae asked, turning to watch Matheson as well as the man disappeared into the elevator.

"Politics. That's why I never want a desk job."

The weight of that dark gaze landed on Malcolm, probing in its curiosity. "You do not intend to retire from active duty?”

“I’ll retire when I’m dead, or when I’m too old to do the job.”

“Ah. Not long now, then.”

Malcolm eyed Seong-Jae. “I can’t tell if that was a threat, or a joke.”

Seong-Jae returned his gaze with bland indifference. “Why not both?”

“…and I am too old trying to figure out if that was a meme, or you being so completely disdainful of pop culture that you have no idea what you just said.” Malcolm shook his head and headed for the door. “Don’t answer that. Let’s just go. This time, we’re going to bag the right Wellington.”

[12: YOU WERE NEVER GONNA LET ME GET AWAY]

SEONG-JAE LEANED AGAINST THE DOOR of Malcolm's car, idly watching the traffic around them yet not really seeing it when his mind was on the case.

The case, and District Attorney John Matheson.

He wondered what the DA had heard about him. Wondered what he knew. How much of Seong-Jae's record he had access to, when reviewing and approving a personnel transfer—whether it was only his record as a police officer, or if Matheson would have been able to unseal and review Seong-Jae's juvenile records.

It didn't matter. The past was the past. His record had been expunged.

It didn't matter what Matheson knew.

Or what he chose to do about it.

He would cross that bridge when he came to it.

As Malcolm pulled the Camaro to a halt outside the Wellington estate, Seong-Jae pulled from his thoughts, lifting his head. "We are not going over the fence this time?"

"Last time we wanted to be shady. This time we have to be direct if we want this to stick." Malcolm opened the car door and levered his bulk out. "Besides, I have a feeling Maximilian Wellington isn't here to bully us off the property anyway."

"Then why are we here?"

"Best place to find out where he is? Is to check where he isn't."

Seong-Jae arched a brow, but sighed and slipped out of the car to follow.

Sometimes, keeping up with Malcolm Khalaji was exhausting.

Malcolm strode up to the gate and, without waiting for a word from the guard at the station—the same from last time—pressed his badge against the window. "I don't want to hear a word about Wellington's orders or private property," he barked. "We have probable cause and an incoming warrant for Maximilian Wellington. Let us in or it's obstruction."

The gate guard blinked, eyeing them both with a mixture of skepticism and nervousness. Seong-Jae closed his eyes, pressing his fingers to his eyelids.

Sometimes, too, keeping up with Malcolm Khalaji gave him a headache.

The gate guard frowned. "I can let you in, but the big guy's not here. He took off early this morning. His driver came for him, so I guess he's traveling and didn't want to leave the car anywhere. They haven't given me the updated schedule yet."

Malcolm swore. Seong-Jae stepped forward, flashed his badge for good measure, then asked, "What of Lillienne Wellington? Is she in residence?"

The guard blinked. "Yeah, I think she's home."

"Then either let us in to speak to her, or summon her forth."

"Summon her forth?" the gate guard repeated. "Dude. What? Are you straight out of Lord of the Rings or something?"

"If you're going to mock the way my partner talks," Malcolm said, "I can probably get you on a half-dozen uniform code violations."

"I'm not even a real cop! You can't cite me!"

"Since you're not a real cop, you don't really have legal authority to explain why you're holding up an active investigation, either," Malcolm snapped.

Seong-Jae repressed a smile.

Because sometimes, too...

The old wolf was not half bad.

The guard made a flustered sound. "All right, all right! I'll pass you through." Muttering under his breath, he smacked the release for the gate. "...wish I'd never fucking taken this job..."

"Let me know if you want a rec for a private security agency," Malcolm tossed over his shoulder, already moving to squeeze through the opening gap in the gate. "I know a few that are hiring."

"Dude, fuck off."

"Language," Seong-Jae murmured, and slipped through the gate after Malcolm, catching up to him in two quick steps. "You enjoyed that far too much."

"I've got a feeling right now. And when I get a feeling, I get a little punchy."

"And what is that feeling?"

"That we're about to lock up the right person, this time." Malcolm's smile was dark and fierce, every inch the feral wolf, his eyes gleaming with the heat of a hunter on the scent of prey. "If I said I wouldn't enjoy taking a bastard like Wellington down, I'd be lying."

"Again, there seems to be some personal component driving you here." Seong-Jae watched Malcolm sidelong. "If I did not know better, I would believe you carried a grudge against the wealthier classes."

"I carry a grudge against rich assholes who think being rich lets them literally get away with murder." Malcolm jerked his chin toward the house. "Focus on the case. Not on me."

"As you say."

Yet Seong-Jae's mind was not on Maximilian Wellington, as they walked in silence up the winding blacktop lane beneath the dapple and shiver of the trees.

But he diverted his attention appropriately as he caught sight of a large, flopping sun hat bobbing to one side of the house, nearly obscured among the garden hedges. Lillienne Wellington bent among the bushes, her face shaded by a massive hat and her eyes obscured by massive reflective sunglasses. Bits of green leaves stuck to her simple white sleeveless tunic and loose, swishing white pants as she clipped roses with gloved hands, her movements agitated and jerky as she gathered each pale peach rose, snipped it, then laid it delicately in a basket. The scent of cut stems and fresh petals was thick, overpowering.

"Malcolm." Seong-Jae nodded toward her, and Malcolm immediately adjusted his trajectory, stepping off the path and onto the grass. Seong-Jae kept pace—but kept his gaze fixed on Lillienne Wellington. A feeling on the wind, a ready and waiting tension, told him she would run.

Even if she wasn't guilty, she was hiding *something*.

She lifted her head, turning toward them—then went stiff, her mouth turning downward in an ugly crease. He could see it: the urge to bolt in every line of her body, the guilt in the flutter of her pulse, the realization that this drama was about to come to an end.

But if she hadn't killed Marion Garvey, why was she so afraid?

He saw, too, the moment she decided against running; she'd been poised like a faun ready to flee the hungry beast, the scissors clutched defensively in both hands, but as they drew closer she seemed to choose pride over self-preservation and drew herself up. The scissors fell to dangle from one hand, while the other rose to rip her sunglasses off. She watched them coldly through red-rimmed eyes that spoke wordlessly of a grief that wasn't theirs to witness, yet it was just another pebble weighting the scales away from the possibility of her guilt.

"What do you want?' she snapped as they drew within earshot. "You already put my husband in jail. What's next? Do you intend to drag me off in cuffs, too?"

She made a bitter sound and flung the scissors down into the basket of roses; without thinking Seong-Jae relaxed, the instinctive part of him that recognized a weapon standing down from alert. Lillienne folded her arms over her chest, staring at them defiantly.

"How much worse can you make this?" she demanded. "You're about to show me, aren't you?"

Malcolm stopped a safe, non-threatening distance away. Seong-Jae held back another step, considering his tendency to, as Malcolm put it, *loom*. Lillienne Wellington was clearly fragile right now, on the verge of snapping, and he did not want inadvertent intimidation to push her to any drastic action.

Malcolm was silent for long moments, but his eyes were dark with regret as he regarded her. "We're not looking for you," he said gently, carefully. "We're looking for your father."

Lillienne paled, her eyes briefly widening before she froze, a statue of motionless dread. If her fear and guilt were an aura, they would be a cloud of brittle orange around her, noxious and hazardous sand nearly screaming the things she wouldn't say.

"Why…" Her voice trailed off in a dry rasp. She licked her lips. "Why do you want my father?"

"Because," Seong-Jae said, "we have reasonable video evidence to believe he is the one who murdered Marion Garvey."

Lillienne sucked in a sharp breath—but there was a curious absence of shock in her expression. Her face crumpled, her eyes welling, and she pressed the back of one gloved hand to her mouth, closing her eyes. Her shoulders shook with soundless sobs, yet there was no surprise, no anger, not even grief.

If anything, Seong-Jae would characterize the sudden laxness of her body and the expulsion of her tears as *relief.*

"You knew," Seong-Jae realized. "That is what you have been attempting to conceal. Both from us, and from your husband."

"You don't understand,' she choked out, voice muffled against the back of her hand. "If I'd told anyone…what if he'd killed Paul, too?" She stared at them with pleading, miserable eyes. "You don't know what he's like. But he's my *father.* I couldn't…I couldn't just…"

"It's too late now," Malcolm said—that gentleness still in his voice, but edged with firmness. "We need to know where he is."

But Lillienne said nothing, looking away, her lips trembling as she scrubbed at her nose.

Malcolm glanced at Seong-Jae. A subtle cant of his head seemed to ask *should I?* He...oh. He was actually checking with Seong-Jae before he took action, instead of diving in as if he was working alone. Seong-Jae faltered. He...didn't quite know what to do with that, but after a moment he nodded.

Do as you will.

Malcolm's lips curved briefly, before settling into a solemn line as he stepped closer to Lillienne Wellington, moving with careful, non-threatening motions, exuding that sense of protective comfort that was so much more like the Malcolm that Seong-Jae had first met.

"Lillienne," he said softly—and when he rested his broad hand to her shoulder, she didn't flinch away. He leaned in until she turned her head to look at him with clear reluctance. "You can't protect him from his own actions. Where is he?"

She only shook her head, mutinously silent, but it wasn't hard to tell she was on the verge of cracking. Malcolm squeezed her shoulder lightly.

"Please," he urged. That hypnotic cadence in his deep, rumbling voice coaxed, assured, promised, enticed—as if he was a bastion of confidence and security, if only she would trust him. It fascinated Seong-Jae when Malcolm did that, yet he wondered if the man was even aware of what he was doing as he continued, "He killed the man you love. He hurt you. You're *afraid* of him, and I think you've been afraid since long before Garvey's death. We can make sure your father finally gets what he deserves for the harm he's done."

Her features twisted, a struggle between grief and doubt and anger in morphing lines, her mouth screwing up, before her body convulsed with another sharp sob. She looked up at Malcolm wretchedly. "Can you?"

"It's what we do," Malcolm promised.

That seemed to be what she needed to hear. She stared down at her sandaled feet. "Is it?" She sniffled, then wiped at her eyes, tossing her hair back and clearly trying to pull herself together. "He's at the airport," she said thickly, yet resolutely. She was crossing that line, Seong-Jae realized, and not turning back—and quietly, he admired her for that. "He's going on a business trip to the UAE."

"The UAE does not have an extradition treaty with the US," Seong-Jae pointed out, and,

"He knows exactly what he's doing," Malcolm finished, then swore. "We have to get moving." But for a moment he fixed his gaze on Lillienne again. "Thank you. I know that couldn't have been easy."

"Like it's easy knowing my father killed my lover?" she threw back bitterly. "No matter what happens, my life is going to fall apart now."

"Then why did you tell us the truth?" Seong-Jae asked.

She turned a wavering, darkly humorless smile on him. "For Marion. I don't even know, maybe even for Paul. Because..." She swallowed. "Because he doesn't get to just get *away* with this like he does with everything else."

"Thank you," Seong-Jae echoed, then, "Malcolm. The airport."

"Let's hit it."

"Indeed."

As they turned to leave, Lillienne Wellington was a small figure against the sprawling backdrop of the estate.

She stood surrounded by roses, watching them in forlorn silence, her hands hanging helplessly at her sides as they walked away.

CURSING UNDER HIS BREATH, MALCOLM hung up the phone with the TSA agent at Baltimore-Washington International and smacked his hand against the steering wheel. Even with the lights up on the dashboard and the siren going, traffic wasn't moving anywhere for them. Traffic to the airport wasn't moving anywhere at *all*, and they were just sitting here screaming uselessly into the motionless wall of packed cars.

"All they'd tell me without the warrant is that Wellington's on a private jet and his flight's fueling and almost prepped for takeoff," he snarled. "Fucking useless assholes wouldn't even consider detaining him."

"Could the Captain perhaps use her influence?" Seong-Jae asked.

"Hoping so." Malcolm was already tapping at his phone, sending a quick message to Anjulie.

I've got a warrant in the works for M Wellington but TSA are being obstructionist bastards

Won't detain him and we're stuck in traffic

Can you call in a favor or two

He waited, tapping his fingers restlessly against the steering wheel, then swore and leaned over, shutting the siren off. It was just giving him a headache, and probably annoying everyone for a hundred yards around. His phone buzzed a moment later.

you owe me

He smiled faintly. Everyone was saying that, lately. He glanced up at Seong-Jae. "Anjulie's going to do what she can. We just have to *get* there."

Seong-Jae frowned. "Considering the state of airport security, you would think your call would bring the entire terminal to a halt."

"The TSA are a bunch of authoritarian assholes who don't work well with other agencies. The dick I spoke to barely even believed I was a cop. If I wanted him to do something, I'd have to call in a bomb threat."

"We may have to consider that as an alternative for next time," Seong-Jae said dryly, then muttered something in softly inflected Korean. "We can see the airport from here. The fact that we are sitting here helplessly is ridiculous."

"Traffic is always like this. You can't have a high-speed police chase around the airport." Malcolm sank down in the seat, glaring through the windshield at the fence surrounding the airstrips, fields of dun-yellow grass and the sun glinting off the curving, swooping white roof sections of the airport, making bright splashes of almost wet-looking glare out of the glass. "We're not going to make it."

"We could leave the car."

Malcolm stiffened. "I am not leaving my car."

"We are close enough to get there faster on foot. Park on the curb. Lock the car." Seong-Jae's brows arched challengingly. "What are you afraid of? A ticket?"

"I'm afraid of someone stealing my goddamned car!"

"You can buy a new car. You cannot forcibly extradite Maximilian Wellington from the United Arab Emirates."

Malcolm stared at Seong-Jae, then groaned, taking the steering wheel hand over hand so he could edge into the next lane the moment an opportunity came. "I hate you."

"I am aware of this."

"No, I really, *really* hate you."

"Hate me when we have Maximilian Wellington in custody." Seong-Jae unlocked and opened the passenger's side door. "I am going ahead."

"What?" Malcolm leaned over and snatched at the hem of Seong-Jae's coat, but it slipped from his fingers as Seong-

Jae slid smoothly out of the car. "Don't leave me here!"

"You will catch up after you park," Seong-Jae threw back, then slammed the car door. Then he was gone, threading through the stalled cars smoothly, before he hit the shoulder and took off, long legs stretching out until he nearly flew along the grassy embankments lining the highway, following the line of the fence with smooth, graceful strides. Malcolm stared after him, frozen in his seat.

"You fucker," he muttered, then slammed down on his horn and flipped the siren back on as he tried once again to wedge the Camaro toward the side of the road.

When he caught up with Seong-Jae, he was going to fucking kill him.

THE MOMENT SEONG-JAE FOUND a break in the fence, he changed direction and sprinted across the tarmac, his chest aching fit to burst as he threw everything into each ground-eating stride. He couldn't let that plane take off—not with Wellington on board. Once he was in the air bringing him down would be impossible, and once he was in the United Arab Emirates he had enough money to stay indefinitely and avoid capture for the rest of his life.

That wasn't happening.

But he barely made it halfway across the massive paved space, airplanes parked in neat intervals, before a sudden boiling eruption of people came swarming toward him— everything from baggage handlers to traffic directors to uniformed TSA officers with weapons drawn. He stopped short, lifting his hands, raising his voice to be heard over the barked orders for him to stop, identify himself, back away, hands up.

He wondered that he felt nothing, with several weapons pointed at him.

Nothing at all.

"My name is Seong-Jae Yoon," he called sharply. He didn't have *time* for this. "I am a Lieutenant Detective with the Baltimore Police Department homicide division. I have a very short period of time to apprehend a fleeing suspect currently boarding a private jet. I would appreciate if you would not delay me."

Several of the crowd quieted, looking at each other oddly, then looking at him as if he had grown a second head. A few others continued barking at him, demands for him to lie face-down on the ground among several other annoyances. Seong-Jae sighed.

"I am going to lower my arms now and retrieve my badge from inside my coat," he said. "Do have the courtesy not to shoot me."

Amidst more shouts and demands, he dropped his arms and slipped his hand inside his coat for his badge. For a moment he saw a trigger finger tighten, before he withdrew his badge and held it up.

"If," he bit off, "you could be so kind as to lower your voices, verify my identification, and get out of my way."

Garbled, confused conversation. More puzzled looks. Then one of the TSA agents holstered her weapon and stepped warily forward, coming just close enough to reach for his badge. "Let me see. ID, too."

Seong-Jae handed over his badge, then pulled his wallet from his back pocket and flipped it open to let her check his license. Irritation made his blood feel like thorns pricking inside him; he was wasting precious minutes on bureaucracy while she took her time squinting at his badge and his license.

Finally she looked up, eyeing him suspiciously, then tossed over her shoulder, "He's legit. Stand down." While weapons slipped away and people milled in confusion, she passed his badge and license back to him. "Who the hell are you looking for and why didn't you come in the front door like a normal person?"

"Time is of the essence," Seong-Jae ground out. "I took the shortest, most expedient route, and considering my partner called ahead and your agents were uncooperative, I had to take other measures. I need to know which runway Maximilian Wellington's private jet is departing from, and I need to know now."

She stared at him. "Maximilian Wellington? As in the big corporate mogul?"

"*Yes,*" Seong-Jae hissed. "Can you help me or not?"

"This way," she said, already turning to stride across the tarmac toward the entrance, unclipping a walkie from her belt and murmuring into it. "Air traffic control, I've got BPD inbound needing eyes on a passenger on one of the private aircraft, name of Maximilian Wellington. Can you put a hold on takeoff?"

The walkie crackled. "One moment," spat out in a grating garbled voice, followed by, "We've got Wellington on runway zero-niner. Pilot is non-responding, but we've removed clearance for takeoff. What's going on?"

"Nothing I have time to explain," the TSA agent said, then shut off her walkie and gave Seong-Jae a dire look. "Runway zero-nine. You want your guy, you better ru—hey!" she cried.

But she was already talking to Seong-Jae's back, as he turned quickly to get his bearings, staring at the numbers painted on the concrete, then took off.

Runway nine.

Maximilian Wellington wasn't getting away.

MALCOLM WAS HALFWAY THROUGH THE terminal before Sade's number buzzed on his phone. He quickened his stride, pushing through the crowds, as he lifted his phone to his ear.

"Talk to me," he said. "Tell me something good."

"I got you one better than the facial matching," Sade said gleefully. "I've got Maxxy-Waxxy Wellington going into the hotel service corridors right before the murder, and leaving them right after. He was wearing a suit coat when he went in, but when he came out he had taken it off and folded it over his arm. There's a few stains on his shirt, though."

"No cameras in the service hallways, and he knew about the shutoff window for Lillienne's meetups with Garvey. He took the coat off to hide the bloodstains. He knew what he was doing. The timing is enough for suspicion, combined with the footage of the murder." Malcolm elbowed past a few lines until he got to the TSA security desk and flashed his badge to the man behind the counter, leaning in to murmur "Here after a suspect, need you to wave me through," before turning his attention back to Sade. "Did you get me a warrant?"

"I had to call in a few favors."

"Favors? To whom?"

"Nobody you need to worry about," Sade replied almost too quickly. "I got you a warrant. I'm emailing you a signed copy."

ID, the officer mouthed, and Malcolm tapped his foot impatiently as he handed it over. "Will an emailed copy hold up under trial?"

"We'll make it work." Sade sounded unusually grim, serious. "We've made harder things work. We've got the signed document on hand before the arrest takes place, so it should be enough. Unless you have time to come back for the paper copy."

"No. No, I don't. I don't have time for anything. Including this asshole carding me like I'm trying to buy beer with a fake ID." He glowered at the agent. The agent glowered right back, and Malcolm turned away. "Thanks, little spider."

"Go get 'em, Mal. And hey?"

"Ah?"

"Be nicer to that pretty partner of yours."

"I'm trying," he said. "I promise I am."

"Good boy," Sade trilled, laughing and sounding like their old self all over again. "Later, baby."

"Brat." Malcolm hung up and immediately dialed over to Seong-Jae's number. The man picked up almost instantly, and Malcolm asked, "Seong-Jae? Where are you?"

"En route to runway nine." Seong-Jae's voice was harsh and panting, as if he was running, the sound from the other end of the line crackling as if the phone was being buffeted by strong winds. "I managed to negotiate a brief delay, but Wellington's pilot is not responding. I had to, as you would, 'bully' a few terminal agents."

"I thought you were against bullying."

"Civilians. I have no particular fondness for TSA agents."

"I'm feeling you. Look, I've got a digital copy of the warrant. Texting it to you now. I'll meet you there."

"Malcolm?"

"Yes?"

"*Hurry*," Seong-Jae said, before the phone went dead in Malcolm's hand. Malcolm couldn't help a grin.

Always rushing him in the heat of the moment.

Malcolm dropped his phone in his pocket, leaned over the counter, and plucked his badge from the TSA agent's hand. The man made an offended sound, then cut off as Malcolm leaned in closer, looking at him eye to eye.

"No bullshit," he said. "No time. Get me to fucking runway nine as fast as you can."

SEONG-JAE HIT THE EDGE OF runway nine just as Maximilian Wellington was climbing the steps to board his private jet.

He was flanked front and back by the same two large, bulky bodyguards who had accompanied him to retrieve Lillienne Wellington from interrogation, nearly blocking him from sight. The long, sleek Gulfstream's engines were already whirring, their buzzing scream echoing over the tarmac and their wind swirling dead grass and leaves about.

Seong-Jae reached into his coat for his Glock, thumbed the safety off, and sprinted toward the plane, raising his voice to shout, "Maximilian Wellington!"

Wellington froze on the steps, looking back with disdainful calm. Seong-Jae skidded to a halt at the foot of the steps, aiming his firearm upward. One of the bodyguards blocked his line of sight, immediately positioning defensively in front of Wellington.

"You are all instructed to descend the stairs away from the aircraft," Seong-Jae said. "Maximilian Wellington, you are not permitted to leave the country when under suspicion of murder."

Wellington scoffed, brushing his bodyguard aside as if he was nothing and looking down at Seong-Jae with contempt. "What is the meaning of this?"

"You are under arrest for the murder of Marion Garvey," Seong-Jae retorted, switching his aim to Wellington, watching him down the length of the barrel.

"I most certainly am not," Wellington scoffed. "I don't

even know who that is."

"We have recorded video evidence of you assaulting Garvey with a kitchen knife and plunging it into his chest," Seong-Jae bit off. "I am warning you for the last time. Put your hands up."

Wellington curled his upper lip in a sneer. "I warned you I would have your badge."

Seong-Jae blindly retrieved his phone from his pocket, keeping his aim on Wellington, and thumbed through in two quick swipes to Malcolm's most recent text, tapping the image of the scanned document to fill the screen and holding it up. "Signed warrant. You cannot rely on your DA connections now."

"That's not a warrant. That's a photograph." Wellington's laughter was incredulous. "You can't use that as grounds for arrest."

"I can, and I will. Do not make the mistake of assuming I will not shoot you if you continue to remain non-compliant." Seong-Jae caught a hint of motion—one of the bodyguards reaching into his coat, trying to be subtle. Seong-Jae transferred his aim to him. Fuck. If it came down to it he was outnumbered...but he'd faced worse. "Inadvisable," he snapped. "I can see the shape of your holster. If you draw on a police officer, you will not like the results. Wellington, tell your men to stand down. Resisting will only add to the charges against y—"

His words ended with the gleam of a silver barrel, the

bright burst of muzzle flash, the gunshot's sharp report.

THIS HAD BETTER BE THE first and last fucking time Malcolm ever drove to an arrest in a baggage cart.

The unfortunate TSA agent he'd commandeered—a man who, ironically, called himself Lucky—had nearly driven Malcolm to violence with calling in security checks with his supervisor, before he'd reluctantly led Malcolm through the terminal at a half-jog to steal a baggage cart and send it careening across the tarmac. As much as a baggage cart could careen, anyway, but at least it was marginally faster than moving on foot.

Marginally.

"Can this thing go any faster?" he growled.

"You can walk," Lucky retorted sullenly, then nodded up ahead. "That's runway nine up ahead."

Malcolm leaned forward, squinting across the tarmac, past a wide dividing band of grass separating one runway from the next. A pristine white Gulfstream jet sat parked on the concrete, engines whirring, several dark shapes gathered on the steps to board, one lone, lanky figure standing at the foot, arms outstretched and—

Oh. Oh, fuck.

He knew that silhouette.

"Seong-Jae," he whispered, his heart thumping hard. He flung himself from the moving baggage cart, stumbling and rolling only to tumble himself to his feet and take off across the grass. The TSA agent shouted after him. Malcolm ignored him, gaze locked solely on Seong-Jae as Malcolm vaulted a ditch in the grassy median, came down hard on one knee, then sprang forward to the edge of the runway. That jackass. That *jackass*, Malcolm never should have let him go alone, never should have—

The sharp *crack* of a gunshot blasted over him. He didn't even look. He just threw himself at Seong-Jae, crashing into him until their sharp angles knocked together with bruising dull points of pain, slamming them both down to the pavement. Seong-Jae started to shove at him, hands curled against his shoulders, then froze, staring at him.

"...Malcolm."

Malcolm pushed himself up on one elbow. "You okay?"

"Yes. Thank you." Seong-Jae's gaze shifted over Malcolm's shoulder. "Wellington is departing."

Malcolm twisted to look over his shoulder. Wellington and his goons were racing up the steps, hustling double-time into the jet. "*Shit.*" He tumbled off Seong-Jae, reaching down to clasp his wrist and haul him up, then bolted for the boarding ramp and vaulted up the stairs. He caught the door just before it swung closed, wedging his hand painfully in, then yanked it open and threw himself inside, Seong-Jae on his heels before the door slammed shut. He lifted his head.

And stared right down the barrels of two drawn pistols.

The two bodyguards stood in the aisle, expressionless, grim, weapons pointed straight at him. Maximilian Wellington stood behind them, little visible other than his smug, smirking face.

"Not a wise decision, Detective Khalaji," he said.

Malcolm flung himself around the entryway wall separating the main cabin from the cockpit, gesturing to Seong-Jae. Seong-Jae hovered on the other side of the cabin entrance, peering around the wall quickly before pulling back, his Glock clasped in both hands. Malcolm slipped his own Glock from its holster, then leaned carefully around the wall, taking in the lay of the cabin before he pulled back again, flattening his shoulders against the wall.

"This isn't going to end the way you think it is, Wellington," he said. "You don't get to draw on two cops. It doesn't work that way."

"And what do you think will happen?" Wellington asked mildly, as if he were taking tea with the queen. "You are outnumbered in a moving airplane en route to a foreign country. Your laws don't apply here."

"Our laws apply until you cross the border of that foreign country. And you're not there yet." He backed away, just enough to rap on the cockpit door. The pilot opened the door a crack, peering back quizzically. "Don't take off," Malcolm said. "Don't you dare fucking take off."

"Gregory," Wellington said calmly, "if you value your life and your family, take off."

The pilot didn't even hesitate. "Yes, sir," he said.

The plane accelerated in an instant. Pure forward momentum rocked Malcolm, sending him stumbling to one side; Seong-Jae swore, falling against the corner between the wall and the door. Malcolm braced a hand against the wall, shoving to his feet, only to reel to the other side as the plane abruptly tipped upward, front wheels lifting off with a screaming whine of the engines, gravity and force combining to send Malcolm tumbling to the ground. He caught a glimpse of Wellington's goons falling, of Wellington himself bracing himself between two banks of seats, before Malcolm hit the ground. Seong-Jae caught him under one arm and hauled him out of the aisle, pulling him back behind the safety of the wall.

Breathing hard, they sank down together, crouching and pressed hard against the wall. Seong-Jae leaned into him, nearly wrapping around him to steal another glimpse into the cabin before he pulled back. "They are regaining their footing," he whispered, leaning in until his lips almost touched Malcolm's ear, warm breaths kicking up the spikes of adrenaline making Malcolm's blood boil. "We cannot risk an open exchange of fire in an airplane in flight."

"Do they know that?" Malcolm muttered.

"Perhaps they should." Seong-Jae's grip tightened on his

Glock. "Are you willing to trust me to handle the situation?"

Malcolm searched Seong-Jae's gaze, then nodded. "Yeah," he said, mouth dry. "I trust you."

"Then take care of the pilot."

Seong-Jae was already standing, one hand flattening against the wall, then spreading his legs sharply and planting his feet to balance himself as the plane leveled off. He caught Malcolm's eye one more time, nodding, then swung himself around the wall to stand in the aisle of the cabin, weapon aimed straight forward.

"I would advise you to disarm yourselves and surrender peacefully," he ordered coolly.

Malcolm took advantage of the distraction to thrust himself to his feet, edging along the wall to the cockpit. The door still hung open. The pilot caught sight of him, glancing back, and made a panicked sound before lunging for the door handle. Malcolm got there first, wedging his foot and shoulder in and pointing the Glock toward the pilot, aimed carefully just to one side. He wasn't going to shoot the man if he could goddamned well help it, but the pilot didn't need to know that.

"Bring this goddamned plane down," he growled, keeping one eye on the pilot and one eye on Seong-Jae, Wellington, and the bodyguards.

Wellington laughed. "Ignore him, Gregory," he said. "Do you think I won't shoot you and dispose of your bodies over the Atlantic?" His sneer was contemptuous—and utterly confident. "Do you think I haven't done worse to secure my empire?"

"The confession is appreciated," Seong-Jae retorted dryly. "However, I feel I should inform you of something you may find disconcerting."

And then he swung his weapon away, off Wellington and the guards, leaving himself exposed.

Malcolm's heart rate ramped up to a frantic speed. Everything in him told him to drag Seong-Jae under cover, to protect him, but he held himself in place.

Are you willing to trust me to handle the situation?

Yeah. I trust you.

Seong-Jae stretched his arm out to his side, aiming the gun toward the wall of the Gulfstream. Coldly, with utter calm precision, he said, "A single shot fired in such an enclosed space may harmlessly puncture the airplane's hull. However, if my aim is accurate—and it is always accurate—it will shatter a window, at which point this cabin will depressurize. Not only will we all be sucked toward the aperture, but we will rapidly lose oxygen and risk the airplane breaking apart in midair. You may attempt to shoot me before that can happen, but I promise you that I will pull the trigger before the bullet impacts my body. Now." He arched a brow, his sharp black gaze challenging. "Will you lower your weapons, or do I take the shot?"

Malcolm's eyes widened.

That was fucking psychotic.

And he goddamned well loved it.

One of the guards barked out, "Motherfucker, are you nuts? You'll fucking kill all of us!"

Malcolm almost laughed. "He's a little fucked up like that," he said. "I'd listen to him."

Wellington's eyes narrowed. "You would not dare."

"Try me," Seong-Jae retorted, finger tightening subtly on the trigger.

It was the guards who broke first—first one, then the other holding their hands up, loosening their grips on their weapons. ""Okay, okay! Just don't fucking fire that thing!"

Wellington's face reddened. "Larry! Zeke! I did not give you the order to stand down!"

One of the men—Larry or Zeke—looked over his shoulder at Wellington with a mixture of disdain and wide-eyed fear. "Motherfucker, I ain't getting blown out a plane for your narrow white ass."

Malcolm exhaled a sigh of relief, and switched his attention back to the pilot. "You heard them. Bring the plane down. Turn it back around and head back to the airport."

The pilot gibbered a faint sound. His face was pasty, sheened in a slick of sweat. "They're not going to let me land without clearance—"

"Then you goddamned well circle until they let you come down. If I could fly a plane, I'd have you in cuffs, too." He eyed the pilot, then slipped forward into the cabin, keeping his Glock angled to the side and at the ready. "All of you. Safeties on, weapons down, face down in the aisle, hands behind your heads." He caught Seong-Jae's eye as the guards complied, lying down head to toe in the aisle, safeties clicking and weapons sliding across the floor. Wellington was slower, looking as if he might try to pull something, before he reluctantly dropped to his knees as Malcolm lifted his Glock and sighted down its barrel, keeping Wellington in his line of fire. "Seong-Jae."

"Understood." Seong-Jae holstered his pistol and edged through the aisle, stepping over the first bodyguard's prone form to straddle his waist, pulling a pair of cuffs from his pocket and drawing the man's arms down to snap them together at the wrists. As he moved to the next, retrieving another pair of cuffs, he said, "I would not advise attempting anything rash. You are all currently charged with resisting arrest and threatening an officer, and you may both be tried as accomplices to the murder of Marion Garvey. Which means that you—"

He broke off, lifting his head, giving Malcolm an inquisitive look and holding up one hand. Malcolm reached into his coat and snagged his own cuffs, and tossed them to Seong-Jae.

Seong-Jae caught them neatly out of the air and angled gracefully around Maximilian Wellington's stubbornly kneeling form. A hand to the back of his head pushed him gently but firmly down, and Seong-Jae snapped the cuffs on he continued, "—will not buy your way out of jail on technicalities regarding the warrant. Your arrogance is your end, Maximilian Wellington."

Wellington arched and flopped like a beached fish, then managed to lift his head, baring his teeth at Malcolm like an angry bulldog, an ugly thing that was half furious leer, half twisted smile. "I won't see a day of jail time," he promised. "I could admit it right now. I could say I stabbed him in the chest and you won't be able to pin me."

"That doesn't mean I won't make you damned uncomfortable trying," Malcolm said.

"You—"

Wellington broke off with a muffle snarl as Seong-Jae pushed down on the back of his head once more, expression almost too bland as Wellington ate a face full of carpet. Malcolm wouldn't fault him on it. Standard procedure to subdue an apprehended suspect without hurting them, after all.

Wellington turned his head enough to spit out, his face florid red, almost purple, "I will *ruin* you! Both of you!"

"Good luck with that." With the three of them cuffed, Malcolm holstered his weapon and stepped over the guards, moving to sink to a crouch near Wellington, looking down at him. "Why did you kill him, Wellington? What was the goddamned motive?"

Whatever composure Wellington had left, whatever intent he had of dissembling, exploded into fragments. "Because *she always picks the wrong men!*" he bellowed, his eyes bulging with fury. "First that filthy trucker—"

"I believe he was a mechanic," Seong-Jae interjected.

"Fuck what he is! I don't care! He's common trash and she only married him to rebel! Then that oily, disgusting, low-class piece of criminal filth—"

"You don't own your daughter," Malcolm said, cutting him off. "You can't keep her caged under glass, in mint condition and untouched. She's not property."

"She's *mine*," Wellington hissed.

"No," Malcolm said, standing and then settling into one of the cabin seats as the hum of the engine changed and the floor began to tilt, gravity sloping them downward. "She's not. And she never will be again. Seong-Jae?"

"Yes, Malcolm?"

"You brought 'em down. You want to Miranda them?"

"With pleasure," Seong-Jae said—and pushed Wellington's face a little harder into the carpet of the aisle as he began, "You have the right to remain silent..."

BY THE TIME THE PLANE landed, Wellington had subsided into rebellious silence. Malcolm had weathered the descent in one seat with Seong-Jae settled across the aisle, both of them keeping a close eye on the handcuffed men between them.

Once the plane landed, Malcolm and Seong-Jae hustled Wellington and the guards to their feet, funneling them down the aisle and down the steps that were quickly ushered up to the airplane door. Malcolm urged them down the stairs—and right into Anjulie's waiting custody, her car slewed to a halt right there on the tarmac along with several other marked cars. She caught his eye and smiled faintly; he returned the smile, exhaustion making him slow, his reactions dulled, before he turned back to the cockpit and pulled the door open.

"Up," he said as the pilot sagged with a groan. "You too."

The pilot stood reluctantly. "Come on, man, I was just doing what my boss said."

"So he pays you well enough that you'll break the law for him?" Malcolm snorted. "Turn around. Hands."

Sighing, deep and aggrieved, the pilot turned and gave Malcolm his hands. Malcolm slid the cuffs on, then caught him by the shoulder and guided him out, trailing him down the stairs.

Anjulie took the handover, gripping the pilot's arm firmly and guiding him toward one of the marked cars, hand on the back of his head until she stowed him away. Straightening, she dusted her hands off.

"That the last of them in this fucking clown car parade?"

"Yeah. They're all in on obstruction and resisting, plus murder for Wellington." He drifted to her side, watching as the uniformed officers locked up. "You're late."

"Like hell I am. Who the hell do you think got you clearance to land?" She leaned over enough to bump him hard with her shoulder, pushing him off-kilter, before straightening with a groan. "God, this is gonna take so much ass-kissing to smooth over. The two of you running around like there are no fucking DHS protocols in an airport...for fuck's sake, Mal."

"How much do you hate me right now?"

"Not nearly as much as I should." She tossed her head, then turned to stride toward a cluster of rather anxious-looking people in suits, voice drifting back. "Go. You're done here. File your report and go do something productive."

The only thing Malcolm could think of that might be productive, right now, was collapsing into bed and sleeping for twelve hours straight. He didn't know why he was so surprised when he was so *tired* after chasing down a perp, once the endorphins wore off and his body crashed like he was coming down from a bad trip. Every time, though, seemed worse than the last.

Then again, it wasn't every day his partner threatened to blow out a goddamned airplane just to stare down a suspect.

And speaking of his partner...

Seong-Jae stood off to one side, near the tail of the Gulfstream. Rather than watch the officers milling about with TSA agents while Anjulie spoke in smooth, authoritarian tones to settle the airport personnel clustered around her...Seong-Jae was looking off toward the end of the runway, where the horizon blurred and turned strange and misty, as if the land and sky forgot where their edges were and just what strange boundaries kept them apart.

Malcolm drifted to Seong-Jae's side, and spent a few moments watching the horizon with him. Heat-wave shimmers against the tarmac told him it was only afternoon, when he felt as though months had passed in the space of minutes. He glanced at Seong-Jae, tracing over the fierce line of his jaw, the high peaks of his cheekbones.

"Were you serious?" he asked. "Would you have blown the window?'

"I considered it," Seong-Jae replied.

"You didn't *know*?"

Seong-Jae shrugged. "I would have known when I made the decision."

"Just when I think I have you figured out…" Malcolm chuckled. "You've got a wild streak, don't you."

Seong-Jae canted a sidelong glance toward Malcolm, lingering, then looked out across the runway again—but for a moment, his lips curved faintly. "I have no idea what you may mean, Malcolm."

"Keep saying that," Malcolm said, as he watched the sun glint silver off the belly of a jet rising high into the sky, lifting its great weight from the earth by sheer force of will only to disappear into a vastness of clouds that made this great thing small. "You just keep right on saying that."

[13: SINKING AWAY]

MALCOLM STOOD OUTSIDE THE GATE of the Wellington estate, looking up at the peaked iron curls and flourishes wrought into the design. The gate guard was watching him strangely; so was Seong-Jae, but Malcolm wasn't ready to walk in there yet.

Wasn't ready to do what was necessary, if he really meant to do his job right.

And wasn't sure if he could go in there and force himself to be the bad guy yet again, when the air still wasn't clear between himself and Seong-Jae.

He sighed, gathering up handfuls of his hair, working his fingers through it. Seong-Jae made a soft, quizzical sound. Almost nothing, but it was enough to force Malcolm's pride out of the way enough to let his voice escape.

"That was a good catch. The cameras across the street," he straggled out, then sighed. "You're right. I was sloppy. I have a lot on my mind, and everything's irritating me right now. That's not your fault. And it shouldn't impact my work." He took a deep breath, then forced himself to say, "I'm sorry."

"I do not require an apology."

Malcolm let out a bark of laughter, glancing at him. "You never do."

Seong-Jae inclined his head, considering, then added more quietly, "...but I do appreciate it."

Malcolm couldn't help smiling, then, no matter how tired he felt. "Thanks."

"Would you like to talk about the things weighing upon your thoughts?'

"No. I don't think it would do any good." And Malcolm didn't want to put that burden on Seong-Jae. Not when some of it was *about* Seong-Jae. "But I guess I'd better go see Ryusaki. At least offload some of it."

Seong-Jae made a faintly amused sound. "That is two people in forty-eight hours who have threatened to suspend you. Technically three, if you consider the Captain and the District Attorney separately. Four if you include Wellington."

"You'd be surprised how often I hear it. It's almost like people don't want me working on the force."

"I doubt that," Seong-Jae murmured. "You are good at your job, Malcolm. Everyone has...what is the term? 'Off days.'"

Malcolm's eyes widened. Only Seong-Jae could deliver a compliment in the same dry, deadpan tone in which he said everything else, yet it was that very cool neutrality that made it clear he meant it, if only because he wouldn't waste words if he didn't.

Malcolm's face burned. He looked away, scowling. "Oy.

I don't need pity."

"It is not pity."

"Then what is it?"

"It just…is," Seong-Jae said simply.

"…I can accept that." Malcolm flicked his fingers at the gate guard. "Let's go do the ugly part of this."

Lillienne Wellington was just leaving the house as if she'd been expecting them, when they strode up the walk to the house. She paused, hand on the doorknob, stylish in a softly shimmering black wraparound dress and gold wrist bangles, her hair perfectly blown out in tumbles around her shoulders. Her quizzical, confused gaze flicked over them.

"Officers? What can I do for you? If this is about my husband, I was on my way to post bail—"

"There's no need to post bail. He's being released as we speak," Malcolm said, ascending the steps. "Lillienne Wellington, you're under arrest."

She paled, eyes rounding. "What? But…but I didn't kill Marion!"

"But you willfully concealed who did. That's obstruction of justice and accomplice liability." Malcolm retrieved his cuffs from his pocket, snapping them open. "You'll probably avoid a prison sentence. But you do have to stand trial."

More than anything, Malcolm hated that moment: that moment when people who'd done nothing but made questionable decisions in a bad situation realized they would have to face the law for it, anyway. And he wondered how sheltered Wellington had kept his daughter, so ground under his heel that she'd probably had no idea what to do other than what he'd told her, when he'd kept her under glass her entire life.

Arresting her after that, after she'd had to lose someone she loved to escape her father's grip, felt like a betrayal of his duty—and of her.

But it had to be done.

And she didn't protest, as he gently guided her to bring her hands behind her back so he could snap the cuffs home with a final and fatalistic *snick*.

PAUL BARKER WAS RELEASED FROM holding just as they finished booking Lillienne Wellington and handing her over to the uniforms for processing. Barker came rocketing down the hall, pushing through people toward the booking desk, and he slammed into Malcolm hard enough to leave a throbbing spot that would probably turn into a bruise as he shouldered past to get to his wife.

"Lilli? Lilli, it's going to be okay," he gasped out frantically.

He caught her by the shoulders. The booking officer started to intervene, but Malcolm caught her eye with a subtle shake of his head.

Let them have this, while they could.

Lillienne strangled on her words. "It…it's not going to be okay," she managed raggedly. "They said…they said because I lied about what Daddy did…"

Barker stared into Lillienne's eyes with such adoring fervor that it almost cut Malcolm's heart in two to see it. Barker pulled his wife into his arms, holding her close. "I'll call the lawyer. We'll post bail and figure out what to do next. It'll be all right."

Lillienne leaned hard into him, her eyes welling, her voice choking. She struggled against her cuffs, then gave up, just collapsing into his embrace. "Paul…"

"I promise it'll be all right," he swore, clutching her tight as the booking officer carefully pulled her free from his grasp, guiding her away.

She strained back over her shoulder, tears spilling down her cheeks. "*Paul!*"

"I'll come get you," Paul promised, staring after her, chest heaving. "I'll be there soon, I promise." Then he rounded on Malcolm and Seong-Jae, glaring at them with a fury that replaced the passive, quiet man who had sat in their interrogation room before. "How could you?" he demanded. "She wasn't trying to protect Max. She was *afraid* of him. That man is a damned tyrant. If she'd gone to the police, he'd have just bought his way out of a sentence and the next person he'd go after would be her." He gestured savagely, tense muscles in his arms bunching and rippling. "You don't know that man. You don't know what living with him is like. You were supposed to protect her. You're supposed to protect the innocent."

"She lied," Malcolm pointed out. Moments like this made him feel so tired. So broken. "And it wasn't to protect herself, or her father. It was to protect you. Even when grieving the death of her lover, she broke the law to protect *you*. Not anyone else. She thought, if her father was desperate enough, he might hurt you."

Barker faltered, his bunched fists falling to his sides limply. "I...what? Doesn't that mean *anything* to you pigs?"

Malcolm closed his eyes, took a deep, slow breath, then opened them again and made himself speak—made himself be careful and calm, because he couldn't do anything for Barker or Wellington if he let his emotions run away.

"I have to obey the law," he said. "Just like anyone else. And the law says deliberate concealment makes her an accomplice." He retrieved one of his cards from his breast pocket and offered it to Barker. "It doesn't leave her without options. The courts aren't heartless. Any judge will recognize she's a victim who just made a few poor life choices. If asked to testify, we'll say the same. They'll grant her immunity for testifying, and her testimony can make sure her father never hurts either of you again." He flicked the card, drawing

Barker to look down at it. "I know everything seems frightening right now, but let due process happen."

Barker stared down at the card—then snatched it from his hand, crumpling it in a thick fist but at least not throwing it away. He turned hard, recriminating eyes on them, staring at Seong-Jae, then Malcolm, as if memorizing their faces. "If anything happens to her, it won't be Wellington you have to worry about."

"I know," Malcolm said. "And I understand."

Barker said nothing.

He only glared at them bitterly, then turned and walked away, the line of his back tense as a stretched wire ready to snap.

Malcolm watched him until he vanished through the door. Then, with a sigh, he slumped against the edge of the reception counter, rubbing at his temples. Seong-Jae settled to lean next to him, their shoulders brushing lightly.

And even if Malcolm felt heartsick and heavy, the contact warmed him just a little.

Just enough.

"How do you do that?" Seong-Jae asked.

"Hm?" Malcolm lifted his head. "Do what?"

"I am attempting to understand how you find the line between patience, compassion, enforcing the letter of the law, and choosing to let infractions slide." Seong-Jae's soft strawberry mouth remained open for a few moments, before struggling words drifted forth. "I..." A frustrated sound. "I have yet to find that balance. I do not understand how to tell someone they have no choice in complying with due process in one moment, only to empathize with their plight and offer comfort the next."

"It's not that hard."

"Oh?"

"Enforcing the law is part of my job," Malcolm said. "Remembering those people are human is part of *me*." He thumped a hand against his chest. "You have to keep a part of yourself that doesn't belong to this job, Seong-Jae. I hope you have that." He met black, stark eyes that still, as always, told him nothing, when some broken and completely fucked up part of him was starting to wish for...*something*. "If you don't, find it."

Seong-Jae only watched him in silence, as if he could see every wayward thought Malcolm refused to speak.

And Malcolm had to drop his gaze first, as he pushed away from the desk and headed toward the stairs.

SEONG-JAE WONDERED IF HE COULD TRULY say there was anything he had, outside of his job.

Perhaps in Los Angeles. His parents. His sister. But anything else…

He didn't have room for that, right now.

Especially when it wasn't safe for anyone else who might get involved.

He finished signing off on his half of the paperwork for the Wellington case, then closed the folder and stood, stretching and cracking his sore, aching neck before pushing the case file across Malcolm's desk. "Your desk is too short," he said.

Malcolm didn't even glance up from his own scribbling, dashing in notes in case files and gaze distracted behind the lenses of his glasses. "Get your own."

"I still like yours better."

"Sounds like a personal problem."

Malcolm paused, though, lifting his head. With his glasses on and his hair caught half-up, half-down in messy trails, suit coat discarded and the sleeves of his shirt rolled up over his brawny, corded forearms to his elbows, Seong-Jae could see who he had been: Professor Khalaji, a man of quiet thoughts and deep study and a curious disposition. What had driven him to change, Seong-Jae wondered?

"You heading home?" Malcolm asked.

"Yes. It would appear we are the only ones left, save for the Captain and Sade."

Malcolm glanced around the empty bullpen as if he was only just aware of the time. The windows were dark save for the flash of tail lights and the glow of street lamps, and the only illumination in the room was Malcolm's desk lamp, the square of yellow spilling through the Captain's open office door, and the multicolored glow emanating from Sade's bizarre tangle of technology inside the room they'd turned into a lair.

"Huh," Malcolm said, then pushed his glasses up and rubbed at his eyes. "I should probably head out, too." Exhaling, he let his glasses fall again and fixed his gaze on Seong-Jae once more. "You okay, after today?"

Instinctive defensiveness had an *I am fine* on Seong-Jae's tongue, but he strangled it back. If he was going to ask Malcolm to *try*, as his partner, then Seong-Jae should try as well.

"I did not particularly enjoy having to arrest her," he said. "Unfaithfulness is not a crime."

"Not one punishable by law, no." Malcolm folded his arms against the desk, leaning on them heavily. "It was a shitty situation overall. That was their personal business, but the second there was a dead body involved..." He fell pensively silent for a moment, gaze dropping to track sightlessly over the desk, before he continued, "Still. She had to walk in on her lover's dead body, find out her father killed him, and we still had to arrest her."

"Regrettable that we could not overlook it."

Malcolm laughed—a low chuckle, softer and sweeter than his usual harsh, wolfish barks of laughter, exhaustion turning the raw edges of his voice from a growl into a purr. "Since when do you break the rules?"

Seong-Jae ignored the strange tingling pulse in his lips, as though a memory had come back to life, and said, "You may be having a bad influence on me."

"I can't say I'm overly upset about that." Malcolm pulled his glasses off, idly tapping the end of one arm against his full, firm mouth. "She'll be all right. There'll be trauma counseling in prison, if she's convicted. If not, she's smart enough to get a counselor on her own. There's her husband, too. He's pretty determined to look after her."

"Do you think they will remain together?"

"I don't know. He loves her, that's for certain. How she feels about him is their business. I've seen smaller things than a murder and an affair break couples apart, but I've also seen larger things push them back together." The tapping stopped, Malcolm falling still, his gaze glassy and distant, a wrinkle appearing in his brow. But then he said, a touch more sternly, almost dismissively, "We just catch the killers. We're not relationship counselors."

"Speaking of counselors…"

"You're nagging me again?" Malcolm scowled, but there was no real heat behind it. "Fine. I'll go before I clock out today, if Ryusaki's still here."

"I only do not wish to see you suspended, Malcolm."

There was something almost charged, then, in the space between them. In the sudden way that Malcolm's gaze focused on him, sharpening with utter clarity. "Yeah? There any reason for that?"

"No reason at all," Seong-Jae deflected.

But he had to look away from Malcolm, to speak again.

Because the weight of slate blue eyes and the keenness of a hunting wolf's stare suddenly made him feel like prey, as if Malcolm could see his vulnerable underbelly, as if his flesh were primed and trembling for a killing strike. Especially when he forced himself to speak the words on his tongue, instead of swallowing them back to keep them in his throat and hold them secret and unsaid as he so often did.

"If…" He felt as if the words inside him were trying to scale walls that only grew taller the higher he climbed. It was easier to discuss a dismembered body than to make a simple casual, friendly inquiry. "If…I wait…do you wish to visit Swabbie's once you are finished with the counselor?"

Even if he couldn't look at Malcolm…he could hear the smile in his voice, when Malcolm replied gently, "Maybe some other time." A low, amused thrum, the sound velvety and compelling, almost demanding Seong-Jae look back, when he *couldn't*. "I'm never really the best company after a visit to Ryusaki. But next time, Seong-Jae. Your treat."

"I find those terms acceptable," Seong-Jae said. "Goodnight, Malcolm."

Then he turned and walked out of the office, before he could give in to the urge to look back and see if the smile on Malcolm's lips was as devilish as he imagined, that one-sided half-smirk that was at once arrogant and patiently weary. He didn't need to see it to know it was there.

And he didn't need the strange feeling that walked soft fingers down his spine as Malcolm called after him, lingering on the familiarity of his given name as though he could *taste* it.

"Goodnight...Seong-Jae."

ANJULIE WATCHED HER NEWEST PROBLEM child leave, and told herself she wasn't stalling on going home.

Not that it made much difference. Home or work, she was just constantly herding difficult people.

The only difference was the amount of blood involved.

Even if, right now, she thought if she went home there'd be more than a little blood and tears before the night was over.

She forced herself to focus on the stack of paperwork on her desk. In the morning she'd have to deal with an angry district attorney and whatever mess of lawyers Wellington sent in the BPD's direction. She might as well clear out her desk so she wouldn't fall behind while playing politics. It was the part of her job she hated most, yet it seemed all she ever did since her promotion.

It was worth it, she told herself.

But she'd never wanted to strangle Malcolm Khalaji and Seong-Jae Yoon for successfully solving a case more in her *life*.

Yoon was supposed to make Malcolm easier to deal with, not worse.

Two weeks with the BPD, and between the two of them they were going to turn her prematurely gray.

"Hey. Captain."

She glanced up as Sade's smooth, almost musical voice drifted into her office—yet they sounded distinctly un-Sade, that omnipresent and wicked edge of unvoiced laughter absent to leave a quiet hesitation, solemnity, that she'd rarely ever heard.

"Sade." Anjulie set her pen down and laced her fingers together. "You've been particularly quiet lately. I feel like that should make me nervous."

Sade fidgeted in the doorway like an errant schoolchild sent up to the principal's office, their ragged ripped tank falling off one curving shoulder and chain-bedecked half-gloves rattling lightly as they twined their fingers together. "I've just been busy. Narcotics confiscated over two dozen fingerprint-protected laptops during a raid, and they want the financials off all of them."

"That's like third-grade homework for you."

"It's pretty sophisticated," Sade countered—but they

didn't seem to be particularly invested in the narcotics seizure, or even to be paying much attention to their own words. Their gaze skittered away from Anjulie, then back, then away again. "I...um..."

Anjulie tilted her head, then exhaled heavily as it clicked. She'd known this day would come again, as it had come many times in the past.

It didn't mean she had to like it.

"You have to go, don't you."

"It's Lumbee homecoming." Sade flashed a shallow smile. "It'll only be a week, maybe. My cousin's getting married during the whole...yannow...and like...have you ever *seen* a Lumbee wedding? I'll be lucky if it only lasts a week."

Anjulie said nothing, because the words choked in her throat with a sudden fury and frustration. The lie of it—the lies she knew were necessary, when Sade wouldn't be standing there with their dusky skin white with fear if they were really going home. They'd be bright with joy, breathless with the eagerness of getting to spend time with their tribe, not pale and quiet and nervous, but Anjulie couldn't even acknowledge the deception when she knew her place in this game as much as Sade knew theirs.

It didn't mean she had to like that, either.

Or that she didn't hate the feeling of sending one of her own off into a situation she had no control over, and couldn't protect them from.

She swallowed back her helpless annoyance, and nodded tightly. "Send my regards to your family, then."

"Yeah." A pallid smile. "I'm sure they'll say hi back."

Sade turned away, but paused when Anjulie said, "Sade?"

"Yeah?"

"Stay safe. Don't do anything too dangerous."

Sade threw back a choked, humorless laugh. "The most dangerous thing I'll do is get drunk and dance on tables."

"Of course." Anjulie sighed. "I'll put in for your leave and see you in a week."

"Thanks." Sade started to move away again, then stopped, one slim hand curling against the door. They stared out across the office, but the lines of their lean back were taut, tense. "Don't...tell Malcolm until I'm already gone?"

"Why?"

"I just..." A tight shrug. "He worries."

"He's protective."

"Yeah." Barely a whisper, thick. "Some things, he can't protect people from."

"I think everyone knows that but him." Anjulie leaned back in her chair. "I'm good at keeping secrets, Sade. It's all right."

"Thank you." Another smile flashed over Sade's shoulder, brighter this time, warmer. "See you in a week, Captain."

"Out, scamp."

Sade slipped away, vanishing in that quiet way they had; for someone so effusive and bold and reckless, Sade had a talent for becoming invisible, gone between one breath and the next, lost in a blink.

Anjulie only hoped this wasn't the last time she saw them, disappeared on that last sighing breath and never to return.

EVERY TIME MALCOLM SAT IN Dr. Karen Ryusaki's office, he hoped it would be the last.

It wasn't Karen herself. Karen was a friend of over ten years, and was the best damned departmental counselor in the BPD. She *knew* him, in ways few others did—knew when to push him, when not to, knew all the old hard ugly knots of pain inside him so he didn't have to unravel and unspool them for a stranger every time.

But that was part of the problem. Karen knew him.

Knew all the things he wanted to forget, and not just the ghosts of homicide victims haunting him, the trauma and stress of the job.

And every time he had to come back here, it was because someone else was dead in horrible enough ways to leave another scar on his psyche.

Every time he had to come back here, it opened up old wounds.

He sprawled on the couch with his hands folded over his stomach, staring up at the ceiling; she was just a faint shape in his peripheral vision, trim and neat with her pad in her lap and her graying black hair swept up in a twist. Her gentle, understanding smile was in her voice as she said,

"Malcolm. It's good to finally see you."

"You threatened to have me suspended."

"I use the means at my disposal." She chuckled. "I see you're still a couch man."

"I'm tired. It lets me take a nap while you drone."

"You know I never drone. And you know your defensive quips never work on me." The faint scratch of a pen. "It's been a while."

"It has."

"That new partner of yours is interesting."

Malcolm tensed. Why was she opening with Seong-Jae? "If by 'interesting' you mean he's going to make the last of my hair go gray."

"Do I?" More scratching, the pen moving across the page. "He frustrates you, then. Why?"

"He's just so…" Malcolm unfolded his hands and gestured helplessly. *"Him."*

"I see."

"Don't." He knew that quiet, neutral tone. "I hate being psychoanalyzed."

"I know this quite well. Why do you think I threaten you to get you in here?"

"It's your job. It's not his. And he's *always doing it*."

"He is former BAU," she pointed out mildly.

"There's got to be a fucking off switch."

"Is that the real reason he bothers you?"

No, Malcolm thought, but god, he couldn't talk about that with her. Couldn't talk about fisting up handfuls of that pretty pianist's hair and wondering if Seong-Jae would gasp the same way, if Malcolm pulled his hair just hard enough to make him shudder, to make his mouth go soft for a hungry, needy kiss.

"You didn't call me in here to talk about him," he said.

"I didn't," Karen answered. "But he reminds me of you a great deal, you know. Or at least, you ten years ago. So very serious. So very determined to carry everything on your own shoulders."

"That was ten years ago."

"And this is now." A faint rustle of paper. Malcolm tilted his head back enough to watch upside down as she set the pad aside on a small table, and suddenly she was *Karen* and not Dr. Ryusaki, watching him with her eyes dark with warmth. "And I'm concerned about you now, Malcolm. Obviously the Park case must have had an effect on you."

"It…" His throat tried to close. "It's left me a little raw, yeah." The faces of those dead boys, the mutilated horror that girl had made of them. "I just. We see it all the time. How bigoted people are. But when they find ways to express it like that, this…this twisted portrayal of hate as love…" He shuddered. He couldn't stop seeing Nathan McAllister's face, the haunted, shattered look in his eyes that said even if he'd survived, he would never be all right again. "It breaks me, a little. And I feel sick with myself that I felt bad for her."

"For who?"

"Sarah," he said. "The perp. She killed a bunch of queer boys and I'm worried about *her?*" He laughed at himself, but it was a scouring and hurtful thing, like swallowing raw gravel. "I should hate her. With everything in me. But she's just a girl, and she fell through the cracks. Someone should have taken better care of her. Someone didn't do right by her."

"Caring for her well-being does not mean you've chosen not to care for the people she hurt. It's not about choosing sides. You can care about both."

"Can I?"

"Why do you feel that you aren't allowed to separate hatred for what she did from compassion toward her as a person?"

"Because *she as a person* murdered four queer boys and traumatized another one for life out of some fucked-up obsession!" Malcolm flared, unable to keep from snarling—

then caught himself, swallowing back, taking several deep breaths and closing his eyes. "I'm sorry. I'm *sorry*."

Karen was silent for a few moments, then said softly, "It's rare that you let me see your temper this way, Malcolm."

"Can you not…" He fumbled helplessly, then flicked his fingers. "That thing."

"Hm?"

"The therapist voice where you say my name at the end of every other sentence and try to make me feel *seen* and *heard*." He grumbled. "You know I hate that."

She chuckled. "I do. I'm sorry. It's a hazard of the job."

Malcolm pushed himself up on one elbow, twisting himself to face her. "Are we done? Is this enough to clear me?"

"I think if I suspended you, you'd ignore me anyway." She watched him shrewdly, but not unkindly. "You don't feel right unless you're on a case, do you?"

"It keeps me busy."

"Why are you so desperate to keep busy?"

"The pointed questions aren't any better than the therapist voice." He swung his legs down and pushed to his feet, reaching for his coat draped over the arm of the couch. "I'm done."

She sighed, but said, "All right. If that's what you want."

He shrugged on his suit coat, settling it into place, and smoothed his tie before heading toward the door. She reached it ahead of him, rising to her feet and drawing the door open for him, looking up at him with her small, thoughtful smile that seemed to forgive everything, even his surliness.

Malcolm stopped, gripping the doorframe, looking down at her, then exhaled roughly. "Karen…"

"Yes?"

"Thank you," he grit out. "I know I'm difficult. But thank you for caring. Even though it's your job."

"It's not just my job. After all this time I'd like to think we're friends, Malcolm."

"Yeah," he said. "We are."

"May I ask you something?"

"Yes?" he replied warily.

"Have you heard from Gabrielle lately?"

Malcolm almost flinched. The doorframe bit into his palm and fingertips as his grip tightened. "…last week." His gaze dropped to the toes of his shoes. "She saw the case on the news. I guess the reporters at the campus killing caught me on the edge of a shot, or something. She was worried."

"And how is she?" Gentle, probing, yet somehow Karen always seemed to know how to touch those old wounds just the right way to make him bleed.

"She's…" He swallowed back the lump in his throat. "She's actually thinking about moving back to Baltimore. But she's living. She's finding her way. It's a good thing."

"And are you, then?"

"Am I what?"

"Living. Finding your way."

That was the question of the century, wasn't it. "I'm trying to," he admitted, and Karen smiled slightly, warm with understanding, with sympathy.

, "And how do you feel, about your ex-wife moving back here? About her possibly being part of your life again?"

"I don't know," he admitted. "I care for her. We're friends. But I feel like apart, we were able to pick up our lives and make something again after..." Fuck. After all this time he should just be able to come out and say it. Finish that sentence without feeling like every word was a spear embedding into his heart. "After..."

Karen's smooth, warm hand landed lightly on his arm: an anchor, a solid point of human heat that dragged him back from the past. "You don't have to say it, Malcolm. I know. It's all right."

"...yeah." Fuck, his eyes were stinging. He sucked in a sharp breath, grinding his knuckles against them. "But with her here again...I don't want to be the reason she loses what she's worked to rebuild."

"And what about what you've worked to rebuild?"

"I don't..." He felt hollow, empty. "I don't know."

"You should think about it."

"Yeah. I should." But not right now. He couldn't stay here for this conversation right now, couldn't endure another minute of this. He pried his fingers away from their death-grip on the doorframe and straightened his suit coat. "I should go home, too. It's late. I'm keeping you here, and you…"

"…are going home to a cat and a quiet apartment. It's all right. My babies are all flown the nest, with Dai in college. There's nothing waiting for me at home but a glass of wine and a few trashy romantic comedies."

"How are things with your eldest? Is he still…?"

"He's still…everything." Her face fell for a moment, before brightening with a brave smile. "Kou is…troubled. And the hardest part of being a therapist and a parent is wanting to fix my children, but knowing I can't do anything for them that they don't want for themselves."

Malcolm managed a smile and gripped her shoulder, squeezing gently. "I hope he works things out."

"So do I." Her hand rose to cover his, clasping warmly for a moment, before letting go. "Thank you, Malcolm. Enjoy your evening."

"Goodnight, Karen," Malcolm said.

Then slipped into the hallway, and left the mausoleum of his memories behind.

SEONG-JAE STARED DOWN AT THE glossy photoprint, and tried

to decipher the message hidden in the single letter streaked in blood against pale wallpaper.

V.

It shouldn't mean anything at all, yet it had been traced in blood along the wall outside the crime scene, in a different hand than the initial bloody smears left behind. The fingertip that had made those marks was slightly thicker than the one that had smeared bloodied streaks in a moment of panic, that frantic stumble as Lillienne Wellington had stumbled away from the crime scene. Someone had entered the hotel room after the killer had departed but before Lillienne Wellington had arrived, and had deliberately used the victim's blood to paint that V on the wall.

That V had been there on the surveillance footage before Lillienne's hand ever made its mark.

The question was who had left it.

The same question he had asked himself at the scene of DeMarcus Shay's murder on the University of Maryland campus, when someone had used the victim's blood to paint an O on the paved front colonnade of the building where the body had been discovered. The O could have been left by Sarah Sutterly.

But Sarah Sutterly was under psychiatric care.

She could not have left the V.

Seong-Jae lifted the color glossy of the photo he'd taken off his printer, lingering on it.

Then he pinned it to the right of the photograph of the O,

and took a step back.

His steps echoed off the walls of his concrete and brick-walled apartment, rising up to the exposed beams of the ceiling with little furniture to catch the sound and absorb it. He fixed his gaze on the letters next to each other, searching for their meaning. For some sort of message. Anything.

O. V.

What did they mean together?

Did they mean anything at all?

Maybe they weren't letters. Maybe he was imagining things, and they were just random blood patterns or some other accident of blood smear and spatter from multiple people contaminating the crime scene.

But those movements were too deliberate, those shapes so clear he could almost run a handwriting analysis on them, following the dips and swoops to create the profile of a chaotic personality, laughter hiding in the intersection of lines and a subtle pleasure in the curve of the O. Seong-Jae pressed his knuckles to his mouth.

"What are you trying to tell me?" he whispered. "What are you attempting to say?"

A clattering rattle came from his fire escape—like feet pattering, running away. He whirled, tensing sharply, searching the long, low line of windows, then crossing the room in quick strides and ripping the window open, leaning out to take in the strange concrete and exhaust scent of a city at night. He searched the street below, then tilted his head back to look at the fire escapes above.

No one there.

No one who could have made that sound. Nothing but the wind sliding silken fingers over his cheeks, and the sounds of traffic calling far and away, the noise of life moving down lonely streets.

Maybe it was a cat, bouncing along the wire grating.

But as he leaned back into the building and shut the window, he couldn't escape the distinct feeling of being watched.

BY THE TIME MALCOLM MADE it back to his desk to grab a few case files he wanted to take home with him, the heavy feeling in his heart and the sick feeling in his stomach had faded to a sort of distant melancholy. The past was the past, he reminded himself.

He'd made a life for himself. So had Gabrielle.

Just because she was moving back to Baltimore didn't mean their lives had to intersect.

Just because they'd be close once more didn't mean they had to break each other all over again.

At his desk, a bit of sticky note paper was tacked on his monitor—neon blue covered around the edges in little stick-figure doodles and handwritten anime emojis with sharp teeth and wide grins.

He knew even before he unstuck the note and read the scrawling writing that it was from Sade.

Hey hey Mal!

Listen I gotta go hook up with my family for like a week or so?

Don't do anything weird with your computer because there's a time bomb inside and if you fuck it up you'll detonate it!!!

Try not to get into any murders that need a cyber-brain 'cause I'm not gonna be here to fish your ass out of trouble.

Also don't worry, okay?

I'm okay. I promise.

Lubs!

<3,
-Little Spider

Malcolm chuckled and glanced up as Anjulie emerged from her office, coat draped over her arm, and pulled the door shut.

"What's this about?" he asked, lifting the note.

Anjulie shrugged, threading through the scattered desks toward him. "You know Sade. Sometimes they just do their own thing."

"When they tell me not to worry, I worry."

"Because you're an overprotective mule." Anjulie stopped before him, studying him with a cock of her head. With her heeled boots she was almost his height, and her wry, piercing gaze met his before she lightly socked his shoulder with a curled fist and one of her tired, razor-edged smiles. "Go home. Even Yoon clocked out."

"You're still here."

"I'm considering sleeping on my desk."

"Anjulie." He arched a brow. "Go home."

"Nngh." With a grimace, she slumped to sit on the edge of his desk. "I'll think about it."

He settled next to her. "What are you avoiding?"

"People who catch feelings when I tell them not to and I don't want to?" she said almost plaintively. "Sex is sex. Love is something…entirely different. It's not my thing."

"If you talked to them and were honest with them, you can't control their behavior," Malcolm said. "All you can do is remind them of what you told them. If they can't handle it, they can leave."

"I don't *want* her to leave. I just…don't…want her making it uncomfortable. Alloromantic people don't *listen*." She sighed, shoulders slumping. "How do you handle it? Being *loved* by someone. It's such an uncomfortable thing. And it's *rude* when I specifically asked her not to."

"It's uncomfortable even for people who want it. It's like holding your beating heart out in both hands and begging someone not to bruise it, and sometimes it's more terror than anything else. But for those of us who want it…" Malcolm shrugged. He didn't know how to explain. Especially when half the time, he thought Anjulie had the right of it. "It just *is*. You learn to live with it, and even embrace it."

She snorted. "Hard pass. I'm good."

"Yeah, you are." He bumped her with his elbow and grinned. "You'll get it sorted."

"I always do." She straightened, slinging her coat on, draping it over her lanky frame. "You allos make life too messy."

"Probably. And you're stalling. Go *home*, Anjulie."

She grinned, lopsided and fierce. "You first."

"Mature."

"The soul of." She settled her collar. "All right. I'm going. I'm going. Get some rest, you."

"Goodnight."

She just flicked him a merry wave, her free-swinging strides taking her toward the door—but she paused, abrupt as if a thought had struck her. "Hey, Mal."

He looked up from sorting through the folders on his desk. "Yeah?"

"Everything okay between you and Yoon?"

"Will be," he said, and it wasn't wholly a lie. "We're sorting it out."

"That's better than trying to kill each other." She laughed, and swung herself through the doorway. "See you tomorrow."

"Bright and early," he called after her, but she was already gone.

Leaving him alone in the cool ghost-light of the near-empty office, the silence his only companion.

HE MADE IT OUT OF the office in time to get out to Pikeville and Seven Mile Market before it closed. He was in the mood for something more traditional for dinner tonight, but didn't feel like dropping in on his parents unannounced. He was a little too raw for their good-natured concern. Something about the gentle way his parents understood him and let him *be* without words could, at times, tear him apart even more than Ryusaki's gentle probing.

He just wanted a proper meal.

Not an emotional breakdown all over the only people who knew him well enough to not need a moment of explanation.

At this time of night the grocery store wasn't overly busy—just a few people browsing the aisles, the deli already darkened and closed but a few fresh prepared dishes sitting in the warmer and waiting to be taken home. Malcolm leaned over the plastic packaging, eyeing a dish of eggplant parmesan. He'd thought about cooking himself, something more traditionally Persian, but he was so damned tired he might just pick up something and go home. He wasn't likely to find anything he wanted premade at Seven Mile when it tended to follow Ashkenazi kashrut and didn't do much for a more limited market of Mizrahi foods, but with the raw materials he could usually put something together for himself. If he was honest with himself, he was missing his father's cholow nokhodow, which was just telling him what he really needed was home.

He'd stop by for Shabbat dinner this week.

Tonight, eggplant parmesan was good enough.

He tossed the plastic container into his basket and steered it toward the beverage aisle, only to draw up short at a somewhat familiar voice at his back.

"Malcolm Khalaji."

He paused, glancing back. The man he'd met at the piano bar last week—not the pianist, but the green-eyed nameless man with the laughing gaze and the pale, near-white platinum blond hair—stood half-in, half-out of the entrance to one aisle, watching Malcolm with a knowing, amused gaze.

Malcolm blinked. "Oh. Hey." That…was odd, running into him here, but not unheard of. Especially when Seven Mile was one of the few strictly kashrut-certified markets in the Baltimore area. "It's unfair that you know my name, and I don't know yours."

"You did leave me alone in your flat," the man lilted, a touch of laughter underscoring his soft British accent. "You also had the chance to learn my name. Now? Now I just won't tell you."

Malcolm chuckled. "Cute."

"You thought so last week."

There was something of an invitation in that soft, sultry purr, in the way green eyes watched him from beneath the thick fan of pale lashes. The nameless man draped himself on the handle of his shopping cart, his lean, angular shoulders thrusting up in pale, smooth mounds from his loose off-the-shoulder shirt, the slouch of his sleek body an enticement. Malcolm remembered leaving bite-marks on those pale shoulders, kissing the taste of sweat from his skin.

But he didn't have anything in him, for the invitation in those sly eyes.

"Mm." He offered a rueful smile. "I don't do second times, my friend."

The nameless man's smile only widened, both sweet and confident and subtly mocking. "But you're intrigued. Admit it."

"A little," Malcolm acknowledged, then diverted the subject pointedly. "You live in this neighborhood?"

"Close enough." One soft shoulder shrugged. "I come to this shop for the challah."

"You're Jewish?"

"I'm many things," the man teased, eyes glittering. "Including nameless."

Little *minx.* "I could just look you up in the public records database."

"Using what criteria?" The nameless man pushed away from his cart and swayed closer to Malcolm, hands lacing together behind his back as he titled his face up to him as if asking sweetly for a kiss. "I'll make you a compromise, Detective Khalaji."

"Malcolm. I don't mind first-name basis for people I've slept with."

Or partners who let me be so free with their name, when

it means so much to them...

He couldn't stand to think of Seong-Jae right now, and kept his focus on the nameless man. This close, Malcolm caught the scent of him: vanilla and rain. He hadn't been able to pinpoint it when they'd been a tangle of limbs and touches and gasping cries, but that was the closest he could label it: vanilla and rain, and it drew him to lean in closer without even thinking about it, drawn by a certain magnetism the nameless man exuded with his whimsical charm and air of playful teasing.

"Malcolm, then." The nameless man purred over his name, turning it over like a cat batting it around, a treat for him to play with. Then he caught Malcolm's hand, warm skin to warm skin, spreading his fingers with a touch that grazed along his fingers and palm with an electric shiver, baring his palm so the nameless man could pluck a pen from his pocket and scrawl numbers across Malcolm's hand in dashing script that tickled his skin. "Here's my number. If you change your mind about no second times, I'll change my mind about telling you my name."

Something about his brazenness, his boldness, or maybe the touch of those soft fingers ignited heat at Malcolm's core. He forced himself to ignore it. If he did anything tonight, it would just be a Band-Aid on the wounds he'd re-opened today, and he'd feel worse for it in the long run. It would just be using the nameless man, and he'd done that once already with the pianist.

But his mouth was dry, his lips aching with the want for contact, as he curled his fingers against his palm and murmured, "Deal."

The nameless man's smile was slow and enticing, and he cast Malcolm a beguiling sidelong glance as he turned away. "Ta for now," he said, retrieving his cart.

And with one last knowing look that said he knew exactly how much Malcolm *wanted*, he sauntered away, narrow hips moving lazily, drawing Malcolm in with hypnotic rhythm.

For now?

All right, then.

For now.

Seong-Jae dreamed:

The smell of an alleyway after a fresh rain. The scent of blood and meat from severed stumps of legs. The stench of rotting, the aroma of death, and the sound of soft, wild laughter. Everywhere he looked were limbs with their ends cut off in ragged shreds of flesh, no bodies attached. Arms, legs, smeared with blood. Severed heads. As if dolls of men had been torn apart, their segments thrown into a bin, every last one of them staring at him with dead, accusing eyes.

Dead, accusing slate blue eyes, familiar and seared on his mind with the knowledge that he hadn't done enough.

He hadn't been able to save him.

His heart split in two, a scream of raw desperation and rage and loss and confusion rising in his throat. His mouth tasted like blood. His pulse threw itself into a frenzy. His body chilled, sickness and terror curling in the pit of his stomach as he fought through the heaps of limbs, the pieces of corpses piled everywhere, filling the alleyway and turned macabrely comical by the dancing rainbow lights of the club's exterior.

But the body parts rose up to swamp him, the heaps growing until he was wading waist-high through the squelch of flesh, the slippery feeling of blood-slick bodies, rubbery waxy skin giving underneath his touch as he pushed through. But they only rose higher, higher, until he was floundering, crushed, reaching for salvation but there was no one to grasp on to, nothing to anchor him, he was drowning, drowning...

And then the garrote snapped around his neck, wire cutting in, and he couldn't breathe. He couldn't scream.

He could only gasp, as everything went dark.

He woke: sweating, panting for breath, his chest in knots and a feeling around his throat like an icy hand had closed in and pressed over his trachea, like a frozen knife had plunged into his heart. He sat upright in bed, staring blankly across the room.

Staring right at the pin-up board, and those two letters next to each other.

V. O.

One drawn in the blood of a dead queer boy, the other in the blood of a man murdered for love.

He saw those bodies, cut into pieces and put together into a terrible thing, a mockery of obsession. Yet in the lens of his dream, those body parts hadn't belonged to the boys surrounding Nathan McAllister.

No. Those hadn't been strangers, in his dream.

Not strangers at all.

He stared at his phone on the nightstand. Just this once, he told himself.

Just this once.

He grasped his phone in shaking, sweat-slicked fingers, and hit Call.

MALCOLM DIDN'T REMEMBER FALLING ASLEEP on the couch.

He woke to the sound of his ringtone and blinked blearily, sitting up. The Yuri Herrera novel he'd been reading fell off his chest, landing open on the rug between the coffee table and the couch. His *everything* hurt from passing out in this awkward position, neck propped on the arm of the sofa, one leg hanging off to the floor, book on his chest and his empty plate and wine glass still sitting on the coffee table.

Fuck.

He dragged a hand over his face, then snagged his phone from the coffee table. Seong-Jae? He almost missed the call, but swiped it quickly and lifted his phone to his ear, scrubbing tiredly at his eyes.

"Yeah?"

"Khalaji," Seong-Jae said. There was something strange in his voice, something ragged and soft. *"Malcolm."*

"Seong-Jae?" Malcolm sat up further, frowning. He'd never heard Seong-Jae sound so...so... He couldn't explain it, but the way he'd said Malcolm's name shot straight to his heart. "What is it? It's two in the morning."

"I know."

"Do we have a new vic?"

"No. I...there is no case."

Malcolm pushed himself off the couch with a wince for the pull in his back, gathering up the dishes one-handed and taking them to the kitchen to deposit them in the sink. "...then why are you calling me?"

"I..." A trembling breath, then, "I cannot sleep."

"You called me because—"

Malcolm stopped short as he realized what Seong-Jae wasn't saying. What he was too proud to say.

That he, like Malcolm, was haunted.

That case had hit Seong-Jae just as hard…and Malcolm wouldn't be surprised if Seong-Jae had woken gasping and broken from nightmares. Sometimes Malcolm did, too. The night after they'd brought Sarah Sutterly in, he'd woken up from a particularly bad one in which she'd cut Nathan McAllister into bits with strings of razor wire, and nothing Malcolm had ever been able to do in any iteration of the dream could save him. He'd kept those dreams to himself, ignored them until they finally stopped.

But they still lived inside him, dark things sinking in his chest like stones.

"Ah," he said softly. "How bad was it?"

Seong-Jae was silent. Malcolm waited him out; he wouldn't force Seong-Jae to say anything he wasn't comfortable with. While Malcolm waited, he headed toward his wardrobe, unbuttoning his shirt as he walked. Finally Seong-Jae spoke, barely a whisper.

"Half of the dead young men had my face," he said. "The other half had yours."

"That's pretty bad," Malcolm said, as he shrugged out of his shirt and hung it over the wardrobe door.

"Malcolm?" Seong-Jae asked, and the note of vulnerability undermining the stiff, frozen pride in his voice cut Malcolm to the core.

"Yeah?"

"Do you ever…?"

"All the time." He smiled faintly, leaning his shoulder against the door and just listening to Seong-Jae's voice: husky, gently accented, that meticulous pronunciation roughened by the dark-edged burr that made deep, quiet music of his words. "Is this your first time?"

"No. But it has been some time. And it was never so...so..."

"Personal?"

"Yes. Personal."

While Malcolm gathered his thoughts, searching for the right thing to say, he finished changing, abandoning his slacks for a loose pair of cotton lounge pants, hitching them up around his hips and tightening the drawstring before settling to sit on the edge of his bed.

Bu the only right thing to say, no matter how long he stalled, no matter how long he searched, was, "It's all right, you know."

"Is it?"

"It's all right with me."

"That is..." Seong-Jae swallowed audibly. "That is no small thing." Then, a touch stiffly, "I am sorry for waking you."

"That's all right, too." Malcolm shifted to stretch out on his back, pulling his hair loose to spread against the pillow beneath him. He looked up at the ceiling of his apartment and thought of Seong-Jae in his own bed, doing the same: lying there with Malcolm's voice in his ear, looking up at the ceiling, this intangible line drawn between them, this connection made of a horrifying experience no one should ever have to share. "Seong-Jae…"

"Yes?"

"You don't have to hang up."

"But I do not have anything else to say."

"You don't need to." Malcolm smiled to himself, closing his eyes until it was just the dark and the sound of Seong-Jae's breaths. "You don't need to say a single word."

Seong-Jae sounded so uncertain of himself. So *young*. "Then we simply…stay?"

"Yeah. It's all right to just stay."

After a considering silence, Seong-Jae said softly, huskily, "As you say."

"Yeah?" Malcolm's smile widened. "Okay, then."

And so they *stayed*, and the chaos that had been eating away the edges of Malcolm's soul finally quieted, as he listened to nothing but the faint sounds of Seong-Jae moving, Seong-Jae breathing. As if in some strange way they were together, even when separated by distance and the walls they had already settled so firmly in place. Like this these moments were a secret, a timeless thing, and in the silence was an intimacy and understanding that eased a tired and aching craving inside Malcolm.

Even when Seong-Jae's breaths evened and slowed and Malcolm knew he had fallen asleep, he stayed. He listened. He held on to this for as long as he could. In the morning,

Seong-Jae would likely pretend this had never happened—and that, too, was all right. Morning was morning. Now was now.

And for now, Malcolm hung on Seong-Jae's every sleeping breath, and wondered if he would ever feel this calm again.

[THE END]

Read on for a preview from CRIMINAL INTENTIONS Season Two, Episode Three: THE MAN WITH THE GLASS EYE!

[DISCOVER YOUR CRIMINAL SIDE]

GET MORE OF THE THRILLING M/M romantic suspense serial everyone's talking about. Follow Baltimore homicide detectives Malcolm Khalaji and Seong-Jae Yoon as they trail a string of bizarre murders ever deeper down a rabbit hole—that, if they can't learn to work together, may cost them both their lives. **Full-length novels released once per month!**

Browse on Amazon and Amazon KindleUnlimited

https://www.amazon.com/gp/product/B07D4MF9MH?ref=series_rw_dp_labf

See the series on Goodreads

https://www.goodreads.com/series/230782-criminal-intentions

CRIMINAL INTENTIONS: SEASON ONE, EPISODE TWO
JUNK SHOP BLUES

[PREVIEW: CI S1E3, "THE MAN WITH THE GLASS EYE"]

[0: TRAJECTORY]

DECLAN LUTZ COUNTS HIS LIFESPAN in sixty-second sprints.

This is how he lives. This is how he dies, his heart stopping at the end of every minute only to start again with a heavy, thudding beat as he realizes he's survived again and again and again.

He dies one thousand, four hundred and forty times a day.

He lives one thousand, four hundred and forty times a night.

Yet now, as he presses his back against the dingy, dirty concrete wall of his apartment, he counts the seconds in time to his beating heart and ticks the minutes over into lifetime after lifetime and wonders if tonight will be the night when the odometer reaches sixty and this time, doesn't roll over to a fresh start at zero.

His apartment is cold and smells like old fried noodles, and next door flickers of light spill into the tiny windowless cubicle where he sits on a wireframe bed and bare, stained mattress, clutching at his naked sweaty feet and rocking back and forth. The light comes from a hole in the wall. That hole, barely larger than pinky finger, was there when he first moved in. It will be there long after. He does not know how it came to be. The neighbor, whom he does not know and yet feels intimate kinship with, likely has no idea either.

He has never seen the neighbor's face. Never spoken a single word. They have never once met, and yet they share an unspoken agreement regarding the hole:

If you don't look, neither will I.

And so he has only seen their shadow dimming the light from their apartment, like a planet passing in front of a distant star and telling astronomers there, far away, is a body with the gravity to bend and sway light.

That hole is why he keeps the lights out. So he can see that single starlit glow piercing through the opening. So he can see this body of gravity making flickers like Morse code, S-O-S.

That hole is why he chose the apartment.

Because he wants gravity to hold him to earth, when his racing, ticking clock is running overtime and counting his life down to nothing.

It's coming tonight. He can feel it. He can feel it the same way he feels the ache of withdrawal making his veins shrink down tight like they're trying to strangle his blood and shrivel his meat, bind it up like a butcher's shank tied up in twine. He can feel it the same way he knows the feeling of first, second, third, fourth, fifth gear through his palms, vibrating through touch until he doesn't need to look to know how his every caress demands more and more speed.

It's what he does. It's what he's good for.

Other people handle the business.

He just drives the car, and counts his life in the click of safeties and the burn of the speedometer and the seconds of asphalt raging past.

The pain is eating him. His heart, throbbing. His clock is moving too fast. Too fast, his *thump-thump*—like Jack Sparrow, ha-ha, *thump-thump*—churning and pumping and slamming around frantically. He clutches at his chest, smearing his loose, stained shirt with the sweat of his palms. He read once somewhere that some doctors thought you only had a finite number of beats in your heart from the moment you were born, hard-coded in your genetics. When your heart rate accelerates, you're using up those beats, shortening your life.

The straining organ in his chest is moving so fast he might only have a few more deaths and resurrections left. One, two, buckle my shoe, bam, pop, gone.

Everything Declan is just...*gone,* in one last wild and frantic beat.

His next heartbeat comes in a gunshot: the shatter-sharp sound of his doorframe rattling with a single harsh impact, and his heart ricocheting in echo. He jumps, curling both hands in the front of his shirt, pushing himself back against the headboard. His gaze fixes on the door. In the darkness the door is nothing but the thin sliver of poison yellow light underneath, and the cleaner edges of the framing picked out by the illumination through the hole in the wall.

The light settles on the handle and glides over its slow turn, gleaming along the edges. Someone on the other side. Left, then right, testing the lock, slow and methodical. There are gravitational bodies blocking the light beneath the door, one and two, left foot right foot, their shadows stretching beneath the door and reaching for Declan like tall, long arms.

He whimpers.

His heart stops, then starts over again at zero.

Zero, one.

The door rattles in its frame again—harder this time. The person on the other side is not knocking, no. Only one slam, as in that of a shoulder, and the wood of the frame bulges and splinters. The chain lock rattles.

Run, Declan's racing blood says.

But there is nowhere to run.

Two, three.

The light through the hole shifts, changes direction. The neighbor's gravitational body has moved its orbit. Perhaps they will help him. Perhaps they will hear, and come.

No one is coming, his blood hisses, and he whines in the back of his throat and huddles back against the headboard, metal tubing biting into his back as though it's trying to break his spine.

Four, five.

His mouth is the sour taste of fear. Another slam against the door, and the hinges squeal.

Six, seven.

Again. Again. Until on the sixth try—*eight, nine*—his apartment door blows open as if ripped apart in a mighty tempest. It hangs by one hinge. The wood around the door latch is chewed and ruined. The remnants of the chain lock leave a scar of white against the dark wood varnish. Declan clutches his knees to his chest, his heart swimming through his rib cage in wild rolling tumbles, and stares.

Ten, eleven.

He knows the man standing silhouetted in his doorway, and does not know him. Only certain people know his name. Declan was never that privileged. He was told only to obey him, always.

Told only to fear him.

Twelve, thirteen.

The man wears a suit of meticulous, neatly pressed black with sharp creases in his slacks. Just as meticulous are his movements, as he steps inside. The hallway is empty behind him. The hall light glints off the pockmarks in his deep brown skin, the burrs of close-cropped hair shaved neatly against the sides of his skull, his wireframe glasses, the glint of one eye behind the glasses, an eye that glimmers just a little more slickly than the other.

Fourteen, fifteen.

That eye chills Declan. It is not human. It has no life, no soul. It cannot actually see, yet as the man turns his head slowly toward Declan he feels as though the heart of that eye is the heart of this man, and that emptiness and soullessness will swallow Declan whole.

Sixteen, seventeen.

The Beretta in the man's hand. Silencer affixed. It is a cold statement of purpose without needing words, without needing threats. The man says nothing. He is expressionless, mild, as empty as that blank handcrafted eye. He knows why he is here. Declan knows why he is here. Little else matters.

Eighteen, nineteen.

Declan shakes his head, whimpering. *Twenty, twenty-one.* "Please, man. Please. It doesn't have to be like this."

The man steps forward. His movements are measured. He steps over the dirty clothing crumpled on the floor with an air of fastidiousness.

Help, Declan wants to cry, but no one here will help him.

If they would, they would have come the moment the crash and rattle of the splintering door banged over the hall. They would have shifted their gravity, brought themselves into his orbit.

Twenty-two, twenty-three.

The man lifts his Beretta, gestures it at Declan. Declan is shaking, but he understands the meaning. The floor. The man wants him on the floor. With clumsy movements, he slides off the bed. His bones are too loose, his joints held together with string fraying strand by strand as fear rockets through him.

Twenty-four, twenty-five.

The scarred, weathered floorboards bite into his knees. He feels inglorious in this moment, pathetic, staring down at his naked thighs, hairy and flabby and lean, protruding from his briefs. His cock is flaccid and shriveled with fear, just a little pouch against the cotton.

Twenty-six, twenty-seven.

He puts his hands behind his head without being told, fingers lacing together and tangled in his hair. He keeps his gaze turned downward. Looking at the floor is better than looking up into that glass eye, better than staring down the slim mouth of a silencer like some fancy, pretty lady's elegant black cigarette holder.

The man with the glass eye still has not said a word.

Twenty-eight, twenty-nine.

"I'm not holding," Declan pleads, trying for reason. Just once. Just once, maybe, if he could just be honest… "I swear I'm not holding. I delivered the last of it. I didn't use any, either. There's nothing in me, I swear."

Thirty, thirty-one.

The *click* of the safety calls him a liar. Whispers of the jitters shaking through his entire body, as if he isn't strung quivering tight with a terror that rocks him deeper than the withdrawals ever could.

Thirty-two, thirty-three.

His sixty-second life is more than half over.

He swallows, licks his chapped lips. His eyes burn, stinging, the pale brown lumps of his legs turning blurry. "I swear to you I'm done. I—I'm done, I just want out, I d-did the job and now it's over and I won't tell no one, I swear. I...I just want to be...I want to be..."

Thirty-four, thirty-five.

He stares at his thighs. At the striations on his inner thighs, red spreading track marks that leave behind bruises and necrotic flesh. At the marks of a thousand lifetimes lived craving every day, while that rot digs deeper. If he lives tonight, he will shoot up again. He will shoot up to forget, and tell himself the crash is worth it just to let go of the fear that will keep him looking over his shoulder for the rest of his many sixty-second lives.

Thirty-six, thirty-seven.

He'll die curled up in a gutter with a rubber hose tied around his thigh, wasted and sniveling and begging for just one more hit.

Thirty-eight, thirty-nine.

He can see it as clearly as if that glass eye is an oracle. A scrying crystal, showing him the future. He looks up, then, past the vacant black stare of the silencer's mouth and into the eyes of the man without a name, the man who is to be obeyed. In the glass eye, its color slightly off from its flesh counterpart, is nothing. Nothing but the promise of a future Declan cannot escape.

In the dark, tired eye that studies him, however, there is

understanding.

Forty, forty-one.

"…free," he whispers, eyes widening. His heart almost loses its count. Another lifespan is drawing near to close. *Forty-two, forty-three.* "You're here to grant my wish, aren't you?"

Still the man says nothing, but the cool mouth of the silencer kisses Declan's brow almost gently.

Forty-four, forty-five.

Declan smiles.

It is a painful smile, as painful as the dark knife of acceptance cutting through his lungs and making it hard to breathe. He almost wishes the man would show some emotion. Some warmth, that says he understands that this is an act of compassion.

But there is only that calm regard, that lined and seamed brown face that speaks of a thousand secrets that will never find voice, held inside the clairvoyant sphere of an empty, shining eye.

Forty-six, forty-seven.

"Don't make it hurt," Declan asks. He is calm, suddenly. Too calm. "Please. I won't run. Just don't make it hurt."

Forty-eight, forty-nine.

The man considers in silence, then inclines his head. His finger tightens on the trigger.

Fifty, fifty-one.

There's a sound almost like a chirp. Declan can't really

quantify it, can't really liken it to anything but that: a shrilling chirp, a thump of impact, and a cold, piercing feeling that should hurt but somehow the pain is there and gone, swallowing up inside itself. Swallowing up inside a great and descending darkness.

Fifty-two, fifty-three.

He stares into the glass eye, until it clouds into nothing. Everything is black. He can feel a dull and distant throb inside his skull, but his thoughts no longer want to connect together. A slick, sticky warmth pours down his face. His body is not his own.

It is only a sack, collapsing to the floor.

Fifty-five, fifty-six.

For a moment more, he is still alive. It is a strange feeling, to be dying yet still alive. To, for a fleeting moment, feel a sense of self independent of a body that has cut itself off from him, alone as it bleeds away, while he…he is something else, somewhere else, but it is gone as soon as he becomes aware of it, draining into the bits and fragments and detritus of himself pooling out across the floor.

Fifty-seven.

His clock stops on fifty-eight, and does not start again. His timer has run out.

Declan Lutz simply…ceases to exist.

Read the rest on Amazon Kindle and KindleUnlimited!

https://www.amazon.com/dp/B07G3FJG5B

CRIMINAL INTENTIONS: SEASON ONE, EPISODE TWO
JUNK SHOP BLUES

[SERIES Q&A WITH THE AUTHOR!]

HI THERE, COLE HERE. I get a lot of
questions about the series, so let's answer
some of the most common ones!

sleep deprived

Q. I don't quite get the "seasons/episodes" thing.

A. The general story arcs are structured less like a
book series and more like a television series. Every
full-length novel is akin to a TV episode in a series,
where you get a single episodic story arc with a
conclusion for that particular plotline while continuing
the overarching storyline driving the entire season—
and getting to know the characters and their
developing relationships a bit at a time.

Q. So how many episodes will there be per season?

A. Thirteen, just like with TV. Most TV series have
either 12-13 episode seasonal arcs, or 26-episode
seasonal arcs. I'm following the hour-long episode
format with 13-episode seasons so that each novel has
the same feel of a more in-depth hour-long show.

Q. Thirteen. Thirteen actual novels per season. Not novellas. Not chapters. 50,000-70,000 word novels. You're kidding. And you're releasing one per month?

A. Yep.

Q. *How?*

A. I have issues.

Q. So how many seasons will there be?

A. I have five loosely planned, but that's not concrete. I may realize halfway through Season Three or Season Four that we're nearing the end of any viable plot and anything else would be reaching/stretching. If that happens, no matter when, then I'll make that season the final season.

Q. Do I have to wait all the way to Season Five for Mal and Seong-Jae to get together?

A. Nah. I won't tell you exactly when in Season One that they get together, but it'll happen. That doesn't mean subsequent seasons won't bring some rocky times, but we'll get them *into* a relationship in Season One.

Q. But I thought these were kissing books!

A. They are. :) But because it's structured like a television series instead of a normal romance novel, you won't get a complete beginning-to-HEA romance arc in a single book. Instead it's like those partner shows where you watch all season as they flirt with and deny the sexual and romantic tension between them, hoping for every intimate moment until it finally happens, watching their relationship deepen (and occasionally fracture) through the work they do together. It also means now and then as long as they're not tied to each other they may get involved with other people to further complicate their romantic entanglement, but it's just part of the arc to help them realize their feelings toward each other.

Q. You write a lot of unprotected queer male sex.

A. Yes, I do. This isn't real life. There's a massive stigma in real life toward queer men in which people treat us like disease bombs waiting to go off, unclean and deadly, along with the subtle insinuation that it's our fault anyway because of societal shaming of the assumed promiscuity of the stereotyped queer male lifestyle plus a deep misunderstanding of the AIDS crisis. While it's a shitty stigma that treats us like we're disgusting and subhuman, safe sex in real life is still important regardless of gender or sexuality.

Fiction, however, provides a safe place to flip the middle finger at that stigma and very pointedly ignore condom usage. Believe me, as a queer man, with me it's entirely political, utterly deliberate, and a rather firm statement in defiance of the outrage that screams "how dare you, unclean creatures that you are, even fantasize about unprotected sex?" It's also a kink for some people—the fantasy of skin to skin and the sensations involved, and one that can often only be indulged either in fiction or with a long-term partner, allowing for a certain sense of intimacy. If you're waiting for mention of a condom, 8/10 with me you're going to be disappointed. I throw them in now and then, but more often than not I don't. Unprotected sex is always mentioned in the trigger warnings, so you can be forewarned and choose not to read it if it's something that upsets you.

Q. What's the deal with the Nameless Man?

    A. ¯_(ツ)_/¯

Q. Hey, man. Glocks don't have safeties. That's not how they're designed.

    A. I know. :) It's 100% dramatic license for the intense moment when the safety comes off, etc. I get why that would kind of twitch people, though. TV does stuff like this all the time (like what a gunshot actually sounds like, etc.) and sometimes it's just fun to fuck around for the sake of the tension of the moment.

Q. Will every book have super-gory, gross, extreme crimes?

> **A.** No. Although this is a rather graphic series, I really want people more focused on the slow development of the character interrelationships and intrigue with the cases as the framing for that, and as an opportunity to find out how our leads' minds work in various situations. Besides, if every crime is super-graphic that leaves nowhere to go as overarching plots escalate to a head—so some things will end up scaled back to make the truly plot-critical ones more impactful. While I will likely always include some explicit detail of every crime scene, for the most part the details are there more to give readers clues to the evidence informing the detectives' thought processes, and less for shock value.

Q. What made you choose vinyl gloves over surgical nitrile when Mal's allergy means he can't use latex?

> **A.** Personal preference. While I don't have a latex allergy, I do have OCD germophobia and sensitive

skin; I use disposable gloves in certain situations to keep from tripping off my OCD, and the second my hands start to sweat in the gloves I'm likely to get rashes, irritation, and cracked skin on the backs of my palms and knuckles if I use latex. (Which…actually may be an allergy, I'm not sure, I just know I don't like it so I avoid it.)

So I started using both vinyl and nitrile as alternatives before dropping the nitrile unless I have no other choice. Vinyl doesn't get as sweaty as quickly, so it stays comfortable longer; vinyl gloves are also a more comfortable fit for larger hands, when nitrile gloves often feel like they're choking off my circulation at the wrists. The looser wrists on vinyl gloves also make it easier to take them off quickly without dirty portions of the gloves possibly making skin contact. Since Mal has large hands like mine and a need to keep from contaminating himself with the things he touches (such as crime scene blood), I gave him my preference just as one of those little quirks I often share with my characters. The only downside to the vinyl is that it tears more easily if it snags on something or is stretched to its limit.

Q. …why does nearly every single person in these books use some model of Android phone? Are you shilling?

[343]

iPhones are a thing, you know. (Yes, someone asked me this. I actually really love how observant y'all are with the little details like this.)

> **A.** So. Though iPhones are hugely popular, I've never had one. Ever. I'm not really a fan of Apple interfaces or hardware as far as my particular preferences for usability and utility, or maybe I'm just holding a grudge from being forced to use really old Apple computers in art school. Point is, I don't know iPhone interfaces, what apps are or aren't supported by the platform, mobile security, user navigation flows, capabilities, etc. Which means I can't write about using them with as much confidence or ease as a more familiar Android phone. Considering the integration of mobile technology into many of these investigations, I'd rather not slip on those details. So everyone gets Androids.

Q. Why don't you always translate foreign language words, such as the Persian or Korean slang Malcolm and Seong-Jae sometimes use?

> **A.** That's a complicated question with an even more complicated answer that involves an in-depth look at privileged expectations—and it's tied into the reason why many authors and readers who speak languages other than English are increasingly against italicizing non-English words, too. To keep it short I will say that

I translate when it's relevant to the dialogue or plot or when another character asks about things said aloud, but for minor words I don't because in a character's POV they normally wouldn't stop to define the word they just thought/said in English.

I'll also say that while the gist is often apparent from context (for example, we knew "jot" was an insult long before Seong-Jae told Malcolm what it meant), in general non-English speakers reading English language books don't have the luxury of having every word translated and explained directly to them. They have to learn the language. So. Again: ¯_(ツ)_/¯ Take from that what you will. You won't lose any of the plot by not knowing those little bits of slang.

Q. But I noticed you sneakily went back and switched "jaji" with "jot" after the first book released.

A. I did. I'm going to outright own this: my Korean is rusty and self-taught, and I messed up. Someone was kind enough to point out that I swapped the anatomical word for penis ("jaji") with the slang insult for dick ("jot"), so I went back and fixed my screw-up. (And thanked that person profusely.)

Q. Why does Sade use they/them pronouns? Are they male or female?

> A. Sade doesn't identify as either male or female. They identify as two-spirit, which is a rather complex concept that differs between Indigenous nations and isn't something to be lightly discussed here. The closest analogue in non-Indigenous western culture is genderqueer, which is a nonbinary expression that may figure in masculine traits, may figure in feminine traits, or may eschew gendered traits altogether.
>
> Not everyone identifies explicitly with the male/female gender binary, whether they're cis or trans, and identifying as genderqueer, genderfluid, agender, neutrois, genderbend, demiboy, demigirl, or many of the other identities along the nonbinary spectrum may be more comfortable. That can often mean ditching the gendered pronouns, too. While many nonbinary people default to using "they/them/their" in the singular, others use pronouns such as "xie/xer" or others depending on what suits them best. I will likely never reveal what gender Sade was assigned at birth. It's just not necessary to their story, and can cause people to start unconsciously gendering them.

Q. Why don't all the Q&As in each book have the same questions?

A. I add new questions and answers as people ask them as the series progresses and sometimes delete episode-specific questions from new episodes, but I don't always go back to update the previous books every time as it can take a while to do that with every new release each month. So newer books will have longer Q&As with more/updated questions. Eventually, though, I go back to refresh the back matter of older books, and end up adding the latest version of the Q&A.

Q. ...your avatar is wearing cat ears.

    A. Yes, yes it is.

Q. *Why?*

    A. ...

    . . . .

    . . . .

    ¯_(ツ)_/¯

[AFTERWORD]

IN THE AFFTERWORD TO CRIMINAL INTENTIONS Season 1, Episode 1, "The Cardigans," I mentioned that my parents, grandmother, and stepmother had all been police officers. I mentioned what it was like growing up with my parents, and watching the jobs they did eat away at their humanity and capacity for empathy.

What I didn't mention was how rarely either of them ever received counseling for the daily work stressors chipping away at them and making them less and less capable of handling the job.

If police officers during my childhood, decades ago, didn't receive enough psychological and emotional support...the problem has only worsened to this day. Lack of understanding of the profound and traumatic effect of police work leaves the psychological damage and PTSD of the job running unchecked, making officers increasingly more volatile and unstable.

Increasingly more dangerous.

That's why it was important to me to show, in this episode, that both Malcolm and Seong-Jae are human enough for the graphic events of the first book's case to have a lasting effect, rather than being brushed off as episodic criminal of the week. Even more important was showing that they had access to and made use of a mental health support network, and even more chose to support each other with empathy, kindness, and understanding.

We don't pay enough attention to the mental health of the people we trust with our safety and well-being; the people we trust with protecting us.

We should.

Police officers should not be more of a danger to private citizens than the people they're meant to protect against, and yet they frequently are.

Which is why it's important to support crisis intervention organizations like **COPLINE**, who provide mental health counseling and support services for officers. I have conflicted feelings about the police, being both the son of two cops and a man of color who firmly believes in #BlackLivesMatter.

But there's nothing conflicted about my belief that we would all be safer if better care was taken with mental health in law enforcement.

-C

[GET VIP ACCESS]

WANT FREE STORIES AVAILABLE NOWHERE else? Subscribe to the Xen x Cole McCade newsletter:

www.blackmagicblues.com/newsletter/

Get SOMETIMES IT STORMS (previously featured in IPPY Award-winning charity anthology WINTER RAIN), Red's story in PINUPS, as well as deleted scenes from A SECOND CHANCE AT PARIS and FROM THE ASHES – and deleted scenes, bonus content, episode soundtracks, and artwork from CRIMINAL INTENTIONS.

Subscribing also gets you release announcements and

newsletter-only exclusives, including early access to new books, giveaways, and more. **Become a VIP!**

www.blackmagicblues.com/newsletter/

[FOR REVIEWERS]

XEN x COLE MCCADE
ARC REVIEWER TEAM

INTERESTED IN ADVANCE REVIEW COPIES (ARCS) of upcoming releases? Apply to join Xen x Cole McCade's arc reviewer team, A MURDER OF CROWS:

http://blackmagicblues.com/join-the-murder-of-crows-arc-team/

CRIMINAL INTENTIONS: SEASON ONE, EPISODE TWO
JUNK SHOP BLUES

[ACKNOWLEDGMENTS]

As always, I'm grateful to the chosen family who have become like sisters to me. To my editor Amanda, who puts up with so much shite. And to the Fight Club, who shall ever remain nameless but whom I can always trust to whip me into shape.

Thank you.

CRIMINAL INTENTIONS: SEASON ONE, EPISODE TWO
JUNK SHOP BLUES

[ABOUT THE AUTHOR]

COLE MCCADE IS A NEW ORLEANS-BORN Southern boy without the Southern accent, currently residing somewhere in Seattle. He spends his days as a suit-and-tie corporate consultant and business  writer, and his nights writing contemporary romance and erotica that flirts with the edge of taboo—when he's not being tackled by two hyperactive cats.

He also writes genre-bending science fiction and fantasy tinged with a touch of horror and flavored by the influences of his multiethnic, multicultural, multilingual background as Xen. He wavers between calling himself bisexual, calling himself queer, and trying to figure out where "demi" fits into the whole mess—but no matter what word he uses he's a staunch advocate of LGBTQIA and POC representation and visibility in genre fiction. And while he spends more time than is healthy hiding in his writing cave instead of hanging around social media, you can generally find him in these usual haunts:

- Email: blackmagic@blackmagicblues.com
- Twitter: @thisblackmagic

- Facebook: https://www.facebook.com/xen.cole
- Tumblr: thisblackmagic.tumblr.com
- Instagram: www.instagram.com/thisblackmagic
- Bookbub: https://www.bookbub.com/profile/cole-mccade
- Facebook Fan Page: http://www.facebook.com/ColeMcCadeBooks
- Website & Blog: http://www.blackmagicblues.com

[FIND MORE CONTEMPORARY
ROMANCE & EROTICA AS COLE
MCCADE]

http://blackmagicblues.com/books-by-xen-x-cole-mccade/

[DISCOVER SCIENCE FICTION, FANTASY & HORROR AS XEN]

http://blackmagicblues.com/books-by-xen-x-cole-mccade/

Made in the USA
Coppell, TX
14 April 2022

76564265R00203